Alison Roberts is a New Zealander, currently lucky enough to be living in the South of France. She is also lucky enough to write for the Mills & Boon Medical Romance line. A primary school teacher in a former life, she is now a qualified paramedic. She loves to travel and dance, drink champagne, and spend time with her daughter and her friends.

Three-times Golden Heart® finalist **Tina Beckett** learned to pack her suitcases almost before she learned to read. Born to a military family, she has lived in the United States, Puerto Rico, Portugal and Brazil. In addition to travelling, Tina loves to cuddle with her pug, Alex, spend time with her family, and hit the trails on her horse. Learn more about Tina from her website, or 'friend' her on Facebook.

Discover more at millsandboon.co.uk.

DR RIGHT FOR THE SINGLE MUM

ALISON ROBERTS

A FAMILY TO HEAL HIS HEART

TINA BECKETT

MILLS & BOON

First Published in Great Britain 2019
by Mills & Boon, an imprint of HarperCollins*Publishers*
1 London Bridge Street, London, SE1 9GF

Dr Right for the Single Mum © 2019 by Alison Roberts

A Family to Heal His Heart © 2019 by Tina Beckett

ISBN: 978-0-263-26984-0

MIX
Paper from
responsible sources
FSC˘ C007454

This book is produced from independently certified FSC™ paper
to ensure responsible forest management.
For more information visit www.harpercollins.co.uk/green.

Printed and bound in Spain
by CPI, Barcelona

DR RIGHT FOR THE SINGLE MUM

ALISON ROBERTS

MILLS & BOON

For every mother (and father),
in recognition of the amazing bonds we have
with our children xx

CHAPTER ONE

'HAS ANYONE HEARD what's happening?' Laura McKenzie slowed down as she pushed an IV trolley past the central desk of Wellington's Royal Hospital's emergency department and then she stopped. 'Has the baby arrived yet?'

One of the department's consultants, Fizz Wilson, was in front of a computer screen, studying the lab results on blood samples. 'Last I heard, it's not far away. Maggie was almost fully dilated. When Cooper brings Harley in for his feed later, I'm hoping we can use my break to go and meet the new arrival.'

'Yes… I'm due for my break at the same time.' Laura nodded. 'I'll come with you.' Maggie was a close friend and ex-flatmate and Laura couldn't wait to meet her baby.

'Where are you off to?' Tom Chapman, the senior consultant in this emergency department, dropped a patient file on the desk.

'To see Joe and Maggie's baby.'

Tom's eyebrows rose. 'Maggie's in labour?' He was already scanning the board that provided the update of all the patients currently in the department, whose care they were under and at what stage of their assessment or treatment they were. 'I was working with Joe at the rescue base yesterday and he thought it was still a week or two away.'

'Nope. Today's the day. They headed into Maternity at about four this morning.'

But Tom didn't seem to be remotely excited and Laura could feel a slightly puzzled frown line appearing between her eyebrows as she let her gaze rest on his profile for a moment longer. She'd worked with this man for more than two years now but sometimes she had absolutely no idea what was going on in his head. He was a brilliant doctor, was warm and kind and completely trustworthy but, at the same time, he could be oddly reserved. Like now, when you might expect him to share at least some of the excitement of imminent parenthood to people he knew well.

Maybe he just had other things on his mind. Like how his emergency department was coping with the patient numbers and the levels of attention they needed. Laura brushed off an urge to reassure him in some way that, as always, he had everything as under control as it was possible to have it but a couple of seconds later she thought that it had been just as well that she hadn't said anything because someone would have blamed her for tempting fate as potential chaos broke out. An ambulance crew was rushing through the automatic doors leading to the vehicle bay, someone was calling for assistance from one of the cubicles and a cardiac arrest alarm was sounding.

Tom was the first person to put his hands on the trolley that contained a lifepack, airway and IV equipment and the drugs that could be needed to manage a major cardiac event.

'Where's the arrest?' he demanded.

'Waiting room,' someone responded.

Tom started moving. 'Fizz, take over here for a minute. Laura? Come with me. We can get there before the arrest team arrives.'

Abandoning the IV trolley, Laura was almost running to keep up with Tom's long stride. Expecting to see an elderly patient who had collapsed in the waiting room, it was a shock to find that the cardiac arrest button had been pushed for someone who looked like a child.

'Help...please...she's not breathing...' The distraught woman who had her arms around the young girl had to be her mother and Laura's heart immediately went out to her. She'd be this terrified, as well, if she was holding her son, Harrison, and he'd just stopped breathing.

'What's happened?' Tom eased the girl from her mother's arms to lay her flat on the floor and then he tilted her head back to open the airway. He put his fingers on the side of her neck as he leaned closer.

Laura was peeling open the pack that contained the defibrillator pads. She cut the neck of the girl's T-shirt and ripped it open to give her access to the point below her right collarbone and then lifted the hem to press the second pad on her left side. She noted the dramatic rash on the child's skin and caught

Tom's gaze to make sure he was aware of it, as well. He was. Of course he was.

'She's allergic,' the mother was saying. 'To dairy. She was eating chips in the car and I thought they were the plain ones and they were safe but they weren't…someone had given her some flavoured ones. Ketchup. She thought that was fine but we could already see the hives starting to come up.'

'We've got a pulse,' Tom told Laura. 'But she's bradycardic. Not breathing.'

He reached for a bag mask, fitted the mask over the girl's face and delivered a breath. And then another. But he was frowning and Laura knew why. This had to be an anaphylactic reaction to an allergen and the child's airways were swelling up and making it harder to deliver oxygen. They needed to move fast or it could become impossible to intubate and secure the airway. The fact that the heart rate was already too slow meant that they could be dealing with a cardiac arrest as well as a respiratory arrest in a very short time.

Tom glanced up and this time it was him who was catching Laura's gaze. It was another moment of silent communication and something they were both so used to now it took only a split second to have a question asked and answered. This was a critical situation and every second counted. They would be losing quite a few of those seconds to take the girl into one of the resuscitation areas on the other side of the swing doors but it was entirely possible that they would need more equipment than they had in this trolley—like a surgical kit to perform a cricothyroidotomy if a tracheal intubation proved impossible.

With no more than a subtle nod, Tom broke the glance, scooped the child into his arms and took off.

'Follow us,' Laura told the mother. She had picked up the lifepack as Tom had started moving and she really was running this time to keep up with him and not break the connection between the pads and the defibrillator.

People in the emergency department stepped hurriedly out of their way. Laura saw the startled expression on Fizz's face and the way she signalled junior doctors to take over what she was doing. She was right on their heels by the time Tom put the girl down on the bed.

'Respiratory arrest,' he told Fizz. 'Anaphylaxis. Known allergy to dairy.'

'Has she had any adrenaline?'

'Yes…' The girl's mother was near the foot of the bed, her arms held tightly across her body as if she needed physical support. 'We used her auto-injector but…but it didn't seem to be working. When she started getting wheezy I just drove straight here.'

She was used to coping, Laura thought. Used to providing her own support. Was she a single parent, like herself?

'Laura? Draw up some adrenaline, please.'

'Onto it.' The personal connection Laura was feeling to this patient and her mother had to be put firmly aside as she focused on what she needed to do.

Other staff members were arriving now, including the two medic arrest team. Laura was pleased to see a new nurse beside their patient's mother, easing her to one side of the room, out of the way, but staying with her as she endured the terrifying sight of a medical team fighting to save the life of her daughter.

There was so much happening. Tom was intubating the girl, using a video laryngoscope so that he could actually see what he was doing amongst the swelling tissues. An anaesthetist who'd been on call for the arrest team was setting up the ventilator that would be attached as soon as the intubation had been successfully completed. He had a kit on standby for creating a surgical airway if the intubation was not possible due to the amount of swelling.

Fizz was working to gain IV access and someone else was setting up the bags of saline and the giving sets that they would need for a fluid challenge to combat anaphylactic shock. Laura administered the first dose of intramuscular adrenaline and then began sorting the other drugs that she knew would be needed. More adrenaline, to set up as an infusion if there wasn't enough response to the first doses, along with an antihistamine and steroids. She filled syringes and taped the ampoules to the barrel of the syringes to identify them. She was keeping an eye on the screen above the bed, too, so that she could warn Tom of any changes that could be significant, like a further drop in blood pressure or heart rate. This would become even more of a challenge if the heart stopped in the wake of the lack of oxygen from the respiratory arrest.

The tension was palpable and, at one point, Laura heard the stifled sob of the girl's mother behind her. She could feel a lump in her own throat. This was every parent's nightmare, wasn't it? She was going to hug Harry so hard when she went to pick him up after work today that she knew he would squeak and wriggle free, probably giggling or groaning at the same time, the way six-year-old boys did. In the meantime, she was going to do everything she could to help save this young life in front of them. The alternative was simply unimaginable.

'We're in…' Tom gave a satisfied nod as he hooked his stethoscope back around his neck after checking the placement of the airway. 'Now, let's get this oxygen saturation looking a bit better.'

'Heart rate's picking up.' Like Laura, Fizz was watching the screen above them. 'And I've got wide-bore access on both sides.'

'Let's start the fluid challenge.' Tom turned his head to where the child's mother was standing. 'How much does she weigh?'

'Um…she was about twenty-six kilos the last time it was checked.'

'And how old is she?'

'Nine. Nearly ten…she's always been small…'

Like Harry, Laura thought. He'd always been small for his age and a bit underweight, as well. It made them seem younger than they were. More vulnerable. She wanted to give this young mother a hug. To try and reassure her. She could actually sense the same empathy coming from Tom, whose face creased in an almost smile.

'What's her name?'

'Elizabeth. We call her Lizzie…'

'She's going to be fine. The immediate danger is over.'

'But she's in Intensive Care…'

'This is the best place to monitor Lizzie for a few hours. Just to make sure that everything's under control and the medications are doing their job.'

The woman closed her eyes as she nodded slowly. 'I can't thank you enough, Dr Chapman.' She pressed her fingers against her mouth. 'I feel like it was my fault. How could I not have noticed that the auto-injector was past its expiry date?'

'I'm sure that's something that will never happen again. And you did exactly the right thing, bringing her straight to Emergency.'

'I could have lost her. I…I thought I had…' She had her hand over her eyes now.

The urge to touch this woman's shoulder, or hug her even, to provide comfort was so strong that Tom had to curl his fingers into a fist.

He didn't get personally involved with his patients. Or their families. If he did, he'd never be able to do his job well enough and doing his job to the very best of his ability was the most important thing in Tom Chapman's world.

The only thing, pretty much…

'Go and sit with her now,' he told Lizzie's mother.

'Or take a break? You probably need one after all that drama.'

'I won't be leaving her side for a while yet. It's you that needs a break, I reckon. You worked so hard to save my little girl.'

'It's my job. And my privilege.' Tom glanced at his watch. 'I am on a late lunch break now. That's why I popped up to see that Lizzie was settled well.'

'I hope you've already had your lunch?'

'Not yet. That's next.'

But he wasn't really hungry at all, Tom decided as he walked towards the café in the Royal's entrance foyer. It was often like that, in the aftermath of the adrenaline rush that came from treating someone so critically ill—even more so when that fight for life was on behalf of a child. All life was precious, of course, but children and especially babies were so vulnerable you couldn't help becoming emotionally involved to some extent. For some reason, the feeling of connection was harder to shake off after this case. Maybe that was why Tom gave in to the impulse to turn into the gift shop beside the café.

Ten minutes later he was standing in front of a door in the maternity suite of the Royal.

Hesitating…

He didn't actually have to go in, did he? He could leave his gifts with one of the nurses. He didn't have to prod that no-go area of his heart any more than it had already been prodded today.

But visiting Joe and Maggie as they basked in the glow of new parenthood was a friendly thing to do.

A polite thing, and Tom Chapman was always polite. Manners that had been developed as a form of self-protection had evolved to be useful under even the most extreme circumstances and he'd learned that there was truth in the old adage to "fake it till you make it". Tom had faked it for long enough to have made it long ago.

So, with the string of the pink "It's a girl!" balloon in one hand and the softest baby toy the gift shop had had available, Tom tapped on the door and poked his head through the gap.

'I can come back later,' he offered. 'If you've had too many visitors already.'

'No, come in, Tom.'

'Just for a minute, then.' Tom shook the out-stretched hand of the paramedic who had become a trusted colleague in recent months. 'Congratulations, Joe. And there you were telling me only yesterday that you thought this was a week or two away.'

'Bella had other ideas.' It was Maggie who spoke. 'I have a feeling we're going to be scrambling to keep up with this little one.'

Tom smiled at Maggie, another paramedic who worked at the Aratika Rescue Base. Her blonde curls looked a little tangled and she looked exhausted but the glow of joy in her eyes nearly blinded Tom.

He'd seen that look before.

He'd worn it on his own face, once.

And yes…it was hard to drop his gaze to the bundle in Maggie's arms. To the tiny, slightly scrunched-up face of a baby who'd been born within the last few hours. The pain never really went away, did it? You'd think it had faded or been safely locked away somewhere but sometimes all it took was something like seeing that tiny starfish hand poking up from out of the blanket folds and there it was again. So sharp, it could have been yesterday.

So poignant, it could have brought the sting of tears if he'd allowed it. But, of course, that was never going to happen.

'Would you like to hold her?' Maggie offered.

'Ah…no…' Tom actually took a step backwards. 'I really can't stay. We're pretty busy in Emergency.'

He knew Joe was watching him. He also realised that Joe had respected the confidence of a personal discussion they'd had a while back now. That he hadn't even told Maggie that he'd learned something about Tom that he never told others. And Tom could feel the understanding in that gaze he was under. Joe knew that this was tough. That being with a couple who were so much in love and welcoming their first child had to be a painfully sharp reminder that he'd lost his own wife and son.

He didn't want that understanding. Or rather, he didn't want anybody feeling sorry for him because he had no desire to start feeling sorry for himself.

But Joe was nodding as he spoke. 'We heard about the anaphylactic shock you guys had to deal with. Fizz said it was touch and go for a while there.'

'It was. I've left her in charge, too, and it's about time she went home.'

'Did Laura come back? With Harry?'

Tom had his hand on the door already, but he turned back. 'Harry? Her little boy?' He was frowning. 'I didn't realise she'd gone anywhere.'

'She got a call from Harry's school and she had to go and pick him up because he was feeling sick. It's been happening quite a bit lately. If you see her, tell her to text me? She said she'd take him to the GP but if she was really worried, she said she might bring him in to see you.'

'Oh?' Tom shook his head. 'I'm not a paediatrician. I'm sure her GP can handle it. Or refer her. Laura knows that Emergency is just for emergencies.'

Laura knew she was bending the rules.

Okay, so a lot of people came to the emergency department when they had problems that could—and should—be dealt with by a general practitioner. And the fact that people did turn up when they had a minor injury or illness could mean that the department could get overloaded and the patients that really needed the attention of the staff might have to wait too long or even miss getting a critical treatment in time.

But this was Harrison—Laura's precious little boy.

And something wasn't right.

He'd had tummy aches before. He'd been sick at school more than once in recent months but there'd been something about him, when Laura had arrived at the sick bay to collect Harry today, that had sent a chill trickling down her spine. Maybe it was his skin colour. Or the air of listlessness about him. Or perhaps it was just the expression in those dark brown eyes he'd inherited from her. A sad look, as if he couldn't understand why life was so miserable right now.

Anyway, it was done. Laura was back at the Royal and had Harry in her arms, balanced on her hip. She was still in her scrubs with her official lanyard on so nobody would question her presence in the department and, technically, she was still on duty so she could tell people she'd come back to finish her shift and Harry was just going to wait quietly for her in the staffroom.

But the first person she encountered was Tom and the way he held her gaze for a moment or two longer than you would with a normal acquaintance provided one of those lightning-fast, telepathic conversations.

You're worried about your boy, aren't you?

Yes.

Too worried to go to your GP?

Yes.

Okay, then...that's fine...you've done the right thing bringing him in.

The lines around Tom's eyes softened and Laura felt herself relax just a little thanks to that understanding and trust in her judgement she could see in Tom's face.

She trusted him just as much and it was a trust that was rock solid because it had grown slowly to begin with when Tom had begun working in this emergency department. On both sides.

Laura was always wary around men she didn't know, especially when they were single and as good looking as Tom Chapman was. She had to make sure they got very clear signals that she wasn't interested in being anything more than a colleague. That she didn't want anyone trying to get close. It hadn't taken long to realise that the new consultant was giving off exactly the same signals but that hadn't stopped almost every other single woman she'd seen him interact with trying to catch his attention. A sympathetic glance on one occasion had cemented the unspoken knowledge that, for whatever reason, they had both built solid barriers to protect themselves.

Maybe that was what had given the level of trust between them such a solid foundation—that they both recognised those barriers and knew that neither was going to attempt breaking through them. They were workmates. Not quite friends, because they didn't choose to spend any time away from work together, like Laura did with Maggie and Joe and Fizz and Cooper, but they were more than simply workmates because there was that trust on both sides. That confidence that it was totally safe to be near each other. And that meant they didn't have to be on their guard on any level, which was probably why it was so easy to communicate, even without any words.

'Let's find him a cubicle,' Tom said. 'You fill in the paperwork and I'll come and check on him as soon as I can.'

He smiled at Harry before he turned away. 'Hey, buddy…who have you got there? T Rex?'

Harry clutched his plastic dinosaur more tightly to his chest and curled closer to his mother. Laura could feel the sudden tension in his small body from being too close for comfort to a man he didn't know. But her heart squeezed hard when her son was brave enough to say something back to Tom.

'His real name is Tyrannosaurus Rex,' Harry whispered.

'It is,' Tom agreed. 'Did you know that he had sixty teeth? And they were all razor sharp and could be this big?' He held his hands with a large gap between them.

Harry's eyes widened and his jaw dropped. Laura grinned at Tom. *Way to go*, she told him silently. He had just won the heart of a six-year-old who was passionate about dinosaurs and he might have even erased much of the fear that this small boy had of men he didn't know well.

She headed towards the central desk, to pick up the forms she needed to fill in and to check the board to see what cubicle might be free.

Fizz was on her way out of the department. 'Oh, no... Harry... Are you still feeling sick, sweetheart?'

Harry nodded.

Fizz caught Laura's gaze. 'Want me to stay? Cooper's just gone with Harley to get the car but we could come back.'

'No...we're good.'

Fizz raised an eyebrow. She knew that Harry was shy with men he didn't know. She also knew that her husband had won Harry's trust very early on, when he'd been one of Laura's flatmates.

'You remember Cooper, don't you, Harry? He helped you when you broke your arm last year.'

Harry nodded.

'It's all better now, isn't it? Your arm?'

Harry nodded again.

'Well, Doctor Tom will help make whatever it is that's making you feel sick all better, too.'

'He will,' Laura agreed. 'And who knew that he knew so much about dinosaurs?'

Fizz chuckled. 'There you go. A match made in heaven.' But her smile faded as she looked back at Laura. 'Text me,' she said, 'if there's anything I can do to help.'

'I'm sure we'll be fine,' Laura told her. 'You go and enjoy the rest of your day with your boys. I'm probably overreacting.'

'I'd be exactly the same with Harley. And we both know that you need to listen when a mum's feeling worried. Instinct should never be ignored.'

'Mmm...' But Laura didn't want to think about a mother's instinct. Because hers was trying to send messages that were too scary.

She just knew too much. She'd seen too much in this department. People that came in, occasionally, with symptoms that should be of no great significance but turned out to be something really awful.

Laura collected the paperwork and settled Harry onto the bed in a spare cubicle. She left the curtain open enough to be able to see what was happening in the department because she wanted to see the moment Tom started heading in their direction.

She wanted him to come and make her feel safe.

More than anything, she needed the reassurance that Harry was safe.

Tom collected the new patient file from the central desk and was reading through the information Laura had provided about Harry as he walked to their cubicle. Perhaps that was why it came as a bit of a shock to look up and see Laura and Harry through the gap in the curtains.

He saw Laura McKenzie almost every day he was at work but he'd never seen her looking like this. She was normally on her feet and always busy, caring for her patients or fully involved in an assessment or resuscitation scene. Even if she was taking a break, she'd be reading while she ate a sandwich, or chatting to one of her friends like Fizz.

Right now, however, she was half on the bed with her son, perched on one side and lying across the pillows so that Harry was tucked under the shelter of her arm. She was gently smoothing the dark spikes of his hair, quietly watching as Harry made his plastic dinosaur hop slowly across the blanket she had tucked around him.

Tom had never seen Laura staying this still, her body language shouting its focus on only one thing—her precious son. Or with an expression like that on her face. That mix of tenderness and concern—the picture of a mother's love—hit him like a punch in the gut and Tom found himself swallowing hard. To get a flashback twice in one day was more than a little disturbing when he'd been so sure he was well past that part of his life. Or perhaps this was simply an aftershock of how he'd felt seeing Maggie and Joe with their newborn baby and getting dragged back into the past like that.

It felt like longing, this sharp twinge of discomfort.

Or a renewed flash of grief for a future that was never going to happen.

Whatever it was, he knew he could handle it but it was certainly giving him a new perspective on this woman he'd worked with for so long. Someone he had learned to trust because she'd never attempted to get past the guardrails he had in place in his personal life. And, in this moment, he felt closer to her than he ever allowed himself to get to a colleague or a member of a patient's family, for that matter. It was already under his skin. That note of tenderness. The knowledge that Laura was very vulnerable right now. All he could do was try and contain it. To make sure it didn't grow any stronger.

'Hey…' Tom pasted a smile on his face as he pulled the curtain shut behind him. 'How's it going in here? Is Tyrannosaurus Rex finding enough to eat?'

Harry hid his toy under the blanket. 'He's not hungry.'

'Oh…' Tom pulled out a chair and perched on the edge of it, so that he wasn't looming over the bed. 'How 'bout you, Harry? Are you hungry?'

Harry shook his head. 'I was sick,' he told Tom. 'At school. I was sick on the mat at story time.'

'Oh, no…' Tom could feel Laura's gaze on his face

but he kept his gaze on his young patient. 'And you've got a sore tummy, too, I hear.'

Harry was silent. His chin was going down and his head tilting further into the crook of Laura's elbow.

Tom raised his glance. 'How long has the cream been on his arm?'

Laura touched the clear plastic cover that was keeping the generous blob of anaesthetic cream in place over the easiest vein to get a blood sample from. 'Needs another ten minutes or so.'

'Okay. So, tell me about what's been happening. This isn't the first time for a sore tummy, is it?'

Laura shook her head. 'It's been happening off and on for a long time. Almost since he started school, which made me think it was an anxiety thing, you know? Not wanting to go to school? The vomiting is more recent, though.'

'What's vomiting?'

'Being sick, sweetheart. It's what we call it here.'

Tom was watching closely as Harry looked up at his mother when he asked the question. Was that a tinge of yellow he could see in the whites of Harry's eyes?

'Can I have a look at your tummy, Harry? Is that okay?'

He could see the visible shrinking back further into his mother's arms but, with Laura's encouragement and reassurance, Harry let the blanket get pushed back and his tummy exposed.

'I won't hurt you,' Tom promised. 'If it's really sore, you tell me and I'll stop.' He eyed the dinosaur in Harry's hand. 'Or T Rex can bite me on my arm, okay?'

Big, brown eyes looked up at him. Exactly like his mother's eyes, Tom thought. Harry hadn't inherited Laura's auburn hair, though. The ruffled spikes of Harry's hair were very dark, almost black, which could be contributing to how pale that little face was. There was a hint of a smile there now, however.

''Kay.' He lay back but kept the toy dinosaur in a raised hand, ready to strike if it became necessary.

Tom was as gentle as possible. His hand looked so large against Harry's abdomen as he carefully palpated each quadrant. He left the upper right quadrant till last, probably because he had that suspicion of possible jaundice at the back of his mind.

'Can you take a big breath in for me, Harry? Like this?' Tom demonstrated and Harry complied.

And there it was…

A firm, irregular edge to this little boy's liver as he could feel it coming down with the lungs filling.

'Ow…' The plastic dinosaur tapped against Tom's arm.

'Sorry, buddy.' Tom lifted his hand but his heart was sinking. That prickle at the back of his neck was something he recognised all too easily and it came from the instinct that there was something significantly wrong here. That Harry could be in trouble and it might be impossible to protect him from painful things to come. Pain that would be felt by his mother, as well.

Tom didn't dare catch Laura's gaze just then. He

didn't want to scare her. Not until he was sure about what his instincts were telling him. Maybe he just wanted to put that moment off for as long as possible because he knew, all too well, how it could turn your world inside out and upside down.

Destroy it even…

Or maybe it was because he was suddenly aware of a desire to protect Laura McKenzie.

Where on earth had that come from…?

CHAPTER TWO

THE REST OF that day became a blur.

A desperate attempt for Laura to hang onto something solid enough to not allow herself to get swamped by a terror that was becoming more and more real as the minutes and then hours ticked past.

Blood tests came next for Harry and they were still distressing despite the anaesthetic cream and how brave her little boy was being. Maybe it was so distressing for Laura *because* of how brave Harry was being. Her love for him was so huge, it was filling her chest to an extent that made it seem very hard to breathe.

There was an ultrasound after that and even though Laura was not trained to interpret the blobby images on the screen, she could see that there was something in Harry's liver that shouldn't be there. That was when the real fear kicked in. Fear that had to be hidden from Harry because Laura knew how sensitive he was to how his mother felt. He had been right from when he was a tiny baby and Laura still felt guilty that his fear of strange men had been instilled in that part of his life due to the aftermath of the trauma from the abusive relationship she had escaped.

Thank goodness Tom was there, at least until Harry was admitted for the raft of other tests he was going to need. It was Tom who introduced Laura and Harry to Suzie, a paediatric surgeon who was absolutely lovely, and he was there when the paediatric oncologist was also called in for a consultation. As Laura's world was being tipped upside down, Tom's presence felt like an anchor. Something safe when almost nothing else could be trusted any more. That something solid that she could hang onto.

'Can I call someone for you?' he asked when an orderly came to wheel Harry's bed up to the paediatric ward. 'Have you got family?'

Laura shook her head, stepping far enough away from Harry not to be overheard. 'No one close. It's just me and Harry.'

Tom was frowning. 'What about his father?'

'Not in the picture. Never has been.' Laura wanted to shut down this line of conversation. She'd been alone for a very long time, apart from Harry, and she preferred it that way. More than preferred it, actually. Changing it had never even been an option to consider.

'Friends, then.' Tom's frown had deepened. 'Maggie? I know she wants to know what's happening. She asked me to tell you to text her when I went up to visit her earlier.'

'She doesn't need to know right now. For heaven's

sake, Tom. She's probably just arrived home with her brand new baby. It's okay, I can cope.'

She could. She'd coped before. Because, when you had to, you just did. You took things one step at a time and did your absolute best. But…it was kind of nice to have someone who wanted to help and the expression in Tom's eyes suggested there was something more than purely professional concern for her as a colleague. As she held his gaze for a moment longer, Laura almost had the impression that he was struggling with something. He felt compelled to offer assistance but he wasn't actually that comfortable about it, was he? Because they'd never stepped out of that "colleague" zone into a "friend" zone?

She needed to let him off the hook.

'As soon as Harry's settled, I'll pop home and get everything we'll need. And I'm sure it won't take long for him to feel happy there.' Laura pasted a smile onto her face. 'It'll probably be an adventure for him with all the toys and games they've got available and with other kids to play with and we both know how wonderful the staff are up there.'

Tom's smile only caught one half of his mouth. He knew how hard she was trying to make the best of this situation. He also knew how difficult it was and he wanted to be able to help. More than wanted, in fact. He looked as though he wasn't about to give up until he could do something. And, suddenly, Laura knew what that could be.

'I've got a day off tomorrow,' she told him. 'But,

if you really want to help, could you look at my roster for the next few days?'

'Of course. Take all the time you need. Just let me know how I can make things easier.'

'Thanks.' Laura simply nodded. She couldn't spare any head space to think about how much paid sick leave she might have available. Or how much she had in her savings account to cover unpaid time off work. She did know that it was unlikely to be enough but that was an added level of fear that couldn't be allowed to matter at this point.

The only thing that mattered was Harry. Finding out exactly what was going on and how they were going to deal with it.

'I'll know more in a day or two and I'll come and have a chat about work then. It could be tomorrow, even. Suzie said something about the possibility of a biopsy straight after the CT scans.'

Even saying the words made the terror of this too real. For an awful moment, Laura felt an urge to throw herself into Tom's arms and just burst into tears. She didn't dare catch his gaze again now. He was feeling uncomfortable enough just offering personal assistance. Forcing him to offer comfort would be doing more than crossing interpersonal boundaries—it would probably irreparably damage the trust they had between them.

Those unspoken rules that had never, ever been broken.

No flirting.

No really personal conversation.

Physical proximity and touching only if unavoidable in professional circumstances.

Laura needed those rules to be in place just as much as Tom did because they were the perimeters that created the safe space she had needed for so long. It was a good thing that Harry's bed was on the move beside her. Even if she hadn't been able to control that urge to seek comfort from the touch of another human, there was no chance to do so right now.

'Mummy?' The anxiety in Harry's voice was more than enough to ensure that Laura took instant control of any emotional weakness that might be trying to persuade her to beg for comfort.

'I'm coming, sweetheart. Just wait until you see what they've got painted on the walls where we're going. I think there's even going to be some dinosaurs somewhere.'

Three days later, Tom emerged from one of the resuscitation rooms in ED to see Laura at the central desk. Fizz appeared to be hugging her friend fiercely.

He'd been expecting this.

He hadn't expected to feel a wash of something that felt oddly like relief at seeing her again, mind you. Had he been missing seeing Laura around the department more than he'd realised? Or was he feeling guilty that he hadn't been up to the paediatric ward to visit them? He'd felt a bit awkward, actually. Caught somewhere in the space between being simply a colleague or someone more like a friend who had good reason to demonstrate the kind of concern he was feeling. He had excused himself by keeping very busy and reassured himself that Laura was getting all the support she needed from her group of very good friends.

It was Fizz that Tom had been relying on for updates about what was happening in the paediatric ward and he always checked to see whether any extra help was needed. He knew that Harry had had all the relevant tests, including a biopsy. He had also been told that Laura was coping amazingly well, all things considered, and that she would be coming to talk to Tom, as head of department, regarding any time off she was going to need.

And here she was.

And, as Tom walked towards her, he wanted nothing more than to do exactly what Fizz was doing. To take Laura into his arms and give her a hug that could convey his empathy and encouragement and offer support all at the same time.

The urge to do so was disturbingly out of character for Tom. So much so that it was probably the reason he found it difficult to find a smile as Laura turned away from her friend. He might have even been frowning, he realised, as he saw the way Laura was collecting under his gaze as he came towards the desk. She was trying to hide any show of emotion that could be considered inappropriate in a work setting, wasn't she? Straightening her back and brushing both her forefingers beneath her eyes as if erasing any evidence of tears being shed.

She looked pale. So pale that Tom could see freckles on her nose and he'd never noticed them before. He could see stray wisps of hair escaping from the loose plait her long hair was in, as well, which was a far cry from the normally sleek way she tied up her hair, but what struck Tom the most were her eyes. Maybe she'd lost a bit of weight in the last few days, which made them look larger. Or perhaps it was the light she was standing beneath that made him notice the subtle variations in colour that made them a really golden brown.

No…in the moment Tom broke the eye contact before it became long enough to seem far more significant than it actually was, he realised it was neither of those things. It was the pain he could see in them that touched a part of his own heart.

He knew that pain.

He needed to straighten his own back now. To remind himself that just because he recognised how tough things were for Laura, it didn't mean he had to go back to that part of his own life and relive something he had finally moved on from. His heart sank a little, however. Even a professional chat with Laura was quite likely to be a lot more difficult than he had anticipated.

'This is good timing,' he said to her, by way of a greeting. 'Come into my office, Laura. Fizz? You'll know where to find me if you need me.'

'Sure thing.' Fizz had no trouble finding a smile for Laura. 'Come and find me again after you've had a chat with Tom. With a bit of luck, we can grab a coffee in the staffroom.'

Tom's office was down a corridor, between the staffroom and the meeting room. It was a small space, lined with crowded bookshelves and a desk piled with paperwork that took up most of the rest of the space. There was a big office chair behind the desk and two smaller chairs on the other side, which were padded but not exactly inviting. He waved a hand towards the smaller chairs.

'Please, have a seat, Laura.'

Closing the door behind him, Tom hesitated momentarily. Putting the barrier of that large desk between them didn't feel right but sitting close beside her on the other small chair was going too far in the other direction—as if he was planning to offer a counselling session rather than the kind of professional discussion about rosters and leave that they needed to have. He solved the issue by shoving a pile of journals to one side and hooking his leg over the corner to perch on the edge of his desk. Then he took a deeper breath.

'So… I heard that the biopsy results were going to be available today?'

Laura nodded. 'It's a hepatoblastoma. They thought it might be hepatic cancer because the age range for a hepatoblastoma is usually under three but…but apparently it's a good thing because the stats are better. The survival rate is…is around eighty-six percent.'

Tom used his nod in response as a cover to close his eyes for a moment. He could actually feel the strength that Laura was hanging onto as she spoke.

This was her own child she was talking about, not a patient they had in common. How hard was it to try and focus on the positive side of the equation?

'And the MRI showed that there's no sign of metastatic tumours so that's really good news, too.' The wobble in Laura's voice signalled how hard it was for her to keep the lid on her emotions but she clearly wanted to give him all the information she could and Tom could only silently applaud her courage.

'Have they done the pretext staging?' The pretreatment extent of disease was an important part of how the team would decide to tackle Harry's treatment.

'It's Stage two, but only just big enough to be in more than one section of the liver. They want to give him a few cycles of chemo to try and shrink it so that it's only in a single sector and then they'll be able to remove it totally with the surgery.'

'So surgery will be at least a few weeks away, then? Or more depending on how many cycles of chemo are needed?' Tom reached for a notepad and pulled a pen from the pocket of his scrub suit. 'Let me make a note of how long you'll need to be away for.'

But Laura was shaking her head this time. 'I don't need to be off work the whole time. They're going to keep Harry in for a few days to see how he tolerates the first dose of the chemo but the aim after that is to keep life as normal as possible for everyone and they tell me that if Harry tolerates it well enough, there's no reason he can't keep going to school at the moment. Apparently most children do tolerate it well and he's desperate to get back to school and his friends and our normal routine. Hopefully I'll just need days off to be with him when he comes in for the infusions and I should have a calendar for that later today.'

Tom's eyebrows rose. 'You really want to keep working?'

'I realise that I will need a lot more time off when it's time for the surgery and that it could be a problem in the next few weeks if I have to cut shifts short or something to collect him from school if he gets too tired or is feeling sick, but it's not simply a matter of what I would prefer... I have to keep working, Tom. I can't afford not to.'

For a split second, Tom thought he had found a way to help Laura and still keep a safe distance. How easy would it be to offer to help her financially through this rough patch? Catching her gaze, however, he just as instantly dismissed the idea. He could read the look in her eyes just as easily as the kind of silent communication they could have regarding a patient. She didn't want financial help. She was fiercely proud of her independence and she intended to cope. Alone, thank you very much.

'We'll work around that, then,' he found himself saying. 'I know I won't be the only person in the department who wants to support you as much as possible, Laura. And...I have to say I think your attitude is...commendable.'

More like amazing, Tom thought. He'd always known that Laura was capable. One of the best nurses he'd ever worked with, in fact. He also knew she was totally reliable and trustworthy and, although he never listened to gossip, he'd picked up that she was a single mother. But he'd never put the pieces of the puzzle together, had he? He'd never wondered how she managed her life or how hard it might have been over the years. He knew virtually nothing about her private life and hadn't wanted to know. Until now...

'You're facing this head-on,' he added. 'I really admire your determination and how positive you're being.'

Laura looked down at her hands, which were clasped in her lap. 'It's not the first time Harry and I have faced a challenge. He was born nearly nine weeks premature and it was a bit touch and go here and there.' Her breath came out in a sigh. 'Apparently a low birth weight is one of the risk factors for hepatoblastoma. I'm glad I didn't know that at the time. I had rather a lot of other stuff to worry about.'

Tom was curious to know what that other stuff had been but stifling any questions was automatic. He hated people asking him personal questions so he'd always made a point of not intruding on the private lives of the people he worked with. Having this conversation with Laura was well out of his comfort zone and it wasn't just the subject matter. She looked different, being in civvies rather than the scrubs he was used to seeing her in.

She actually sounded different, too. 'I learned then that you just had to get on with it,' she said, her voice soft enough to make Tom lift his gaze to catch hers. 'You get to choose some of the cards you play with in the game of life but others just get dealt out, don't they? There's nothing you can do about that except to play the absolute best game you can. And you have to fight for the people you love. For yourself, too.'

It was impossible to look away from those warm, brown eyes. She totally believed in what she was saying. Laura McKenzie was quite prepared to fight to the death for someone she loved. There was real passion there, mixed with that courage and determination. He was seeing a whole new side to the person he was so comfortable to work with and it was more than a little disconcerting because it was making him curious. Apart from being an amazing nurse and clearly a ferociously protective single mother, just who was Laura McKenzie? No… It was none of his business, was it?

The half-smile that tugged at one corner of her mouth made it seem as if she could read his thoughts and sympathised with his small dilemma.

But she was just finishing off her surprisingly passionate little speech. 'I guess that's the same thing, isn't it? If you're fighting for yourself that means you can't do anything other than to fight for the people you love.'

Okay… That did it. Tom had to back off fast before he got sucked into a space he had vowed never to enter again. He didn't want to think about what it was like to live in a space where you could love other people so much they became more important than anything else in life. That space that was too dangerous because, when you lost those people, you were left with what felt like no life at all...

He had to break that eye contact. And he had to move. Making a noise that was somewhere between a sound of agreement and clearing his throat, Tom slid off the corner of his desk.

'I'd better get back to the department.' He opened the door and there was an instant sense of relief. Escape was within touching distance. 'As I said, we'll work around whatever you need. Send me a copy of the chemotherapy calendar and I'll make sure Admin's on board for when you're rostered.'

Laura nodded as she got out of her chair. 'Thank you very much.'

Her formality was just what Tom needed to make things seem a little more normal. 'It's the least I can do,' he said. 'The least we can do. You're a valued member of this department, Laura. We'll all do everything we can to support you.'

Oh...help...

Where had that all come from?

Laura was cringing more than a little as she made her way back to the paediatric ward, where she'd left Harry happily watching a movie with his new friend, Aroha—a little girl with Down's syndrome who had been admitted to be reassessed and prepared for heart surgery.

Prattling on about playing the best game you could with cards being dealt in the game of life had made her sound like the kind of inspirational quotes that went around on social media.

And what about the way Tom had been looking at her while she'd been saying it all? She'd never seen an expression like that on his face. As if he understood. As if that whole conversation had been very, very personal. That had felt weird.

Okay, Laura was well aware of how attractive Tom Chapman was. She'd heard plenty of women—staff members and even patients—who'd sighed over that combination of height, wavy hair, dark eyes and that killer smile. It wasn't just his looks, either. He had a way of focusing on people that made it obvious he was really listening. That what you thought or what you had to say was important.

That he cared.

Surely there wasn't a woman on earth who wouldn't have her heart touched by feeling that someone really cared. Maybe that was why she had stumbled into saying things that were too personal. Too emotional. For the first time, Laura had been affected by this man's personality on a level she'd never encountered before. She'd never thought of Tom as anything but one of the best doctors she'd ever had the privilege of working with. And a man she could trust not to come too close.

She took the stairs rather than stand with the group of people waiting for a lift to arrive. It could have been worse, she reminded herself as she began the climb to the third floor. She could have broken even more personal barriers and told him why Harry's premature birth and the months that had followed had been such a challenge—a fight for her own survival as much as her precious baby's.

It had been a long time since Laura had allowed herself to remember the horror of what had happened but it was inevitable that being on a staircase right now would set off those flashbacks she'd thought she'd conquered long ago.

The fear of believing that she was about to be hurt. Again. That the baby she was carrying could be in danger from its own father. Stepping back to try and find safety, only to feel that there was nothing beneath her foot, that she was falling and knowing in that same moment that the accusation that would come— that this was all her own fault—would certainly be true this time. Brent's voice when the paramedics had arrived.

'She just missed the step somehow... I tried to catch her but I couldn't... She fell all the way to the bottom of the stairs... Is she bleeding? Is she going to be okay? What about the baby?'

Laura's breath hitched as she pushed herself up the last flight of stairs. "The baby"—her precious Harry—had survived the emergency Caesarean and those weeks in the paediatric intensive care unit. He would never know about the night, just before he'd been allowed to come home, when Laura had stood up to his father during one of his alcohol-fuelled rages and threatened to call the police, and told him that she would do whatever it took to make sure her baby was safe from him. He had vanished from her life by the time she took her baby home and that was the start of a whole new struggle where Laura had to try and ensure that they both not only survived but thrived.

The early years had been incredibly tough but when she'd chosen to live with flatmates so that she and Harry weren't cooped up in a tiny flat and so isolated, life had settled into something that was as good as it could get, as far as Laura was concerned. Harry had been so happy at home, especially after he'd started at the nearby school. Laura had found great friends in her flatmates and then their partners, and had two jobs that she loved equally—being a senior nurse in the Royal's Accident and Emergency department and being Harry's mum.

Laura pushed open the firestop door in the stairwell and walked towards the brightly decorated entrance to the paediatric ward. Totally out of the blue, she had a new challenge that was every bit as terrifying as when she'd sat beside that incubator in Intensive Care, praying that her baby would make it. And yeah... Tom probably thought she was flaky, talking about playing the best game of life that you could with the cards you had been dealt and how you had no choice but to fight for the people you loved, but...those words of hers had been true, hadn't they?

At least Laura knew how to fight and that it was possible to win in the end.

She'd never been more determined that she was going to win a battle, either. Previous experience was helpful in reassuring her that she did have the strength. That, even if it felt like an impossible ask and you were on the brink of losing absolutely everything, you just had to keep going somehow—one step at a time—and eventually you'd find yourself on the other side. And it was going to be the winning side. It had to be.

For Harry.

And for herself.

CHAPTER THREE

THE FLUTTER OF excitement deep in his gut, as the helicopter skids lifted off the landing pad, was very familiar now but it would never get old. Joining the team at the Aratika Rescue Base as a HEMS doctor had definitely been the best decision that Tom Chapman had made in a very long time. You never really knew exactly what you were going to find at the other end of the flight, how serious the injuries or illnesses might be or what conditions you could have to work in to try and save a life. It was challenging, often thrilling and always enormously satisfying.

That disconcertingly personal conversation he'd had with Laura a day or two ago drifted into the back of his mind yet again but Tom found himself smiling this time. He *was* playing the best game of life he could, having included the extra dimension of his shifts at Aratika as a personal choice of one of his cards. And here he was, on a gloriously sunny afternoon, heading towards an isolated coastal area of the Marlborough Sounds—a beautiful area off the top of the South Island of New Zealand and only a short hop by air from the bottom of the North Island.

'Eighty-two-year-old patient who's fallen,' Joe mused. 'What are the odds that we're going to an NOF?'

'Pretty high,' Tom agreed. Fracturing a neck of femur in a fall was one of the more common injuries for elderly people. It wasn't something a rescue helicopter from Wellington would normally be dispatched to deal with but it was going to take too long to get any land-based local emergency service to the isolated area and a nearer rescue helicopter was tied up on another mission. 'With a view like this one, though,' he added, 'I'm certainly not complaining. Some people pay a fortune to see scenery like this from the air.'

'They do. It's stunning, isn't it?' Tom peered out of the window. 'Maggie's going to be so jealous when I tell her about this run. She's missing work.'

'How long till she comes back?'

'We're working on juggling rosters, maybe as soon as next month, so that we can share Bella's care. Cooper and Fizz seem to be managing well by doing that. They only need outside help with childcare about once or twice a week.'

'Hmm…' Tom was still focused on the pattern of green islands surrounded by deep blue water stretched out below. There were people living in places where the only access was by boat. He was only half listening to Joe as he wondered if loneliness could outweigh the peacefulness and beauty of the locations.

Conversations about babies and childcare, or school, or whatever were so irrelevant to his life he often tuned out automatically but heard enough to make appropriate comments.

'We've got the advantage of having Maggie's mum wanting to help but I've got to get a spare bedroom sorted so that she doesn't have to travel late at night. And the place has been a mess ever since we started knocking the two apartments back into one house.'

'I can imagine.'

'Almost wish we had waited a while to start on that huge project. Maggie's a bit upset that we can't help Laura out at the moment and we could have if the place was still in two separate dwellings.'

'Sorry, what?' Tom turned away from the window, his attention suddenly caught. 'What's that about Laura?'

'She's going to have to find a new place to live. Couldn't be worse timing, could it, with everything else she's got to deal with at the moment?'

For a heartbeat, all Tom could think of was Laura's face when she had been looking up at him and making that brave little speech about taking the cards that life dealt you and playing the best game you could. About the courage and determination and…yeah… that capacity for passion that he'd seen in her eyes that had made him curious about the rest of her life.

He shook his head enough to clear that image. 'I don't understand,' he said. 'Why does she have to move?'

'She hasn't been able to find new flatmates and the house is way too expensive for her on her own.'

Tom could hear the echoes of Laura's voice from yesterday.

'...it's not simply a matter of what I would prefer... I have to keep working, Tom. I can't afford not to.'

That urge to help Laura kicked in with renewed force but, remembering how disconcerted it had made him feel to be aware of her personal life that had nothing to do with work, the need to keep his distance was already fighting with the desire to provide assistance of some kind.

Could he do something secretly? Like helping to pay her rent while she had to cut back on her working hours? No...he couldn't see how that could possibly work. If he had to make enquiries to find out who her landlord was, it was bound to get back to her and there had been a large element of independence as part of that determination to cope that he'd admired in her attitude to facing this crisis. Instinct told him that Laura McKenzie would not appreciate someone assuming they could undermine that kind of independence.

'There must be plenty of people looking for a place to live,' he suggested aloud. 'Has she put a notice up in the staffroom at the Royal? We could put one up at Aratika, too.'

Joe looked doubtful. 'I can't imagine she'd even want to be interviewing people at the moment. Or having strangers in the house when Harry's not well and facing surgery in the near future.'

'No… I guess not.'

'And I've always had the impression that it takes a while for Laura to trust anyone and there's not many people she lets get close. Maybe because she's super-protective of Harry.'

'Hmm…' But, again, Tom was thinking of the way Laura had been looking at him yesterday. Of the way they could always communicate so easily when they were working together. She trusted him, didn't she? As much as he trusted her. Perhaps that level of trust was even more special than he'd realised.

Andy, their pilot, cut into their conversation. 'We're nearly on target. Keep your eyes peeled for an orange school bus on the road. It was the driver, Bernie, who called for help and he's stayed on scene. It's a fair way from any houses.'

'I can see it.' Less than a minute later, Tom pointed and Joe leaned to look over his shoulder. 'Three o'clock.'

'No powerlines,' Joe added as Andy circled back. 'But those trees look close and it's an unsealed road. We'll be throwing up a bit of gravel.'

'We'll head to that beach, I think,' Andy responded, banking the helicopter to the right. 'Looks like it's low tide and there's plenty of space. You boys will just need to get a bit of exercise and run up the hill.'

They didn't run, of course. You never ran when approaching any accident scene because that could interfere with taking in important details like any clues about how serious the situation might be and any potential hazards that needed to be mitigated. They did walk swiftly, however, especially when they heard the distressed cries of their elderly patient.

'That sounds like more than an NOF,' Tom commented. A hip fracture was often not particularly painful as long as the patient remained still. And these were the cries of someone who was terrified as much as being in any pain.

It was Bernie the bus driver who came to meet them.

'It's Maureen,' he told them. 'Ed's wife. She wandered off again and she must have slipped on the gravel and fallen over and hurt herself. He's having a bit of trouble trying to calm her down.'

'Wandered off?' Tom repeated. 'Again?'

'She's got Alzheimer's.' Bernie nodded. 'Should've been in a home long ago but Ed's having none of it. He manages pretty well and we all try and do our bit but...' He was shaking his head now. 'This doesn't look so good.'

The frail, elderly woman was sitting on the side of the road. Her husband was trying to support her by keeping an arm around her shoulders but she was pushing him away, her frustration obvious.

'Go away, go away, go away...' Her voice rose as she saw Tom and Joe coming towards her. 'I wanna go home,' she shouted. 'I wanna go home, I wanna go home...'

Joe's glance was a query about whether Tom had any idea of the best way to approach this situation. He nodded in response. It wasn't that long ago that he'd attended a useful workshop in dealing with various forms of agitation, including that of dementia patients.

He crouched down in front of Maureen and mirrored her distress enough to let her know that he understood it.

'Oh, no,' he said. 'This is terrible. You want to go home, don't you, Maureen?'

She reached out to him, sobbing. 'I want to go home…'

'I know you do.' Tom took her hand in his and then put his other hand over the top of hers. 'I know you do.'

He started taking deep breaths and blowing them out in an exaggerated manner. Maureen was watching him. Clinging to his hand and still endlessly repeating her wish to go home, but she began to mimic his breathing pattern. Tom kept a hold on her hands, squeezing them rhythmically, like a slow heartbeat. Maureen's voice became quieter until it was little more than a whisper. Ed, her husband, was finally able to put his arm around her without being pushed away.

'Dunno how you did that,' he muttered. 'I don't think she could even hear anything I was saying.' He pressed his lips to his wife's silvery hair. 'It's okay, darling. It's all going to be okay now.'

Tom was still holding Maureen's hands. He spoke slowly and very clearly. 'Did you fall over, Maureen? Is something sore?'

She nodded. 'It's my leg. But it's better now. Can

I go home?' She looked around. 'Where's the dog? I came out here to find him because he ran away.' Her head tilted up towards her husband. 'Who are you?'

'I'm Ed. I'm your husband.'

'I don't have a husband. Have you seen my dog?'

This had the potential to become a heartbreaking job, Tom realised as he saw a single tear escape and roll down Ed's face. Being able to distance himself by focusing on a clinical perspective was a relief. He turned to Joe.

'Let's get a set of vital signs,' he said. 'I'll keep holding her hands and talking to her and if you move slowly it should work. An ECG would be good, too. She might have had a medical incident rather than simply slipping on the gravel.'

Joe had been observing their patient carefully while Tom calmed her down. 'I can see she's got rotation and shortening on the left side,' he said. 'We were right about the NOF.'

Tom turned to bus driver. 'Can you go down to the beach, please, Bernie? We're going to need our stretcher. And an extra pillow so that we can splint Maureen's hip. Our pilot, Andy, will help you.'

'No problem. I'd better head off after that, though, if that's okay. Don't want to be too late getting all those kids home from school.'

Bernie was able to continue with his school bus duties and the decision was made to transport Maureen, along with Ed, to their nearest hospital rather than going back to the Royal. Well splinted and secured on the stretcher, with pain relief having been administered, Maureen was drowsy enough to sleep during the short ride to hospital but woke up as she was unloaded. Looking frightened and bewildered, she searched the faces above her and then saw her husband. She reached out both hands.

'Teddy…where am I? What's happening?'

He was at the head of the stretcher in seconds, leaning down to take her hands, to touch her face, to lean even further so that he could kiss her.

'It's okay, my love. I'm here. I'm looking after you.'

The look that passed between the two of them was something that would stay with Tom for ever. In that moment of lucidity for Maureen, he could feel the strength of the love they'd had between them. A lifetime of memories.

It had gone by the time they got to the emergency department of the hospital and handed Maureen's care over to the receiving team.

'I want to go home,' she told them. 'Please let me go home. I have to find my dog.'

Ed thanked both Joe and Tom for their help as they left a short time later. Tom shook his hand.

'All the best,' he said quietly. 'I can't imagine how hard this is for you.'

'They'll want me to put her in a home,' Ed said. 'But it's not going to happen. Not while I've got breath in my body. And not while there's any chance of those moments.'

Tom nodded. He knew exactly what Ed was talking about. That moment of recognition. Of shared love.

'I heard once that dementia is the longest funeral you'll ever attend,' Ed murmured. 'But if that's the price to pay for all the good years we had together, then I'll pay it. They were worth it.'

Wow…

Tom barely registered that the gorgeous landscape below was even more stunning as the sun was setting on their journey back to the rescue base. His mind—and a large part of his heart—was still with his patient's husband. Thinking about how hard it would be to watch a loved one slip away like that but to still be living. He was also thinking about how many years the couple had had together to build that kind of a loving bond that meant Ed was going to fight to be able to continue caring for Maureen.

He was fighting for the person he loved.

Like Laura was fighting for Harry.

He didn't have anyone like that, Tom realised. Not any more. Nobody close enough to inspire the kind of self-sacrifice Ed was making to fight for his person. It made his life safer, certainly, but…

But, for the first time since he'd lost everything, Tom could feel the empty space around him. The loneliness.

What the heck was going on here? Had he spent the last few years since he'd lost Jenny and Sam in that horrific car accident too numbed by grief to feel things like this? Or had he built protective barriers that were somehow being undermined? There was a common element to the emotional tugs he'd been experiencing recently.

Laura McKenzie.

He felt too connected to someone who was facing the possibility of losing their son. It was her words that were running through his head when he was thinking about the battle Ed was more than willing to fight so that he could keep protecting Maureen.

'You okay, Tom?' Joe's voice almost made Tom jump. 'You're very quiet.'

'I'm always quiet.' Tom threw him a grin. 'Haven't you noticed?'

'True enough. Hey, are you coming to the training session tonight? The coastguard guys want to get us up to speed with their new boat and where to find everything.'

'Absolutely.' It sounded like the perfect antidote to any notion that the loneliness in his life might need to be dealt with. 'I was going to work on a paper but that sounds way more interesting.'

It was late by the time Tom was heading home after attending the training session but he felt good. He'd made the right choice in surrounding himself with base personnel and coastguard crews for the evening and it had been a great opportunity to get on board a rescue ship and learn about how things worked. He was going to keep his fingers crossed that he got a job with the coastguard before too long—like the one Joe had told him about, where he and Maggie had been taken out to a ship to rescue a fisherman with a dislocation and fracture of his elbow.

He was still imagining the excitement of getting

out of the coastguard boat and onto a larger vessel in rough seas when he noticed he was walking past the gates of the Royal on his way back to his apartment. It wasn't that late, Tom thought. He might as well pop into his office and pick up the data he needed to start work on that paper he intended submitting to a medical journal.

It was quiet around the main entrance. A security guard stood just outside the semicircle of glass doors. He clearly recognised Tom but seemed to be unde-cided about whether to say anything.

'How's it going?' Tom asked.

'Fine,' the guard responded. 'For me, anyhow. I'm starting to wonder about her, though. She's been there for a long time. D'ya reckon I should find someone to go and talk to her?'

Tom turned to look in the direction the guard's head tilt indicated. He'd walked right past that fig-ure sitting at the far side of the wide bottom step. Someone who was hunched over, with their head in their hands, looking utterly miserable. Someone with hair that had a reddish gleam to it under the artifi-cial lights.

Oh... God...

It was Laura. And it looked as if she was crying. As if she'd been crying for a very long time.

'I've got this,' he told the guard.

He hoped he did, anyway. Despite his head issu-ing a warning about getting too involved, his heart was overriding the message. He could feel a misery that was close to despair hovering over Laura and it was touching him too close to his own heart. Tom had no idea how he could possibly help if Laura had had more bad news about Harry or something, he just knew that he had to try.

'Hey...' He sat down on the step next to Laura. 'I didn't expect to see you here.'

She raised a tear-streaked face, the expression in her eyes making Tom feel as if a giant hand had just taken hold of his heart and squeezed it hard. Then she groaned and scrubbed at her cheeks with her hands.

'Oh, no... I didn't want anyone to see me like this.'

'What's happened? Has something happened with Harry?'

'No...well...kind of...' But Laura couldn't say anything more. She just shook her head, squeezing her eyes tightly shut in an obvious attempt to stifle any further tears.

Tom tried to think of something that might help. Anything. 'Can I take you home? You must be exhausted.'

'I can't go home.' She was still making a visible effort to control her distress, gulping in some air. 'I have to go back to Harry but...but I can't let him see me like this, either.'

'Is he awake?'

'No...but...'

'You need a break. Coffee, maybe.'

'I can't go into the cafeteria. Not like this...'

'No.' Tom was aware that the security guard was still watching them. Other people arriving had turned to stare, as well. Whatever was happening for Laura right now, it was a private thing. She needed protection. That meant that taking her into his office where people from the emergency department could see her was also not an option.

'Come with me,' he said. 'I know where we can get a coffee. Not far from here, so you can be back in no time.' He held out his hand and tried to sound as encouraging as possible. 'Come on…'

She took his hand. He had only wanted to encourage her to get to her feet but as he led her away, Tom found she was still clinging to his hand. A bit like the way Maureen had clung to it when she'd been so lost and distressed. He could pull his hand free, Tom decided. It was quite possible Laura wasn't even thinking about any implications of the handholding, she was just needing that human contact. But he didn't pull it away. It was only a few minutes' walk to his apartment block, after all.

Besides, he'd forgotten how good it felt to have that comforting sense of connection to another person. He didn't really want to let go just yet.

It had been a lifetime since anybody had held Laura's hand.

Brent's grip had always been a little too tight. Controlling, even. But Tom's hand just felt…solid and warm. Protective. The way her own hand felt to Harry, perhaps, when she took hold of it to cross the road.

Whatever. The sensation of being led and not having to think about where she was going was a welcome relief in the middle of a meltdown that had happened because there were just too many things to think about and they were all just too big. Focusing on putting one foot in front of the other and the warmth of that hand holding hers was allowing her to step away from the overwhelming spin of her thoughts and it felt like that flood of tears was finally drying up.

Until she found herself going through an iron gate towards a small apartment block that clearly didn't contain anything like a café that would be providing coffee at this time of night. Confused, Laura's steps slowed and she pulled her hand away from Tom's.

'Where are you taking me?'

'Home,' he answered. He offered a half-smile. 'That's not a problem, is it? I thought you might appreciate a more private space. And…I can make good coffee.'

Silently, Laura followed him up some steps, through a front door and then into the door on the right. It was an old building and the apartment was spacious, with high ceilings and polished wooden floors scattered with rugs. Shelves overflowing with books and even a guitar propped up in a corner. It looked like a home, she thought as she heard Tom closing the door behind her. A place where a family could spend time together and relax. And, suddenly, that spin of scary thoughts sucked her in like a whirlpool and she burst into tears all over again. Silent, painful tears this time. She had to wrap her arms around herself to try and control the shuddering of her body.

She had her eyes tightly shut but she could feel

how close Tom was. She would never have expected him to take her into his arms like that—not in a million years—but in the depths of the despair she was feeling right now, it didn't matter. It was just…so kind. Offering a whole-body version of that protective handholding. She wasn't going to fall into the abyss while she had someone hanging onto her like this. Letting her rest her head against his chest. Rocking her a little, even. Murmuring something soothing, although she couldn't hear the words, she could just feel the rumble of his voice beneath her ear.

She didn't wrap her arms around him—that would definitely have been a step too far but this seemed to be okay, even when she could feel Tom's hand moving in small circles on her back. It was simply one human being offering comfort to another.

The fact that she was beginning to wonder about how appropriate this was meant that Laura was finally escaping the whirlpool in her head. She could actually feel control returning, as if she was mentally pushing things into place and slamming doors. She moved physically, as well, and Tom released his hold on her body the instant he felt her muscles tense.

'Can I call someone for you?' he asked. 'Someone you could talk to, like Maggie or Fizz?'

Laura shook her head. 'I'm not going to disturb them at this time of night. If they're not asleep by now, they're probably wishing they were.' She tried to find a smile but she could feel embarrassment creeping in rapidly as she remembered where she'd been only moments before. Wrapped in Tom Chapman's arms? She'd never even seen him hug anyone. 'And… I'm sorry about that.' She looked away so that she couldn't catch his gaze. 'I guess it was just a case of the straw that broke the camel's back. I'm okay now.' This time she could find something closer to a real smile. 'Or I will be, after a coffee.'

'Onto it.' Tom's tone was brisk—as if he was relieved at the opportunity to change the subject completely. He walked towards the kitchen that opened off the living area. 'Make yourself comfortable, I won't be long.'

But Laura found herself following Tom into the kitchen. Because it felt like something was pulling her to stay close to him. A remnant of the comfort he had provided by holding her when she was crying perhaps. There was a table in the kitchen and a couple of chairs so she sat down and watched as Tom switched on a flash-looking coffee machine and then busied himself with coffee beans and a grinder. In a very short space of time, Laura found a very professional-looking cup of coffee being placed in front of her.

Tom sat down on the other side of the table and, for a minute, there was a slightly awkward silence between them.

'I have to apologise again,' Laura said, finally. 'I can't believe I cried all over you like that.'

'It's okay.' Tom was smiling. 'My shirt's almost dry already, see?' He patted his chest but his smile was fading. 'I'm just sorry to see you so upset. I wish there was something I could do to help.'

'You've done heaps. I might have sat on those steps

for a lot longer if it wasn't for you, and you were right.'

'What about?'

'Needing a break. I haven't been outside the hospital buildings or grounds for days now.'

Another silence fell, less awkward than the first one. It was Tom who broke it.

'You've got a lot to deal with at the moment and it's hard to stay strong all the time by yourself. You've got some very good friends, Laura. Don't feel guilty about leaning on them.'

'Mmm…' Laura scooped a bit of froth from her coffee cup with the teaspoon. 'I can cope, you know. It's just been a lot of things in a very short space of time.'

'Joe mentioned something to me today. About you maybe needing to find somewhere new to live?'

Laura nodded. 'I'll get onto that. It's not a disaster— just bad timing. If I can find something I can afford, it would be so much better to move before Harry's due for surgery. That's if…' Oh, no… Laura could feel tears threatening again.

She picked up the teaspoon again and blinked hard as she focused on the froth still clinging to the edges of her coffee cup but she could feel Tom's gaze on her, like a physical touch. Questioning. Sympathetic. After his kindness, he deserved to know what had caused her meltdown, didn't he?

'I…um…had a meeting with the whole team this afternoon,' she said quietly. 'Our paediatrician, the paediatric oncologist, a radiologist and a nurse—even a social worker. I had a lot of questions, like what would happen if the chemo didn't shrink the tumour enough. If…you know…it didn't look like a complete resection was going to be possible.'

'Oh, Laura…' The tone of Tom's voice brought a huge lump into Laura's throat.

'They said I'm getting ahead of myself and that we can do several cycles of chemo, if necessary, before having to think about something like a transplant, but… I've been doing some research and if Harry needed a transplant I would want to donate part of my liver.' Her breath came out in a huff that was dangerously close to a sob. 'I'd give him the whole thing if that was going to save his life.'

'Of course you would.'

'But I can't even give him a piece of it and…and I think that's what the final straw was today. With my blood group, I'm not compatible.' She wasn't crying again. She wasn't. There were just leftover tears that were somehow sneaking down her cheeks. 'I'm A. I could only donate to types A or AB. And…and Harry's O. He can only receive a donation from type O.'

Tom sounded a little hesitant but calm. 'I know you said his father wasn't in the picture but…'

Laura shook her head. 'He's dead.'

'And his family?'

'They never knew about Harry. And I don't want them to.'

Tom still sounded calm. Reassuring. He wanted to help fix her problems. 'It might never come to that,

Laura, but if it does, there'll be a donor available. I promise.'

Laura stared at him. A bubble of something like anger was forming in her chest. How could he make a promise like that? How could she keep trusting him as much as she did, if he was going to say whatever it took to reassure her when it might have absolutely no basis in reality?

'How can you say that? You have no idea whether that's true.'

'I can be fairly sure.' Tom held her gaze. 'I know there are other tests that need to be done but the first box has been ticked.'

'What are you talking about?'

'My blood group is O,' Tom said quietly. 'I'm a universal donor.'

Laura just kept staring at him. 'I don't understand,' she said. 'What's that got to do with Harry?'

'I'm saying that, if a transplant is needed at some point in the future, I could do that. I could donate part of my liver to Harry.'

'Why?' The word came out as a whisper. 'Why would you do that for someone you barely know? It's not like donating blood, you know. It's risky. The kind of risk you'd take for your own child, but for someone else's?'

She knew she was searching Tom's face, looking for an answer. Or checking to see whether this incredible offer was genuine? Who was this quiet, clever man she'd been working with for so long? Laura felt like she didn't know him at all in this moment.

'Maybe that's why,' Tom said softly. 'I can't do it for my own child because I lost Sam a long time ago—in the same car accident that killed my wife.'

'Oh, my God, Tom... I'm so sorry... How could I have not known that?'

'It's not something I talk about. I find life's easier that way.'

The ground had just shifted beneath Laura's feet. He really did understand what she was facing. He'd been in an even worse space himself. She desperately wanted to reach out and touch him and her hand actually moved on the table but something stopped her. Perhaps it was because his words were personal enough and already breaking an unspoken barrier between them that made this space feel fragile. It felt like touching Tom when he was stepping into the new space for the first time might be enough to push him back into hiding.

'That's...unimaginable,' she said slowly. 'How old was he?'

She could see the muscles move in Tom's neck, which made it look as if it was painful to swallow. 'He was two. And it was about four years ago so that would make him about the same age as Harry if he was still alive.'

Laura closed her eyes. She was thinking back to that conversation she'd had with Tom in his office that day. When she'd had the impression that he really understood what she was going through as she'd grappled with Harry's diagnosis and upcoming treatment. How personal it had felt.

Of course it had. He must have been struggling with his own memories of losing a child.

'I don't know what to say,' she said softly. 'Except that I'm so sorry that it happened.'

'Yeah…me, too.' Tom said. 'I'm used to life on my own now, but I still miss them every day. Jenny. And my Sam.'

It didn't seem to matter that Laura hadn't reached out to touch Tom in any way. The eye contact they were sharing was having the same effect.

Connecting them.

As parents. Acknowledging the depth of love you had for your child. As medical professionals, as well, knowing the lengths that you would go to in order to save a child's life. And perhaps there was something else connecting them now that had never been there before.

Something that had been born in that bubble of time when Tom had been holding her in his arms and letting her cry. Laura wasn't at all sure what it was but she could feel its presence. Something fundamental had changed between them. The barriers that kept personal things safely enclosed were shifting. Getting blurred. It almost felt as if she and Tom were becoming real friends rather than simply colleagues but, on top of everything else she was grappling with emotionally, it was too much to think about at the moment.

'I'd better get back to the hospital,' she said. 'I don't want Harry waking up to find I'm not there.'

'I'll walk back with you.'

Laura opened her mouth to protest. To tell him that she was perfectly capable of walking by herself and to pull her cloak of independence more tightly into place, but the words failed to emerge. Because the cells in her skin were reminding her of what it had felt like when Tom had taken her hand as he'd led her away from the Royal's front steps. Of how protected she had felt when she'd been in his arms. Not that she was going to hold his hand on the way back, mind you, but if he wanted to offer his protection— how could she refuse?

It was heartbreaking that he didn't have the people he really wanted to protect in his life any more.

'That would be great,' was what Laura said instead as she got to her feet. 'Thanks, Tom.'

CHAPTER FOUR

NOTHING WAS QUITE the same.

On the one hand, it felt wonderful to be back in the emergency department of the Royal for the first shift that Laura had managed to roster since Harry had become sick. It was a slice of "normal" in a life that had been turned upside down and was still being shaken at regular intervals. More importantly, it was a slice of normal for Harry. He'd been itching to get back to school and see his friends and he seemed to be tolerating this first cycle of chemotherapy so well it had been decided he could try a return to school and he was loving it.

The staff of both the school and its aftercare facility were being incredibly supportive and, as she'd donned her scrubs and walked through into the working space she loved so much, Laura realised just how valuable this was going to be to her own mental health as a distraction from everything else going on in her life at the moment. She just had to try and put this new tension to one side so that it didn't interfere with her focus on patients—the tension that was caused by her half expecting a call at any moment to say that she needed to be with Harry because he had suddenly become very unwell again.

At least she could put it to one side here and she hadn't been able to do that at home in the few days since Harry had been building up the time he spent at school. He might have been out of sight for an increasing number of hours but he'd never been out of her mind. Not even for a minute.

She'd spent the last ten minutes focusing completely on six-month-old Alfie, however, and hadn't thought about Harry at all. She'd been too busy taking the baby's vital signs again and reassuring the anxious mother that a doctor would be available very soon to examine her son.

That it was Tom Chapman who came into the cubicle made Laura aware of something else that was different about being back at work. They'd always had a great working relationship and had been able to communicate so well that sometimes it didn't even require words, but it felt different now. He had done more than simply look after her the other night when she had been so upset. He had shared a part of his private life with her and, as far as she knew, he'd never shared that with anyone else he worked with and that made her feel trusted. Special.

And because of what he'd shared, Laura could now see Tom as a man quite apart from Tom as a doctor and trusted colleague. She could see him as a husband. As a father. As someone who had endured unimaginable grief. And as someone who had extended a hand of kindness to her. Quite literally, in fact, when he'd taken her hand and led her to his home that night.

Even more than any of that, he had actually offered to get himself tested and be available as a living donor if Harry ended up needing a liver transplant. What kind of person did that? Someone selfless. Altruistic. Possibly the kindest person on earth so the warmth that Laura was feeling towards Tom was really not surprising at all. It was, however, a significant shake-up in her life on top of everything else. A not unpleasant shake-up, mind you. It was just that Laura didn't ever feel like this any more. Not when a man was involved, that is. A single man.

She'd never had the slightest desire to look for another relationship after Brent had vanished from her life. That was partly because her baby had become the centre of her life and she had told herself that was all she needed, but the real reason had more to do with the damage that had been done to her self-esteem. There were only so many times you could be told that you were stupid or ugly or that everything was your fault before you started believing it.

And, even if she'd had moments of knowing it wasn't true and of believing in herself, there was the inescapable fact that she had fallen in love with Brent and then stayed with him for far too long, believing in those apologies and promises that it would never happen again. It had been preferable to stay single than to risk trusting her own judgement when it came to men. Imperative, actually, because it wasn't just herself that she'd be putting at risk if she got things so badly wrong again and there was no way Laura would ever, ever put Harry at risk.

Ever since she had freed herself from her disastrous relationship with Brent, even an appreciative look, let alone an invitation for a date, had been enough to raise her hackles and prompt her to reinforce her protective barriers. Any attempts to let a friendship develop with a single male had always failed because they always ended up wanting more than friendship so it had become an automatic way of life not to let men close. It had been so many years since she Laura had felt this kind of warmth for a man that just thinking about them, let alone being physically close to them, could provoke, but she was feeling it now as Tom came closer.

Not that it was hard to hide it, thank goodness. This was a professional setting after all and, even if it wasn't, Laura knew that Tom would not welcome any move on her part to demonstrate her new appreciation of him as a person. She could actually sense the slight tension in the air between them, as if he was expecting her to do or say something unwelcome. He might have held her hand when she'd been blinded enough by her tears to not see where she was going properly, but there'd been a perfectly normal distance between them when he'd walked her back to the hospital. He wouldn't even talk any more about his offer of being a donor.

It might never come to that, he'd said. *So we don't have to talk about it any more at the moment and I'd really prefer it if no one else knows about this. Let's just wait and see.*

It was hardly surprising, though, that Laura had such a squeeze happening around her heart when she saw Tom being so gentle with little Alfie, as he took the baby from his mother's arms and laid him on the bed beside her. The knowledge that he had been a father himself couldn't be shut away and ignored.

'It's okay, little man,' he said. 'We just want to find out what's making you unhappy.' He glanced over his shoulder at Laura, one eyebrow raised.

'Blood pressure, heart and respiration rate and temperature all within normal limits,' she told him. 'He hasn't vomited again but he was sick four times at home this morning.'

Tom turned his glance to Alfie's mother. 'Does he seem more lethargic to you at the moment? Is this his normal colour?'

'No. He looks really pale to me. And he's kind of floppy… He's never usually this quiet. And he was screaming his head off all morning. It sounded different, too…'

'In what way?'

'I don't know. Kind of high-pitched, I guess. As if he was really in pain. And he was pulling his legs up. I've read online that that's supposed to mean they've got a sore tummy. That was when I got really worried and decided to come here.'

Baby Alfie had caught Tom's thumb and wrapped his tiny fingers around it. Tom's face softened.

'Wotcha got, little man?'

He joggled his hand, which made Alfie's arm bounce and made the baby smile for the first time A toothless grin that made Tom smile back and Laura could feel another squeeze on her heart. He would have been like this with his own baby once. Delighting in every smile. Comforting him when he was distressed. Having dreams of the future when he would be playing with a toddler who was taking his first steps or a child who could run and kick a football or a teenager, maybe, who wanted to learn to drive a car. Dreams that Laura had had with Harry and she was still clinging to them.

She couldn't afford to let herself imagine how devastating it would be to have them ripped away from her, the way they had been for Tom. He hadn't just lost his child, either, he'd also lost the woman he'd loved enough to marry and promise to spend the rest of his life with. Laura's heart had been aching for Tom ever since he'd told her that small part of his story. How hard was it for him to deal with babies and children as patients?

He seemed to be coping just fine with Alfie. Enjoying it, even. He had retrieved his thumb and was gently examining the baby's abdomen.

'It's nice and soft,' he told Alfie's mother. 'I can't feel anything that could be a problem and it's not upsetting him enough to make me think he's in any pain at the moment.'

'He seems so much better,' she said. 'I hope I'm not wasting everybody's time by having brought him in.'

'Not at all.' It was Laura who stepped in to reassure her. 'We always take notice of a mother's instinct about how unwell her baby is.'

Like Tom had done that day she'd brought Harry in. In that last bit of time before her world had tipped upside down. He'd been so good with her little boy that day, as well, winning his heart almost instantly by bonding over dinosaurs. It said a lot about him that he could interact so well with his youngest patients. Surely there had to have been a time when it must have been the most difficult thing in the world to do.

'You did exactly the right thing,' Tom agreed. 'We're going to keep our eye on Alfie for a while and do some tests to rule out any kind of infection. I'm afraid that means a blood test but we'll be as quick and gentle as we can.'

'The anaesthetic cream has only been on for twenty minutes or so,' Laura said. 'It'll take an hour to be really effective.'

'Oh…okay. We'll leave it a bit longer then.'

Tom's glance told Laura that he wanted a careful eye to be kept on Alfie. Her smile and nod told him she would let him know if anything changed. It was a very familiar sort of communication between them.

But it felt different. Bigger, somehow. Special…

Well, that was a bit of a relief.

Tom had wondered, since the last time he'd seen Laura, whether telling her about his tragic past or making that somewhat impulsive offer about being a living donor for Harry would affect their working relationship in some way. He fully expected that it would, by giving them the kind of personal ground that he'd avoided so carefully for so many years with any of his colleagues. Even without inviting a woman to share any part of his private life, he was often on the receiving end of a look he'd come to know all too well. That invitation to share a lot more than simply a conversation. It would be such a disappointment if he ever saw a glimmer of that look in Laura McKenzie's eyes.

He'd shocked himself a little, to be honest, by making that offer of being a donor, but he'd given it a lot of thought since then and he hadn't changed his mind, even after reading up on the extensive check-ups he would need to determine his own state of health, the potential complications and how long his recovery could take. It still felt like the right thing to do because Tom could imagine how it might have made the world a much better place if somebody had been able to do something to try and save his own son's life.

It wasn't that he was singling out Laura, or Harry for that matter, as being particularly special in his life, it was just that the opportunity was here in front of him. A little boy had been lost but he could do something to save another little boy. An act to balance a tiny part of the universe, perhaps, and move on with his own healing.

Quite apart from never wanting Laura to look at him with any hint of sexual interest, he didn't want her premature gratitude for something that might never happen, either. He didn't want her sympathy for the huge loss he had suffered in his life and he certainly didn't want her looking at him when he was dealing with babies and children and wondering whether it reminded him of what he'd lost. Of course it did at times. In the early days it had been unbearable but that was precisely how Tom had learned to control what he was allowed to think about and, more importantly, the feelings he was allowed to acknowledge. If he hadn't, he felt like he might not have survived.

It had been there the day that Laura had brought Harry into the emergency department here. And it was here, to some extent, when he was examining baby Alfie simply because of that background concern that Laura might have read too much into the fact that he'd taken her home to give her a break from the hospital. That he'd held her hand. And especially that he'd made an offer that was clearly above and beyond what most colleagues would do for each other.

But, if anything had changed, it hadn't made Laura look at him in any way that had made alarm bells of any kind ring and that was definitely a relief. A big relief. She was looking a little more tired than usual, perhaps—and who wouldn't with the amount of stress she was still dealing with—but their working relationship appeared to be exactly what it had always been. They could even communicate by no more than a glance, like when he'd wanted to tell her to keep a very close eye on this baby but he hadn't wanted to alarm Alfie's mother by saying anything aloud.

She was there to hold Alfie's little arm still when he went back to take the blood sample. Working together on the delicate task of inserting a cannula into such a small vein and getting the sample they needed made Tom relax even more concerning their professional relationship and hopefully that would extend to any personal relationship, as well. Nothing had really changed. He could even dismiss that nagging memory of how he'd felt during that conversation in his office that day and that it could have been responsible for that new, unwelcome notion that his life was lonely.

He still felt safe with Laura and that was enough of a relief to put a smile on his face when she came into the staffroom just as he'd finally found a chance to go and grab a cup of coffee.

'Tom? Have you got a minute?'

He could hear the note of urgency in her voice and instantly abandoned his hot drink. 'Of course. What is it?'

'Alfie. He's clearly in pain again and I've just found a significant amount of blood and mucus in his nappy.'

'Sounds like it could be intussusception.'

'That's what I was thinking. Shall I get the portable ultrasound machine? Or call the radiographer for an X-ray?'

'Let's have another look at him. And chase up any blood results in case it's an infection we're dealing with.'

There were no smiles from Alfie this time, and his mother was looking just as distressed.

'He seemed to be feeling so much better...'

'The symptoms can be intermittent,' Tom explained. 'It's looking like this could be what's called an intussusception. It's where a part of the intestine folds inside another part—like a telescope—and causes an obstruction.'

'Is it dangerous?'

'Only if it's left untreated, and the earlier we deal with it the better. There's an enema intervention that could mean he won't need surgery but I'm going to call a paediatric surgeon in for a consultation and it'll be their call what happens next. Try not to worry too much. I'm going to give Alfie something to help the pain and Laura's going to look after you until the paediatric team takes over. You're lucky—you've got our best nurse to take care of you both.'

Maybe the casual compliment had been a subconscious test. When he received only a subtle headshake and hint of a smile, rather than any significant eye contact, Tom knew he was right to feel safe. He had this—whatever it was between them that didn't quite fit within professional boundaries—completely under control. Okay, Harry—and his mother—had got under his skin more than he normally allowed because there was some kind of connection there, but he could still keep a safe distance. It didn't mean that he was making a big mistake in offering the kind of support that being a potential donor entailed. Or that he had to stamp on any urges to do whatever else he might be able to do to help Laura.

Yes, it had been disturbing, during that oddly intimate end to his conversation with Laura in his office, to feel that pull towards the kind of space where you loved someone enough to do whatever was necessary to fight for them. The kind of space he'd inhabited when he'd had his own small family and one that he had been quite sure he would never be in again. A space he didn't even want to risk getting close to because he never wanted to risk having to climb out of that abyss of loss ever again.

But keeping a safe distance didn't mean that he wasn't allowed to care a little more than usual in this case, did it? Or that he couldn't allow himself to be involved? He would know if he was getting too involved and then all he would need to do would be to step back.

Yep. He had this pegged. He was at a new stage in his life, perhaps, where part of him had healed. Or scarred over enough to offer him all the protection he needed. You could help someone build a house, for example, he reasoned to himself. You could even wish that things were different and you could live in a house again yourself, instead of being isolated in a small apartment. It didn't mean that you had to move in and live with them, however, and it would not change the knowledge of where you now belonged. But you could visit, if that person was a trusted friend.

That's what had changed.

It felt like he and Laura had become friends.

'They've taken Alfie to Theatre.' Laura was pleased to see that Tom had finally found a moment to make himself a fresh cup of coffee. She reached for a mug from the staffroom cupboard herself, dropped in a teabag and poured boiling water on top. 'I'll try and pop up to see his mum and find out how it went before I go to pick up Harry. How long will the surgery take, do you think?'

'That will depend on whether there's any intestinal damage that needs to be removed.' Tom glanced up at the wall clock. 'It could well take longer than you might expect. I was planning to follow up on the case myself. I can let you know the next time you're on duty, if you like.'

'That would be awesome.' Laura added a splash of milk to her tea and then sat down and took a sip.

'When are you working again?'

'Not sure. This will have been Harry's longest day at school today so I'll see how it went. We've got a session in the oncology day unit tomorrow for another infusion, too, so that might change things.'

'How's he doing?'

'Remarkably well. He gets tired and there are some foods that make him feel sick but the side effects are pretty well controlled. He is starting to lose his hair, though, and he's worried that the kids are going to tease him.'

'Hmm…'

It was no more than a sympathetic sound. Tom wasn't even looking at Laura when he made it—he was peering into his mug as if to check how much coffee he had left—but she felt the sound resonate as it travelled a lot further than simply her ears. She could feel it expanding inside her body and triggering one of those waves of warmth.

'Let me know if there's anything I can do to help,' he added. 'Anything at all, okay?'

The sincerity in his tone gave Laura a lump in her throat. This was getting a bit weird. Tom wasn't even a friend, really. She shouldn't be feeling this…close.

But then he looked up and there was something different about the way he was looking at her. They were so used to having those lightning-fast, silent communications about professional things. It wasn't the first time they'd had one on a more personal level, though, Laura realised. There might not have been clear words involved in the way he'd looked at her in his office that day but she'd been right in knowing that he did understand exactly where she was com-ing from.

And, way back, there'd been that time when they had first been working together when she'd let him know that she understood how much he disliked women coming on to him in any way and, in that mo-ment, the trust between them had probably been born.

This message was something very different. It was acknowledging that they were closer than they had been but there was nothing remotely threatening in that look that might have reminded Laura why it never worked to be friends with a single male. He might be seeing her as more than a colleague now but it would never be as more than a friend. She knew he had his own safety barriers and she could be sure that they weren't going to be taken down any time soon, if ever. He had loved his wife and child so much he was still missing them every day.

She was still safe.

If there'd been a particular moment when the trust between them had been born, she might look back at this moment and realise it was when a friendship had been created.

One that felt like it could last a lifetime.

CHAPTER FIVE

THE RELIEF TOM had been aware of all day made him feel very content with his life as he finally clocked off and headed home after a visit to the paediatric intensive care unit to check on the excellent progress baby Alfie was already making.

As he popped into the supermarket for a few supplies, he reminded himself that Laura would want to know about the baby. He could tell Fizz tomorrow perhaps and she could pass on the positive result. Or he could even take a minute to find her in the oncology day unit, because it really did feel like they were friends now, and not just colleagues.

Perhaps it was making that mental note that made him think about Laura again, as he walked past the bargain bin offerings the supermarket had on display. Or rather it was Harry that he was thinking about now. After what Laura had said about him being worried about losing his hair, the contents of one of those bins caught his eye immediately. It was full to the brim with baseball-style caps. A bright red, with a shiny green dinosaur embroidered on the front. He could tell Laura about these caps when he saw her tomorrow. Better yet, he thought as his steps slowed and he reached into the bin to grab one of the caps, he could take it with him. It would save Laura a trip to a supermarket she probably didn't use and, right now, Tom was imagining the smile that might light up Harry's face if he liked the cap as much as Tom thought he would.

Carrying his bags into his apartment, he noticed the daughter of his elderly neighbour coming out of the door on the other side of the wide corridor.

'Carla! I haven't seen you for a long time. You've had Eileen staying with you since her hip surgery, haven't you? Is she back home now?'

'No.' The middle-aged woman shook her head. 'And it's not going to happen. We've had to move Mum into a retirement village with a good level of care available. I've been here for the last couple of days getting the apartment cleared out and ready.'

'You're going to sell?'

'Eventually. We want to rent it out for the moment, though, and see how that goes.' Carla smiled at Tom. 'You don't know of any nice, quiet, reliable people who are looking to rent a small apartment, do you? It's only got one bedroom but the sunroom can be a spare if it's needed. My kids used to sleep over when they were young. There's even a sandpit in the garden left over from those days, so it's perfect for grandparents.'

Or for a young, single mother, come to that. Tom blinked. This was getting to be a bit of a habit, having Laura popping into his head like this, but having to find a new place to live was one of the issues she was facing at the moment and passing on the information of something ideal being available was the sort of thing a friend should be only too happy to help with.

'I might know someone,' he said slowly. 'How much are you asking for rent?'

Carla named a figure that made him shake his head. 'Ah…that's a shame. I don't think that's within her budget.'

He turned to unlock his door. He could hear Carla locking up behind him and it suddenly sounded like a potential solution for Laura and Harry was being locked away. Not just any solution but one that was perfect at this time—a small apartment that wouldn't require so much time to look after so Laura would have more time to focus on Harry, and it was so close to the hospital for the many visits they were going to have to make. Or in case of any emergency. He would be next door, for that matter, in case of an emergency.

'Carla?'

'Yes?'

'I've got an idea.'

One that was rapidly gaining traction in his head. When Joe had told him about Laura's housing problem and the financial stress she was facing on top of everything else, he'd had to dismiss the idea of helping her because he knew how independent she was and that she could very well be offended by his offer. This time, however, it would be possible to keep it secret. For a while, anyway. Hopefully until this incredibly difficult patch of her life had been dealt with and after that…well, he didn't need to worry about that yet.

'It's a bit unusual,' he warned Carla, 'but you might be able to help me help someone else who really deserves a break. If you've got a minute, come in and I'll tell you all about her.'

'Is she a friend of yours?'

'We work together. She's a very impressive young woman and…'

Tom paused for a moment as he thought about how much he trusted Laura McKenzie and how today had proved that that trust was not misplaced. Of course something had changed between them by him stepping out of his comfort zone in order to offer her support. By holding her when she'd been so upset and by trusting her with his own personal story. But he still felt safe with her and he was confident that Laura felt safe with him, too.

'Yes,' he added firmly. 'She is a friend. And I know that she would be a perfect tenant. I just need to find out if she would be interested in living here.'

It wasn't far to go to find the paediatric oncology day unit in one of the Royal's wings when Tom had a break during his shift the next day. He had expected this area to be a very child-friendly space, with murals on the walls and bright colours everywhere. He hadn't expected to find Harry in a playroom surrounded by toys, games and other children, with his IV infusion on a pole that he could push around himself.

He also hadn't expected that Harry would recognise him. Or that he'd have a smile, albeit a bit shy, on his face even before he saw the gift that Tom had scrunched up in his hand. Laura was smiling too but her eyebrows were raised.

'What brings you here, Tom?'

'A few things,' he admitted. 'Firstly, I found something I thought Harry might like.' He shook the cap to restore its shape and then put it on his own head. 'It's a bit small for me, isn't it?'

Harry was grinning as he nodded.

'Do you think it might fit you?'

The nod became more enthusiastic so Tom put it on Harry's head. He tugged it into place and then looked up at his mother.

'It's gorgeous,' she said. 'And you know what? I think your teacher might let you wear it to school. How cool would that be?'

Tom couldn't help noticing that Laura's eyes looked shinier than normal when she caught his gaze over the top of Harry's head and mouthed, *Thank you*. He had to clear his throat. And then he shrugged so as not to make Harry's hair loss a big thing. Or to make too much out of the small gift.

'I also wanted to let you know that our intussusception case from yesterday is doing very well. It got caught before there was any major intestinal damage.'

'That's good to hear.' But Laura's attention was still on Harry, who had taken his cap off to look at the dinosaur embroidery and was now pulling it firmly back over what remained of his wispy hair. He walked off, pushing his IV trolley to where another small boy was watching a video on a television screen in the corner of the playroom.

'There was something else, too.'

'Oh?' Maybe Laura could hear the slightly tentative note in Tom's voice, because her eyes darkened a little.

'You remember my apartment block?'

'Um…yes?' Her gaze slid away from his instantly.

'What did you think of it? As a place to live, I mean?'

Laura was frowning now. 'I didn't take that much notice, to be honest. But it seemed nice. And it's nice and handy for work for you. Why do you ask?'

'Because there's an apartment that's become available to rent and…and I know you're looking for somewhere smaller for you and Harry.'

Laura's breath came out in a huff of amusement.

'You're in a pretty exclusive part of town, Tom. I'd never be able to afford to live there.'

'You might be surprised. I think the rent is quite reasonable, actually.' Tom told her the amount he and Carla had agreed was believable and Laura's jaw dropped.

'No way…that's no more than I was paying for my room when we had four people living at my place.'

It was Tom's turn to avoid looking directly at Laura. 'Well…just between you and me, I know Carla would ask more from someone else. She's more interested in having a reliable and careful tenant and I told her that I might know just the person. A friend of mine that I'd be happy to recommend.'

Laura's mouth opened and then closed again. She was absorbing the word, wasn't she?

Friend. It had felt good to say it aloud but was he overstepping a boundary?

Apparently not.

'At that price I'd be very stupid not to be interested,' Laura said. 'It's perfect timing, too. With Harry only just starting his second cycle of chemo, we've got a bit of time up our sleeves to make a shift and get settled.'

'Here's Carla's card. She's the owner. The place is ready to go so she's keen to get a tenant in as soon as possible. She'll be delighted to hear from you.'

'Thanks…' She took the card. 'Maybe Harry and I can go and have a look at it on our way home this afternoon.' She glanced over to where Harry was sitting on the floor. 'And thanks again for the cap. It was a brilliant idea and I know he loves it. He'll probably want to sleep in it for ever.'

'It looks as though Harry has been sleeping in that cap.'

'He has. It's his most treasured possession.' Laura unwrapped another mug from the sheet of newspaper and reached up to put it in the kitchen cupboard of her new apartment. 'Apart from his new sandpit, of course. As soon as he saw that, I knew I had to sign up for this place. He's got every one of his plastic dinosaurs out there already.'

'I saw him out there. It's nice to have the doors of the sunroom opening into the garden, isn't it?'

'It's a perfect bedroom for Harry.'

'You might want to check where we've put his bed.'

'You were so lucky to find this place.' Maggie pulled a potato masher from one of the stacked boxes. Baby Bella was asleep in her car seat beneath the kitchen table. 'What drawer does this go in?'

'The one under the cooktop. And it was Tom who found the apartment.'

'Good job, Tom.'

'It was hard to miss when I live right across the hall.' But Tom was enjoying the appreciation from both Laura and Maggie. Especially that smile from Laura. He hadn't her seen smile like that in a long time and the fact that he had made her life a bit happier made him feel very pleased with himself. He was enjoying a bit of a physical workout, as well, helping Joe shift the heavier pieces of furniture Laura was moving into her new apartment.

'Come on, Tom…' Joe was calling from the living room. 'You haven't earned your beer yet, mate. We need to empty this van. There's a couch calling.'

Mate…

It felt good to be part of this group, doing something that had nothing to do with work. Maybe he hadn't actually realised how isolated he'd made himself over the last few years. Or maybe this was just confirmation that he'd been right in thinking he'd finally dealt with his grief enough to be able to let people a bit closer. To step back into a life that would offer more than just work.

When Cooper and Fizz arrived with baby Harley, it felt like a party was happening.

'Sorry we couldn't get here early enough to help with the heavy stuff,' Cooper apologised. 'But some of us had to work.'

'You've brought the food.' Laura was beaming at the new arrivals. 'I can't believe we're having a taco night for our housewarming. It's been way too long.'

Tom eyed the cooler in Cooper's arms. 'Really? Like the tacos you had for your wedding breakfast?' The unconventional feast had been memorable. 'They were fantastic.'

'It became a flat tradition,' Laura explained. 'We got into the habit of taco nights once a week and anyone who wasn't on shift was welcome. You should have let us know you were a fan.'

Tom just smiled. Even a few months ago he would have shied away from being part of a group like this. It was Harry that had been the catalyst for change. The jolt of feeling connected to a small boy who was potentially sick enough to be in danger had oddly not sucked him back into his past but pushed him forward into becoming more involved with people around him.

He hadn't expected that the change would have

affected him so much but he was happier than he remembered being in a very long time. If he had to define the change, he'd say that he was feeling more alive with every passing week.

He'd needed people in his life. People that were more than simply work colleagues. He had walled himself off for so long, he'd clearly forgotten how important friends were.

Tom could still see through the open doors of the sunroom into the small, courtyard garden. An old tractor tyre had been used to create the sandpit in the corner of the garden and Harry had his dinosaurs lined up around the edge of it at the moment.

'You must have finished the second round of chemo by now,' he said to Laura.

'We have. And the AFP levels have fallen more than expected.'

'That's good news.' Alpha-fetoprotein levels were an important marker in monitoring treatment in liver cancer.

'It is. We've got another scan scheduled at the end of this week.'

'Oh, wow!' Fizz turned to join in the conversation. 'Does that mean that surgery could be close?'

Laura nodded. She was smiling but everyone could see that it was enough of an effort to look wobbly. It was such a double-edged sword, wasn't it? The surgery was the best hope for curing Harry completely but it wasn't something anyone wanted their child to have to go through.

'Oh, hon...' Maggie came out of the kitchen and

wrapped her arms around her friend. 'It's going to be okay, you'll see.

'What's wrong with Mummy?' Nobody had seen Harry come inside and he was standing in the doorway, with two very sandy plastic toys in his hands.

'Oh…' Laura swiped under her eyes with her fingers. 'I'm just happy, sweetheart. We've got a lovely new house to live in and…guess what?'

'What?' Harry sounded suspicious. He edged closer to where Tom was standing.

'Cooper and Fizz have brought tacos for dinner. You love tacos, don't you?'

'Not tomatoes.' Harry took another step closer to Tom as if he was looking for some kind of protection. 'I hate tomatoes.'

'Me, too,' Tom said. 'Unless they're cooked. Raw tomatoes are kind of slimy.'

Harry looked up at him, tilting his head so far back his cap almost fell off, his mouth open with astonishment. His dark eyes looked huge, probably because they were such a focus in that small, pale face that had no hair to frame it now. But then the sides of his mouth curled up into a smile that made Tom's throat feel oddly tight.

It wasn't just a group of adult friends he'd been accepted into. This little boy thought he was okay, too, and that was enough to almost make Tom feel proud that he was not fond of raw tomatoes.

Laura was smiling, too. 'You're both excused tomatoes,' she said. 'But not lettuce, okay? Green food is important. Now, come on…' She beckoned Harry. 'Let's get those sandy hands washed.'

Over the next week or two, as Laura and Harry settled into their new home, Laura found that any worries she might have had about living as Tom Chapman's neighbour also settled. It wasn't as if she hadn't lived near workmates before. Maggie and Cooper had both been flatmates and, although they worked for the rescue base and not in the emergency department, she had seen them often enough in a professional setting. And Fizz had been a friend for a long time. It wasn't as if she and Tom were sharing a house, either—only a building—and it seemed as if they weren't even going to see that much of each other given that her hours were all over the place at the moment.

Laura glanced at his front door as she waited for Harry, who had gone back to find the library book he needed to return to school. It was nice knowing that Tom was there. Just across the hallway. That she had a friend nearby, if she needed one. It really did feel like a genuine friendship now. That emotional evening when they'd both shared things that were close to their hearts had opened a door into a space that was something to be treasured. A "friend" space, where it was perfectly safe to love people and care about what was happening in their lives. To help if it was ever needed.

Mind you, that help only seemed to be going in one direction currently. On top of everything else he had already done to help Laura, Tom had not only been directly responsible for solving both her housing and financial issues, he had pitched in and helped with the actual shifting process.

Although…now that Laura thought about it, that day had been the first time that Tom had been included into her wider group of friends in an informal social setting and that had to be a good thing for him, surely? He'd kept himself separate for as long as she'd known him and, while she could understand why he didn't want to let anyone too close, everybody needed friends, whether they realised it or not, so maybe she was helping him, as well. He had certainly seemed happy that day and had formed even more of a bond with Harry over their shared dislike of tomatoes.

'Harry? Hurry up, darling. I can't be late for work.'

He finally appeared, but without a book in his hand.

'Where's your library book? It needs to go back to school.'

'I don't want to go to school today.'

'Why not? Are you feeling sick?'

Harry didn't say anything but he shook his head. And then he reached up and pulled his hat off his head. A woollen beanie today, because someone at school had stolen his dinosaur cap yesterday. He'd cried himself to sleep and it had been hard work to convince him that another hat would be just as good. Now he was crying again.

'I hate this hat,' he sobbed. 'It's itchy…'

Laura looked down at his baldness and her heart broke. She stooped to gather her son into her arms.

'It's okay,' she told him. 'I'm going to ask Tom today where he got your cap and we'll go and find another one after school. It's just for one day. How 'bout I find your summer hat?'

But Harry shook his head again. He sat down by the front door, wrapped his arms around his legs and buried his face. Laura left his schoolbag beside him and sped back into the apartment to look for both the library book and a different hat.

She could hear voices as she came back and slowed down as she spotted Tom crouched down beside Harry. He was wearing a singlet and shorts and trainers and looked as though he'd just come back from an early-morning run. Having never seen him with so much bare skin, her steps faltered even more. This could be a little embarrassing for both of them. She could hear what Tom was saying now.

'Maybe it was because you were cool and some other boy wanted to look just like you.'

'But it was *my* hat.'

'It was. And whoever took it shouldn't have done that and I'm sorry it's made you unhappy, but you know what?'

Harry's intake of breath was a gulp. 'What?'

'I know where those hats come from. And I reckon there'll be another one there. You want me to see if I can find one?'

Laura couldn't hide out of sight any longer or she really would be late this morning. She couldn't pretend not to have heard what Tom was saying, either.

'There's no need to go to that trouble,' she said. 'If

you tell us where to go, we can go after school. I'm finishing before three p.m. today so Harry doesn't need to go to afterschool care today.'

'It's no trouble.' Tom straightened and Laura was even more aware of all that bare skin. She focused on slotting Harry's library book into his schoolbag. 'It came from my supermarket and I'm going there today for groceries anyway. I'm on a day off.'

'I don't want to go to school.' Harry was crying again. 'Not without my special hat. My hat that Tom gave me…'

Laura caught Tom's gaze, trying to apologise for this early-morning inconvenience. But Tom didn't look bothered. He looked as though, like Laura, he was finding a small, bald and unhappy boy a heart-breaking sight.

'Tell you what, buddy. Let's make a deal.' He bent down again. 'You go to school with Mummy now. Mummy can tell me where your school is and when I've done my shopping I'll come to school and give you a new cap.'

Laura was shocked. 'You can't do that.'

'Why not?'

'It's your day off.'

'Which means I get to do exactly what I want.' Tom's gaze held hers a heartbeat longer and she got the message. He wanted to help. Who wouldn't want to help a sick child?

And that look on Harry's face as he looked up at Tom. Hero-worship, that's what it was. Tom was going right into his school, in front of all the other kids, like a knight in shining armour, and make Harry feel like the most special boy in the world. It would make them both feel good, she realised. All that she needed to do was shut down the uncomfortable feeling that she was letting Tom do far too much for them. For *her*. Maybe this was her problem, anyway, because it was so heart-warming to think that others cared and she couldn't afford to let herself start depending on that kind of support because it held the risk of undermining the independence she'd fought so hard to achieve.

Her hesitation made it impossible to protest any further. Harry was tugging at her hand.

'I want Tom to find me the new cap,' he said. 'He knows where the best ones are.' He scrubbed at his nose with his hand. 'Come on, Mummy…it's time to go to school.'

Standing outside the school gates as the bell rang at three-thirty p.m., Laura found she was thinking about Tom Chapman.

Again.

She'd been thinking about him on and off all day. Even though she knew he was having a day off, she'd found herself catching a glimpse of a tall, male figure in scrubs and feeling a beat of disappointment that it wasn't Tom. She'd been watching the clock, too, and wondering whether that precious replacement hat had been delivered in time for playtime. Or the lunch break. She'd warned the teacher that a strange man would be coming to find Harry at some point and, when she'd explained why, Harry's teacher had been delighted.

'Oh...what a lovely thing to do,' she'd said. *'We were all so upset when we couldn't find Harry's special cap yesterday.'*

She'd thought of Tom again when a young boy had come in with a broken arm from falling off his scooter. His mother was carrying a baby and that made her remember Tom and how gentle he'd been with baby Alfie. As it had then, thinking about him produced that lovely warmth that squeezed her heart and then trickled into the rest of her body.

Laura even wrapped her arms around herself, as if to hold onto that warmth, as she watched for the junior school children to start pouring out of the doors as the bell rang, heading for the gates and their waiting parents. She'd be able to spot Harry instantly if he was wearing his new bright red and green dinosaur cap. She'd had a moment of real anxiety at work today, wondering if that supermarket might have run out of the caps. Would she still have a sad little boy to try and comfort this afternoon?

No...there he was, running out of the door the moment the bell rang. She could see the red cap even before he got out of the junior school building.

But then Laura could see another red cap. And another.

There was a surprised murmur running through the group of waiting parents. It seemed that every child coming out was wearing a red cap with a green dinosaur on the front. This wasn't a huge school but there had to be at least a hundred children in red caps filling the playground.

The first child to reach her mother was beaming. 'Look at my hat, Mummy.'

'Where did it come from?'

'A man came with a big box. We're all in Harry's club. We're allowed to wear our hats until he's feeling better and his hair grows back again.'

A man...

Laura was fighting back tears as she watched Harry coming towards her, with the proudest smile she had ever seen on his face. He was more than just special. He had a club of his own. Harry's club.

It wasn't just "a man" who'd dreamt this up. It was the nicest man in the world. That warmth that always came when Laura thought about Tom had just exploded into something that was totally overwhelming. He hadn't just totally won a small boy's heart for ever today. He had won a huge part of hers, as well.

She could feel it happening, singing in her veins and filling her heart so much it felt like it could explode.

Laura knew this feeling but recognising it was a shock.

Was she falling in love with Tom Chapman?

CHAPTER SIX

HOW HAD SHE not seen this coming?

The warning signs had been there all along, maybe from that very first connection Laura had felt with Tom which, ironically, had been that neither of them were interested in any kind of personal relationship. The safety net that had provided had been a breeding ground for the kind of trust that would never have been there otherwise.

And then Tom had become involved with Harry and he'd been there when Laura had been grappling with a parent's worst nightmare, facing a challenge that could mean she might lose her precious child. More than that, he understood what that was like because he'd been there himself and, unbelievably, he'd been prepared to risk his own health if it could save the life of a little boy that wasn't even his own.

She probably could have fallen in love with Tom at that moment if she hadn't been so overwhelmed by her own fears. She'd known something had changed between them but had wrapped it up in part of that safety net that made friendship perfectly acceptable and friendship with this particular, single man perfectly safe. Good grief…she had even convinced herself that living as his next-door neighbour wouldn't pose any kind of problems.

'Look, Mummy.' Harry held up a folded sheet of paper. On the outside there was a green shape that was obviously a T Rex and it now had colourful blobs surrounding it that had been covered with glue and then showered with a generous supply of glitter. 'Do you like my flowers?'

'They're gorgeous,' Laura said.

'Is Tom going to like my card?'

'He'll love it. Do you want me to help you with the writing to go inside?'

'No. I want to do it all by myself.'

'How 'bout I write the words on a different piece of paper and then you can copy them?'

'Mmm…' Harry looked up from under the brim of his new cap. ''Kay.'

'What do you want to say?'

'Thank you for my hat. I love you. From Harry.'

Laura swallowed hard. 'That's a lot of words. You could just say "Thank you from Harry" if you didn't want to do so much writing.'

Harry shook his head. 'Write it down, Mummy. What I said.'

Biting her lip, Laura wrote the words in big, clear letters on another piece of paper. She had to close her eyes for a moment after she wrote, 'I love you.' It wasn't the end of the world, was it? She loved her friends Maggie and Fizz and that was never going to be a problem. Maybe she just "loved" Tom and she wasn't actually in danger of being "in love" with him at all.

Harry used a pen and then did his best to copy the letters, working so slowly and carefully they wobbled enough to be only just legible. It was taking a long time, too. Enough time for Laura to let her mind put more effort into dealing with what was going on in her head. Or, possibly, her heart. Thoughts of Tom were never far away these days so it was easy to summon up a bit of a slideshow.

Like that look on his face when she'd told him about Harry's diagnosis. How gentle he'd been examining baby Alfie that day, with those long, clever fingers of his looking so big on such a tiny belly. The way he'd held her hand that night when he'd taken her to his home for coffee and how comforted she had felt being held in his arms. How disconcerted she'd been only this morning to see him in his running gear with all that skin exposed.

And…there it was.

She had some very clear images in her head now, of those surgeon's hands and those long, bare legs and arms—the skin dusted with dark hair and muscles outlined with a faint sheen of perspiration. The effect was that of a match was being scraped against sandpaper to light a tiny thrill of sensation as Laura's body and brain co-operated to make her wonder what it would be like to be touched by those hands. Or to run her own hands over the shape of those muscles.

The pull of desire was so compelling, it actually stole her breath away.

This wasn't the kind of love that happened in a friendship. This was a magnetic pull that was far more powerful than any passing sexual attraction to someone because this had all the weight of a real relationship backing it up. The weight of trust. Of real kindness and caring. It wasn't that, as a single male, Tom had managed to slip past her barriers and into the space that her friends occupied in her heart. He was crashing into an even more private space. One that, until now, had only been occupied by Harry, as the most important person in her life.

And that was not acceptable, was it?

Not now, when Harry had to be the only thing that mattered.

Not ever, if she thought about how Tom would feel if he knew.

'I've finished, Mummy. Look…'

The prickle behind her eyes was pure pride that her little boy had put so much effort into this masterpiece with its spidery words inside.

'It's perfect, sweetheart. Let's get tidied up and then it's time for your bath.'

'But I want to go and give it to Tom.'

'I think he's still at work.' Laura had no idea where Tom actually was. She just knew she couldn't face him right now. What if he could see something in her face or feel the remnants of the kind of heat she had just created by thinking of him like that…?

Laura's heart was sinking fast. This new awareness had to be buried. Any twinge of physical attraction had to be stifled so thoroughly it wouldn't happen again, that's all there was to it. Compared to every other challenge Laura had going on in her life at the moment, surely this one should be completely manageable?

'Tell you what,' she said to Harry. 'We're going to be in the hospital tomorrow for your scan, remember? I can go and put it on his desk and then it'll be a lovely surprise.'

She could see that Harry was torn between wanting to hand over the card but knowing how much he liked surprises himself. The choice he made was a testament to how much of a hero Tom was to him now.

'You can put it on his desk. I think he likes surprises.'

The emergency department of the Royal was extremely busy when Laura took a few minutes away from Harry the next day to go to the ground floor area. The sedation Harry had needed in order to have the MRI scan had worn off but they had to wait for the results of the scan to be discussed and then Laura had an appointment with Suzie the surgeon and Hayley the paediatric oncologist.

Harry was very happy to have some time in the playroom in the paediatric ward, especially when he found that his friend Aroha was there. They curled up on some bean bags in front of the television screen and held hands as they watched a favourite movie, but Laura couldn't sit still with them. She was too nervous about the results she was going to hear about later. Had the chemotherapy shrunk the tumour? Were they going to schedule surgery or start another cycle?

'They're so cute, those two.' A nurse smiled at Laura. 'I'll be in here with them if you want to go for a walk. You look like you could use a distraction.'

So here she was, entering the ED and blinking a little at the controlled chaos she could see. It wasn't that unusual to see police officers or the hospital security guards in here but it advertised that there were potentially uncooperative or violent patients in the department and that was always enough to put Laura on edge. She could hear angry shouting coming from more than one of the cubicles.

On the plus side, with full cubicles and resuscitation areas and staff moving swiftly between too many patients, it was highly unlikely that she'd even be spotted going to Tom's office near the staffroom.

She could drop off Harry's card and be out of here in no time. The sooner the better, as far as she was concerned, because she wasn't quite ready to come face to face with Tom yet and test how difficult it was going to be to stifle how she felt about him now.

One of the junior doctors passed her in the corridor that led to the staffroom. 'You're not working today, are you, Laura?'

'No... I'm only here for two minutes to drop something off.'

'Just as well. It's crazy in here right now.'

'I can see that. What's going on?'

'There was a nasty fight in town between two gangs. We've got a lot of knife wounds and a few broken bones to sort out and some of them are as high as kites on meth or something. They're not exactly happy to be sharing the same ED, either, hence the reinforcements.'

Laura had already been nervous about what was going to be revealed in the meeting with Harry's doctors this afternoon and about whether things between herself and Tom Chapman were about to get awkward. Now she could throw in a dollop of anxiety that was a little too close to fear as the extent of the simmering violence in the department got a whole lot more real.

She took another few steps towards Tom's office but then she stopped dead in her tracks. What if Tom was in his office for some reason instead of out there in the department? Or what if he misinterpreted the thank-you message and thought that Laura might be using her son to get closer to Tom?

This was a bad idea. She could just tell Harry that Tom had loved his card—he didn't need to know that it hadn't actually been delivered, did he? Instead of going into Tom's office, Laura did an about-face. At the end of this corridor, she could turn left to go towards the reception desk in Emergency, right to go through the double doors that led to the main waiting area, or straight ahead to the doors that led into the rest of the hospital. Suddenly Laura couldn't wait to get back to the relative peace of the paediatric ward and to have a cuddle with Harry before she had to go to an appointment that had the potential to change her life again, for better or worse.

Without thinking, she walked purposefully straight ahead, only to find herself in the path of three leather-clad gang members who had obviously got past security in the waiting area and were storming in to find either their friends or their enemies in the treatment area. One of them swore viciously at Laura. Another one grabbed her arm.

'If you know what's good for you, you'll get out of our way, you stupid bitch…'

The grip of his hand on her arm was painful enough for Laura to know it would leave bruises but it was the tone of his voice and his words that made Laura freeze. Words that, if repeated often enough, became almost believable.

'You're so stupid…'

'It's your own fault, you ugly cow…'

'Just get out of my way…'

Words that took her back in time instantly. She was about to be shaken. Or hurt. Or pushed down a set of stairs that would threaten both her own life and that of the baby she was carrying. Part of her knew perfectly well that this was only a flashback but it felt utterly real. Worse, even, because another part of her mind was telling her that these men could well be carrying knives or other weapons. She might be about to die and there was a silent scream in her head that was a name. A plea, perhaps.

Harry…

The huge man had both his hands on her now and

Laura could feel the pure rage transferring itself into his grip and the force of the sideways shove that sent her flying, pushing against a stainless-steel trolley that crashed sideways with the sound of breaking glass. Through the blur of the noise and movement and her terror, she could sense action amongst the shouting around her and could see uniformed men converging on the group of intruders. It wasn't one of the policemen or security guards that broke her fall, however. It was one of the staff members in blue scrubs.

'Laura… Oh, my God, are you all right?'

It was Tom.

Tom, who was one of the people that Laura trusted the most in the world but right now he was gripping her arms to steady her balance and she hadn't yet processed the terror that the gang member had instilled.

'Let me go…' She could hear the panic in her own voice. 'Let me *go*…'

He let go instantly. Behind him, Laura could see that the gang members were being forcibly removed from the department but the damage had been done for Laura. She was shaking like a leaf. When her gaze raked Tom's face a heartbeat later, he was looking shocked enough for her to know that he was seeing far more than he should in her face.

Not what she'd been afraid he might see—that she'd thought she might be falling in love with him—but something much darker. Something she didn't want anybody to know about because she was so ashamed of that part of her past.

'I'm fine,' she told Tom. 'It was my fault—I wasn't looking where I was going.'

Oh, help...even her voice was weak and shaky. Laura pressed her hands to her forehead as she tried to take a deep breath. She hadn't actually been hurt in any way. She was overreacting and Tom wasn't the only person who was staring at her.

Somehow Laura gathered the strength she needed to lift her chin and raise her voice.

'I shouldn't even be in here.' She gave her head a sharp shake. She even managed a huff of something like laughter. 'I'm due in Paediatrics for an appointment with Harry's doctors. I've really got to go...'

She turned and took a step. And then another. From the corner of her eye she could see the way Tom was stretching out his hand as if he'd wanted to prevent her leaving just yet but nothing was going to stop her getting out of there.

It was all she could do not to start running, in fact.

He couldn't get it out of his head.

That look in Laura's eyes. That note of pure fear in her voice. She'd been afraid. He had felt that tension in her body as he had held her arms to make sure she had regained her balance. The very idea of her being so scared had been shocking. Yes, she'd just had a nasty fright by being abused by those gang members, but he had been the one holding onto her then and she had seemed just as terrified. Of *him*?

Tom couldn't understand it.

He'd known since he'd first met Laura that she had

barriers up in her personal life and it had been a good thing for him because it meant that she was safe to work with. To be a friend, even, and it had been such a pleasure to be able to help her—and Harry. To finally able to be close enough to someone to feel connected and involved had added something to his life that he knew was important. Ever since Laura had brought Harry into the emergency department that day, Tom had known he was being pulled back into an engagement with life that was on a different—and more meaningful—level than the way he'd been living for the last few years.

It was bewildering to think that Laura could be afraid of him in any way.

Disturbing.

Unacceptable.

He needed to find out what was going on here. And to reassure Laura that she could trust him.

It was nearly nine o'clock that evening before Tom got home. He hadn't eaten but he wasn't hungry. He wouldn't be hungry, he decided, until he had found some answers to the questions that had been plaguing him since the incident in the department.

He knocked softly on Laura's door, not wanting to wake Harry if he was asleep. The moment she opened the door, his immediate thought was that Laura probably needed to be asleep herself. She looked so tired. Pale and…and far more vulnerable than Tom had ever seen her look. Maybe that was partly because her hair was hanging in soft waves to her shoulders instead of being tied up, the way it always was at work. Or perhaps it was because she was wearing an oversized sweatshirt over her jeans and that made her look smaller. Younger.

Whatever it was, it triggered a powerful, protective instinct in Tom and all he wanted to do was to gather her into his arms and stroke her hair and tell her that everything was going to be okay. That he would make sure that everything was going to be okay.

But, of course, he didn't do that. He cleared his throat instead.

'I just wanted to check that you were okay,' he said.

Laura nodded.

'And Harry's okay?'

She nodded again.

'You said that you had a meeting with his doctors this afternoon?'

'Yes.' He could see the muscles in Laura's throat moving as she swallowed hard. 'It was good news. The tumour's shrunk a lot. They're confident that it can be completely resected with surgery.'

Tom took a beat to process that news. It was the best news to have this soon—after only two cycles of chemotherapy. It also meant that Harry would be facing major surgery, probably very soon, however, and that had to be terrifying for Laura.

'How soon?' he asked quietly. 'For the surgery?'

'Next week.' Laura pressed her fingers against her lips as if she wanted to stop them trembling. Or to stop herself bursting into tears.

'It's good news.' Tom found a gentle smile to try and reassure her. 'He's going to get through this.'

Laura nodded again. 'I know… He's not even scared. He's excited by the idea of spending time in hospital because his friend Aroha is having her heart surgery next week, too. They'll be in the ward at the same time.'

'And you? How are you doing?'

'I'm okay.' Her smile was unconvincing. 'It's nice of you to ask.'

'I was worried about you after what happened in ED today.' He tried to hold Laura's gaze, willing her not to look away from him.

She didn't look away but she wasn't saying anything out loud. What was it he could see in her eyes? It felt like some sort of apology, but why?

'You know you can trust me, don't you, Laura?'

Another nod. She still wasn't breaking the eye contact. There was more than an apology to be seen. Now it felt like she was searching for something. And it felt as though he was the only person that might be able to give it to her.

'I know there's something going on that you're not talking about,' he said gently. 'So, talk to me… please. I can't go away until you do because I'm not going to stop worrying.'

The silence was even longer this time, but then Laura stepped back, pulling the door open a little further. 'You'd better come in,' she said.

He'd told her about his past, hadn't he? He'd shared something that she was pretty sure he'd never shared with anyone else so he deserved the same level of trust. Laura knew he'd been shocked this afternoon, as well. That he had seen her fear. She remembered how instantly he'd taken his hands off her body and it occurred to her now that he might have thought she was afraid of him as well as those gang members. He deserved to know that that was the opposite of the truth. That he was probably the person she trusted more than anyone else on earth.

As a bonus, if she needed a test to see if her feelings could be stifled, then here it was. And after the emotional exhaustion of the tension of waiting to hear about Harry's scan and the huge fright she'd got when she'd been pushed around in ED, how she felt about Tom Chapman was only a background buzz. Laura couldn't decide whether that made it rather nice to have him here or whether it was going to be the final straw in a tough day.

'I think I need a glass of wine,' she said, as Tom followed her back into her small living room. 'It's been quite a day.'

'Let me.' Tom took the bottle from her hands and then the corkscrew. 'I'd love one myself. Is Harry asleep?'

Laura took a peek into the sunroom and then quietly shut the door so they wouldn't disturb him. 'Out like a light. It was a big day for him, too. Plus he's still got some sedatives in his bloodstream, I expect.'

She took the glass from Tom and he followed her example to head for the couch. For several minutes, they sat sipping their wine in what started as a companionable silence but then it became loaded. Without even catching his gaze, Laura knew that Tom was waiting for her to say something.

'I guess I kind of overreacted today, didn't I?'

'When you said that what happened was your fault? Yeah…' Tom turned his head and she was forced to meet his gaze. 'I wouldn't say overreacted, exactly. It seemed to me more like a reaction that you might have been forced to have.'

His dark eyes were full of concern. A hint of anger, even?

'It wasn't your fault, Laura. Not in any way, shape or form. You had every right to be there. And, even if you didn't, the only person at fault was the lowlife who assaulted you.'

'Mmm…' Laura took a large swallow of her wine. 'I know that… It's just…'

She could feel Tom's gaze still on her. 'It's just that you've been hurt before, isn't it?'

Laura bit her lip. She didn't want to admit it.

'Was it Harry's father?'

A sideways glance reassured her that Harry was blissfully unaware of anything that was being said out here. 'He wasn't like that to begin with. He was really charming. Easy to fall in love with. But he started drinking more and more and then his mates got him into drugs.'

It sounded like Tom was speaking with a clenched jaw. 'How bad was it?'

'He just got angry a lot at first. Shouted at me. Said a lot of nasty stuff. He made it seem like it was my fault. I was still in love with him so it was easy to be made to feel…I don't know…worthless, I guess. I tried to change. To make it better…'

Tom made a sound like a soft growl. 'As if you would ever need to change, Laura. You're super-smart. Kind. The best mum and…well, look at you. You're gorgeous.'

The praise was more than comforting. Did Tom really believe that? And, if he did, was there actually a possibility that they could end up being closer than just friends? Laura didn't look up to meet his gaze but she was looking at his hands and she could feel the tingle of strong emotions that were gathering force.

Sheer longing. To be touched. Not sexually, neces-sarily—just the contact. She desperately wanted the reassurance that touch could be trusted. That it was safe to love someone, perhaps.

'I only stayed with him as long as I did because he promised to get clean. After I found out I was preg-nant. He said he couldn't do it without my help and I think he really tried, too…but…'

'But?'

'He got high. When I was six months pregnant. He got angry. I…ah…fell down some stairs. That was why Harry was so premature.'

Tom was silent for a long moment. 'You said he was dead when we were talking about finding a donor for Harry if it was needed. Was that true?'

'Yes. He died of an overdose—not long after I'd told him it was over. He was drinking again, just be-fore Harry was due to come home from the hospital, and I told him I was going to do whatever it took to keep my baby safe from him.'

'And you did.' Tom touched her arm, just letting his hand settle there for a heartbeat, warm and heavy and solid. 'You still are—doing everything to keep your son as safe as possible.'

The physical touch was more a congratulatory gesture than anything else. It shouldn't have made that longing kick up so many notches that it was almost painful. Laura drained the last of the wine in her glass.

'Can I get you another one?'

She shook her head. 'I'd probably fall over. I'm so tired.'

'I'm not surprised.' Tom got to his feet. 'I should go, too.'

Laura stood up, as well. It had to be more the exhaustion and stress of the day that made her wobble slightly because one glass of wine would never do that. It wasn't even that much of a wobble but it was enough for Tom to notice. For him to turn and put his hand on her arm again.

They were so close. Laura could see the thick tangle of Tom's eyelashes, how dark his eyes were, and the concerned frown line between those eyes. For a moment she was transported back to that time in his office when she'd felt as if he understood her fear for her child better than anybody else could. Now it felt as if he understood exactly why she had reacted the way she had to the violent situation in the emergency department today. And that he didn't think she was stupid. Or ugly. Or any of the things that had once undermined her self-esteem so badly. It also looked as though he'd meant every one of those nice things he'd said about her.

'It was never your fault,' Tom said quietly. 'Not back then and not today. You do realise that you deserve so much more than feeling like that, don't you?'

Laura couldn't say anything. She could feel the warmth of Tom's breath on her face and she was fighting the urge to lean closer to his body. Like the touch he'd given her on her arm moments ago, Tom leaned down and gave her a one-armed hug, made slightly awkward by the wineglass he had in his other hand. Laura responded but tilted her head to check where her own wine glass was and somehow her face brushed his.

Or rather her lips brushed his.

Just for a nanosecond, she froze in shock, because that touch was so electric she could feel it throughout her entire body. Almost as fast, however, her head jerked back.

'Oops... Sorry... That wasn't meant to happen.'

Tom was straightening slowly. 'It was my fault, I think. Clumsy.'

Laura shrugged. She found a huff of laughter, even. 'It's like when you try to move aside for someone in the street and they move the same way and you do that awkward little dance.' She took the wineglass from Tom's hand. 'Let me take that. Thanks for popping in to check up on us.'

Us. Because he'd asked about Harry, too. Because they were neighbours. Friends.

She just needed her entire body to shut down that ache. The one that was telling her how much more she wanted from Tom right now. Something that she was never going to get, judging by the way he was avoiding looking directly at her now. He picked up the laptop bag he'd put down when he'd come in.

'You sure you're okay?'

Laura's nod was brisk. 'Just tired.' She needed to be alone. She suspected she might want to have another glass of wine. Or cry. Or to think about that almost, accidental kiss. Probably all of the above. 'Goodnight, Tom.'

CHAPTER SEVEN

WELL…WHO WOULD have thought a single glass of wine could have that much of an effect?

Tom Chapman shut his front door behind him and then leant against it, his hand against his forehead, middle finger and thumb massaging his temples.

Even after a couple of deep breaths, he could still feel it, though.

That…tingle. The first real signs of life in that particular part of his anatomy since he'd been hurled into that world of grief and loss. And, yeah…maybe he'd been aware that it wasn't normal not to have sexual awareness or needs for this long but he'd never bothered seeking any advice or therapy.

Life was easier this way. Like it was to not tell people about his past.

Or it had been, anyway. Until he'd had an ill-advised glass of wine on a completely empty stomach after a somewhat challenging day. Until that moment when Laura had turned her head in an unexpected direction and their lips had brushed each other's. Awakening of any kind of physical needs was not only a bit of a shock, it had been utterly inappropriate, given what Laura had just been telling him about her previous relationship with Harry's father.

Okay…this was better. Tom pushed himself off the wall. He was feeling slightly sick now and he couldn't blame that on a single glass of wine. It was the thought of Laura having been in an abusive relationship that was turning his stomach and there was a central core of anger there, as well. How could anyone have treated her like that? To hurt her… Not just physically, although the implied violence of her having been pushed down some stairs that had ended with Harry's premature birth made that knot of anger white hot. No…it was the more insidious damage that had been done to Laura's self-esteem that was disgusting him.

Any decent human being would be so horrified by that they would want to offer sympathy and reassurance but Tom hadn't just been saying whatever he thought might help. He had believed everything he had said to Laura, especially that she deserved so much more than that. She was an extraordinarily intelligent woman and such a caring mum.

As he put a frozen meal into his microwave and hit the buttons to get his overly late dinner on the way, Tom found himself remembering that day she'd brought Harry into the emergency department. That moment when he'd reached the gap in the curtains around that cubicle and had seen her almost on the bed with Harry, her arm around him and that look of pure love on her face as she smoothed back his hair. He could even feel an echo of that punch in the gut it had given him. The flashback to knowing what it was like to feel that kind of love for your child—and for your partner. To be…a *family*…

It still felt like longing. Hunger, even.

Of course it does, you idiot… Tom shook his head as the microwave pinged and he took out the plastic container. He hadn't eaten since breakfast and his blood sugar had to be rock bottom. It was no wonder his body was given off strange signals.

He needed food. And sleep.

Tomorrow was another day and Tom happened to know that Laura was not rostered on to work.

Which was a good thing, he decided as he took his first mouthful of a sadly unappetising meal. He needed to push a reset button of some kind in his life that would take him back to where things felt normal. And safe. To a time when Laura McKenzie and her son did not occupy this disconcerting amount of space in his head.

Or his heart, for that matter. Like always, when you decided not to think about something so much, it popped into your head with renewed strength and this time, it was that shocking memory of how frightened Laura had looked when he'd caught her arm after she'd been pushed by that thug. And it definitely wasn't his head that was generating such a powerful urge to offer his protection. That could only have come from his heart.

Tom took a moment, during the next afternoon, to congratulate himself on a plan that was definitely coming together. It had been a busy morning in the Royal's emergency department and he hadn't been distracted in any way from doing the best job he could. Life felt perfectly normal.

One case in particular, a challenging multi-trauma from a car that had rolled as it left the road and then wrapped itself around a tree, had kept him and the rest of the resus team flat out for well over an hour as they'd stabilised the young man enough to get him to Theatre.

'It was touch and go, that surgery,' Fizz told Tom when he found her snatching a break in the staffroom. 'He went into cardiac arrest twice.'

'Doesn't surprise me. I was amazed that we got him to Theatre. He must have lost his entire blood volume with that pelvic fracture slicing his artery.'

'He was in Theatre for hours but it sounds like he's stable now. He'll be in Intensive Care for a while, though.'

'I might go and visit later. I'd like to have a chat to the surgeon and see what he found. I'm sure some of that blood loss was coming from other internal injuries but it was hard to tell on the ultrasound. Do you know if they took out his spleen? Or had to repair a liver laceration?'

Fizz shook her head. 'Speaking of livers, did you know that Harry's got his surgery date now? For next week?'

'Oh?' Tom busied himself making peeling off the plastic from a packet of vending machine sandwiches. He didn't want to admit that he'd been talking to

Laura late last evening. Part of today's plan was to try not to even think about it.

'Wednesday.' Fizz nodded. 'I was talking to her last night.'

Tom raised an eyebrow. Had that been before or after his visit? he wondered. And what had the good friends discussed? Maybe Laura had told Fizz that Tom had almost kissed her?

Dammit...that was the one thing he was really trying not to think about and now it was too late. Even as he pushed the thought from his head, he could feel that damned tingle again. At least Fizz didn't seem to think anything was out of the ordinary so maybe Laura hadn't said anything.

'I had a chat to Maggie, too,' Fizz continued. 'We're going to try and arrange things so that one of us can be with her the whole time that Harry's in Theatre. A liver resection can take quite a few hours sometimes.'

'It's a major operation, all right.'

'They're taking his gall bladder out, as well, because the tumour's on the right side of the liver. But they're only taking one section, which is good. It'll probably only take a few weeks to regenerate completely.'

Tom was listening but his attention wasn't a hundred percent. He could still feel the echoes of that tingle. Maybe it was only natural that his body was waking up again after so long. It didn't mean he was going to lose control and end up back in the kind of space that made it possible to fall in love with some-

one and start making plans for a future together. No…
all it meant was that he might need to allow the physical release of sex back into his life and it would be easy enough to do something about that. It wasn't as if he'd ever been short of opportunities.

Like Hannah, there… He returned the smile of the young registrar who had just come into the staffroom. Blonde, blue-eyed and—as far as he knew—single, she had given him the impression for quite a while that she might welcome a chance to spend some time together away from work. He'd need to be careful, of course, and make sure that he was very clear right from the start that he wasn't looking for anything serious or long term.

But…

But Tom realised that that tingle had faded completely in the short space of time that he'd been considering that option. Perhaps it was simply because he'd never been open to the idea of casual sex with colleagues, not even before he'd met and fallen in love with Jenny. He had long ago accepted that he would never have another relationship like that. Did this mean he might have to accept living like a monk for the rest of his life?

'So…do you want to be on the roster?'

'Sorry?' Tom looked up as Fizz pushed her chair back and stood up.

'I heard about the dinosaur caps.' Fizz was smiling at Tom. 'That was such a cool thing to do and it's no wonder Harry thinks you're a super-hero. I thought you might like to be on the roster we're making so that we can make sure that Laura's got all the support she needs while Harry's in hospital and then recuperating at home.'

Tom had a new image in his head now—that smile on Harry's face when he'd turned up at his school with the carton of supermarket baseball caps. Now, that had been special. He could feel the same squeeze in his chest again just remembering it. A mix of something very warm and poignant enough to give him a bit of a lump in his throat but it wasn't a pull back into heart-wrenching territory. It was a positive thing— part of the new involvement with life that might be throwing up some left-field challenges but Tom knew it was healthy. He just needed to give himself time to adjust.

'I'll do whatever I can to help,' he told Fizz. 'You can count on that.'

It was the longest day of Laura's life.

They had warned her how long Harry's surgery might take but what she hadn't been prepared for was that time seemed to slow down so that every minute felt more like an hour and the hours were interminable.

Even after Harry came out of Theatre, it was another couple of hours before he was settled into his bed in the paediatric intensive care unit and the medical team was happy that every monitoring device was functioning perfectly and that the recordings being made were not raising any concerns.

It was only then that Laura could take a breath

and shift into the next phase of this ordeal—the one where she sat beside Harry's bed and kept watch over her precious son. Following every rise and fall of that small chest for the longest time but then letting her gaze rest on his face, searching for any sign that he might be in pain despite the sedation. Becoming attuned to the soft beeps of various monitors, she could be alert for any change in their patterns of sound at the same time.

Harry's nurse came in at very regular intervals to take note of his heart rate and blood pressure and oxygen saturation levels, to check drainage tubes for any sign of haemorrhage and to record fluid input and output. So many things to keep an eye on but she took note, also, of how Laura was coping.

'When did you last have something to eat?'

'I'm really not hungry.'

'Come into the staffroom and have a cup of tea and a biscuit, at least.'

'I'm drinking water. I'm fine.' If anything, Laura edged closer to Harry's bed. 'I can't leave him. Even going to the loo stresses me out. What if he woke up and I wasn't here?'

'That's not going to happen. He's well sedated and I'm checking on him often enough to see any signs of that lifting. We've got his pain management well under control at the moment' Her face creased with concern. 'You need to rest, too, Laura. You know what we always tell the parents—that you've got to look after yourself if you want to be able to do a good job looking after your child.'

'Yeah, yeah… I know. I'll rest, I promise. I've slept in a chair before.'

That had been back in the days when Harry had been in his incubator in the neonatal ICU, mind you— such a tiny baby who shouldn't have needed to struggle because of an untimely entrance to the world. It felt like a lifetime ago but the feeling of being sucked into an occasional doze, giving her brain a brief respite from the exhausting anxiety, was very familiar.

It was in those moments as she slipped towards unconsciousness that Laura remembered—and felt very grateful for—the support her friends had given her throughout this longest ever day. How blessed was she to have so many good friends? Fizz had brought coffee and doughnuts to the waiting area before she'd started work today and Maggie had stayed for hours, with baby Bella snuggled into her sling, being the most perfect baby in the world. Cooper had come in that afternoon, with little Harley, who'd played with the toys in the corner, and Joe had managed to sneak a few minutes to come and visit after delivering a patient to the emergency department.

It had been Tom who had been the last visitor to come and keep her company in that small waiting room and…and it had been fine. There hadn't been the slightest awkwardness left over from the last time they had been alone together when that accidental, almost kiss had happened, despite how often it had replayed itself in Laura's mind since then. Right now, it might never have happened as far as any effect it was having.

It had actually felt astonishingly appropriate that it was Tom who was with her when the surgeon himself came to tell her that it was all over and that the surgery had gone as well as they could have hoped for. It was, after all, Tom who'd been there when the shocking diagnosis had been made in the first place— who'd been responsible, in fact, for it being picked up as early as it had been.

What if someone else had missed feeling that abnormality in that child-sized liver and the cancer had had a whole lot more time to spread? That was something else to be grateful for. Not only that, it was Tom who'd put up his hand to be a potential living donor and that had felt almost like an insurance policy at a time when Laura had been feeling so helpless in not being able to provide that gift herself if it ever became Harry's only hope of a cure.

And...of all people, it was Tom who could really understand the emotion of that moment when she'd heard that the surgery was over and had, apparently, been successful. The connection Laura felt to Tom had never been as strong as it was in that moment. The depth of her love for him was just as profound but there was no fear at all of him reading too much in her face because that intense connection and the emotion that went with it was simply a background to the only thing that mattered here, to both of them.

Harry.

Tom had stayed with her during that tense time of transferring Harry from Recovery to the paediatric ICU and Laura was enormously grateful for that. She was grateful to all her friends for their support today, of course, but it was Tom whom she was thinking about most often as exhaustion pulled her towards sleep.

And then her head would drop and she would jerk into wakefulness again. It always felt as if she'd had a fright so she would have to start checking everything all over again. Listening carefully to the steady beeping of all the monitors. Watching Harry breathe. Touching his cheek or his hand with a gentle finger to check that he wasn't too hot or too cold. Trying to analyse any perceived flutter of his eyelids or twitch of his lips.

By the next morning, Laura had that spaced-out sensation that came from a total lack of sleep and she was more easily persuaded to take a short break in the relatives' room just outside the intensive care unit, when Fizz arrived with hot coffee and breakfast muffins. Due to the risk of infection, visitors to Harry's bedside were very restricted.

'Tom called us all last night to let us know how Harry was doing. He sounded very positive.'

'It's looking good so far.' Laura managed a few bites of the bacon and egg muffin but it was the coffee she really needed. 'They're going to keep him in the unit for another twenty-four hours or so—mainly to make sure his renal function is good and that pain management is adequate.'

'I'll let Maggie know that she'll need to text when she comes in today. I think she's planning to bring you some lunch but I'll make sure she knows you won't want to be away from Harry for too long.'

'Thanks, Fizz.' Laura hugged her friend. 'I'd better get back now, actually. I know he's far too sleepy to really notice whether I'm there or not but it makes me feel better.'

'Of course it does. Make sure you get some sleep sometime, though. I bet you didn't get much last night.'

Fizz wasn't the only person to be concerned about Laura's lack of any real rest. By early that evening, it was the consultant in charge of ICU who was trying to persuade her to get a few hours of sleep.

'I'd give you one of the on-call rooms here but we've got extra staff on at the moment and they're all reserved, I'm sorry.'

'It's fine, honestly. I'll be able to sleep in the chair tonight. I was just too stressed last night.'

'But you live pretty close to the Royal, don't you?'

'Yes, she does.'

Laura's head swung to see Tom coming through the door of Harry's room. 'Five minutes' walk away, in fact. A two-minute run. Is there any reason she needs to stay close at the moment?'

'No.' The consultant was smiling. 'We're delighted with Harry's progress and we're going to lighten his sedation and look at transferring him to the ward but we won't be doing that before tomorrow morning. Which leaves plenty of time for Laura to get a bit of proper sleep. We'll let you know if there's the slightest change.'

Tom's smile was persuasive. 'Think about it, Laura. Home for a hot shower and some clean clothes. A few hours in your own bed.'

'I…can't…'

'You want to be on top of your game in the morning, don't you? When Harry wakes up?'

'Of course I do…but…what if I fall asleep and don't hear my phone if they text or call me?'

'Okay…' Tom nodded, as if the matter was settled. 'That's no problem. I'll leave my number as well and they can call me. I'll be right next door and I promise that I'll hear my phone if you don't. Consider me an insurance policy.'

That penetrated the fog in Laura's brain. She'd used that phrase herself, thinking about Tom, hadn't she? She knew she could trust him and, given the vague confusion that was always part of total physical and emotional exhaustion like this, it was actually very comforting to have someone else taking charge like this. Rather like that night when she'd been sitting on the hospital steps, so upset, and he'd taken hold of her hand to lead her somewhere more private.

'You'll be there, Tom?' she checked.

'I'll walk home with you. I'll bring you back first thing in the morning or whenever you feel you have to be back here, as long as you've had a good few hours' sleep. I'll be just across the hallway. You'll only have to knock on my door.'

Laura let her gaze soak in the peaceful expression on Harry's face as he lay there, deeply asleep. She listened to that steady beat of the monitors and then caught the gaze of Harry's nurse.

'I'll be here,' the nurse promised. 'We'll have someone with him the whole time, I promise. Please, Laura. You need to rest before you fall over or get sick. Harry needs you to look after yourself.'

Her feet felt wooden as she walked out of the unit—as if she really could fall over far too easily. But she didn't have to stop moving because she had Tom walking by her side and, if she did fall over, he would be there to pick her up. It was amazing how a human safety net like that could give you so much more strength, wasn't it?

It felt as if she could cope with anything as long as she had Tom Chapman walking beside her.

'I don't think I can cope with this.'

Tom closed the door of Laura's apartment behind him, having followed her inside to make sure she was okay. Clearly, she wasn't, because she had walked into the living area and was now frozen in one spot, staring at the door to the sunroom that was Harry's bedroom. When she turned her head, Tom could see how overwhelmed she was. There were tears gathering in her eyes and her voice was trembling.

'It feels too empty,' she added in little more than a whisper. 'I don't want to be here on my own… without Harry.'

'No problem.' It felt good to recognise a problem and be able to solve it so easily. 'I'll stay here with you. I can sleep on the couch.'

'I can't ask you to do that.'

'You're not asking, I'm offering.' Tom could sense that Laura was relieved, as she had appeared to be when he'd taken charge at the hospital and persuaded her to come home for a break. 'You have a shower and I'll find something for us to eat.'

'I don't think I've got much in the fridge.'

'That's not a problem, either. I've got a freezer full of microwave dinners. You have the choice of lasagne, spaghetti bolognaise or possibly a fish pie.'

If nothing else, he'd succeeded in distracting Laura for a moment. 'Microwave dinners?' There was even a hint of a smile on her face. 'When this is all over, Tom, I might have to teach you how to cook. Spaghetti bolognaise is one of Harry's favourites so it's become one of my specialties.'

'It's a deal. Okay... I've got my phone in my hand, see? I'll be back in five minutes and I expect to hear that shower running.'

He could, indeed, hear the shower running when he returned with the frozen, boxed meals in his hands. Because Laura hadn't made a choice, he'd brought the whole selection and he put them in the oven to heat up, rather than the microwave, so that he could do them all at the same time. It would take nearly an hour but...yes... Laura had half a bottle of white wine in her fridge. A glass or two of that and she'd be out like a light as soon as her head hit the pillow.

The image of Laura with a wine glass in her hand generated another one of those disturbing tingles because it reminded him of the last time he'd been in this apartment with her but it was stronger this time, probably because Tom was aware of the sound of the shower running in the bathroom of this small apartment.

Okay…make that rather too aware that Laura was standing beneath that water, totally naked. Possibly with soap bubbles cascading over her skin as she shampooed her hair… Tom had to close his eyes as he fought off that image. What was going to happen later, he wondered, when he was lying on that couch in her living room, aware of her in her bed, on the other side of a thin wall? At least she wouldn't have to worry about him not hearing a phone call, he decided. It was very likely going to be his turn tonight to not get a very restful sleep.

Laura emerged from the bathroom with her hair hanging in damp curls over a rust-coloured sweatshirt and her long legs encased in black leggings. Her feet were bare and her face free of any makeup and she looked nothing like Tom had ever seen her look, either at work or in civvies. Was that why he was suddenly aware of so many details of how she looked? Even with her hair damp, the overhead light was picking out the auburn tints, making it come alive as if it was full of tiny flames. Warm brown eyes were the perfect colour with those autumn-coloured waves and Tom could see the smattering of soft freckles dusting her pale skin.

He'd told her she was gorgeous, that night he'd been trying to reassure her that she deserved something so much better than she'd had with Harry's father. He had been telling the truth, that was for sure. Laura McKenzie had to be one of the most beautiful women he'd ever seen. Especially when she smiled like that…

'That feels so much better.'

'Can you stay awake long enough to eat something? It's going to take a while to heat up.'

'I could use the time to pack some things that Harry's going to need when he's feeling a bit better. Like some books and toys and videos.'

Tom could see her hesitating in front of the door to Harry's room so he walked towards her. 'Need some help?'

'Sure…'

When she moved again, Tom was close enough to feel the brush of air on his skin from her movement. He thought he could feel the warmth of Laura's freshly clean skin, even. He could definitely smell the scent of her shampoo or soap or whatever it was that was flowery and fresh at the same time, like how he imagined the blossoms of a lemon tree might smell.

'Oh…some of his dinosaurs are out in the sandpit.' Laura suddenly turned. 'I mustn't forget them…'

She hadn't stopped her forward momentum as she turned and Tom hadn't stopped his, either, so it became one of those clumsy moments of accidental body contact, like that awkward, one-armed hug had been when they'd both been holding wine glasses. Their lips had been the point of the accidental contact that time but this time it was their bodies, with Laura's breasts brushing against his arm. Even more startling than the unexpected touch, however, was the flare of something he could see in Laura's eyes. It looked a lot like…

…like something he was feeling himself but he didn't know quite what it was.

A connection that was too powerful to ignore?

A need for physical contact that was born from a very particular kind of loneliness?

Just plain, simple desire?

Whatever it was, they were both feeling it. That had to be what made them both move at the same time, turning towards each other rather than away and, a heartbeat later, to be touching lips in a kiss that was the absolute opposite of accidental. It was also totally different from any kiss Tom could ever remember having and it was so utterly astonishing he knew it was going to be very difficult to stop.

But that was exactly what he had to do. Laura was not only his friend, she was exhausted and very vulnerable right now. However powerful this wave of physical need was suddenly becoming, what kind of man would take advantage of a vulnerable woman?

'Noo…' Laura's tiny groan echoed one that Tom hadn't uttered as he eased the pressure of his lips on hers. He still hadn't opened his eyes when he felt her wrap her arms more tightly around his neck.

'Don't stop…' Her whisper came from lips so close to his own, he could feel her breath as if it was his own. 'I need this, Tom… I need it *so* much…'

He heard the way she swallowed—as if it was painful. 'Just this once,' she said, so quietly it might have been in his imagination. Something that he was thinking of saying himself? 'Just tonight...'

How could he pull away now?

Yes, Laura was vulnerable right now. And exhausted. She needed comfort. A break from the unbearable tension she'd been under for so many weeks, let alone the exacerbation of that in the last two days. If he could provide distraction and comfort in the form of a physical release, was it so terrible that he wanted it so much himself?

Whatever argument was going on in his head was rapidly getting muffled as he kissed Laura again and, this time, the intensity of the kiss spiralled into a headlong dive into sheer passion. When he dropped his hands from her back to her hips and then slid them upwards again over the silky smooth skin beneath her sweatshirt, to find that she hadn't bothered putting a bra back on after her shower and Laura pressed herself into his hands with a tiny moan of need, Tom knew he was lost. That he needed this as much as Laura did. That this was exactly how powerful this needed to be in order for him to break through a barrier he'd believed was there for the rest of his life.

Oh... Dear Lord...

He was being so gentle with her that it made Laura want to cry but, at the same time, she could feel the strength behind that touch. Those kisses...and it made her feel safe.

Loved, even.

This was about so much more than just sex. It was

about more than about a release of unbearable tension that had been building ever since she'd learned how sick Harry was. This felt like an acknowledgment of the connection she had found with Tom. About feeling understood. Worthwhile. It didn't matter that it was just this once because this was exactly what Laura needed right now and she shut off any thoughts about anything else and just let herself sink into the sheer deliciousness of physical sensation.

Pleasure that built and built until it exploded into wave after wave of ecstasy. Somehow it wasn't surprising to find that her cheeks were wet with tears as she tried to catch her breath but they became a release all of their own when they wouldn't stop easily.

'It's okay…' Tom used the sheet he'd pulled over them both to mop up her tears and then he pulled her more closely into his arms. 'It's okay…'

And it was. Because she was lying here in his arms and she could feel the steady thump of his heartbeat beneath her cheek. She could also feel the blessed reprieve of a deep sleep just a breath or two away. Tom was saying something about food that would be ready to eat but Laura could only murmur her total lack of interest. She wasn't hungry.

She had everything she could possibly need for now.

CHAPTER EIGHT

'YOU SHOULD WRITE this up for a paramedic journal, Tom.' Joe was shaking his head as he studied the ECG graph on the table in front of him. 'Just look at that massive ST elevation. Most people would assume that this guy was having a cardiac event.'

'ECG changes from traumatic brain injury are pretty well documented now,' Tom responded. 'But it is a dramatic difference when you look at how normal the ECG is once we intubated him. Why don't you write it up? Never hurts to have a few publications on your CV.'

'For when I go hunting for a new job, you mean?' Joe grinned at his crew partner for the day. 'I'm quite happy where I am, thanks, mate.'

Tom smiled back. 'Me, too.'

In fact, he realised that he hadn't felt this happy in…well, he couldn't actually remember how long it had been. He did know that, at least in part, some of this new contentment with life had something to do with that night he'd spent with Laura.

Not immediately, mind you. The early hours of the

morning after had had its moments of uncomfortable awkwardness when he was sure they were both thinking they might have made a terrible mistake. Then they'd walked back to the hospital together and agreed that it had been special—a kind of gift, even—but it had been simply a one-off extension of their friendship that nobody else needed to know about. Laura had been the one who'd broached the subject.

'It was the last thing I expected to happen but exactly what I needed,' she'd said. 'A total distraction and the ultimate physical comfort, but I know it was above and beyond the call of being a friend. Don't worry… It won't happen again…'

Being that close had brought them closer together, of course, but they both still knew that their boundaries were in place. They might have made an exception and stepped over them once but perhaps the only reason they'd both felt safe to do that was because they both knew they had that safe space to step back into.

Tom would never be ready to abandon that safe space, and Laura? Well, she had Harry to care for and he was the centre of her world. Even if she was prepared to risk her own heart and look for more in her life, Tom was quite sure she would never do anything that might risk Harry's happiness. Especially now, when it seemed that he was going to have a second chance at a real future.

As the days had passed, with Harry coming out of Intensive Care and Laura able to share his room in the paediatric ward, any anxiety that their friendship had been damaged by that one-off night of physical comfort had gradually evaporated completely. And that was making Tom's life exactly how he wanted it to be.

Hey…' Joe looked up as someone called a greeting from where the stairs from ground level led into this staffroom area of the Aratika Rescue Base. 'Maggie… this is a surprise.'

'Oh…' Shirley, the rescue base's volunteer housekeeper, dropped what she was doing at the kitchen bench and rushed towards Maggie, wiping her hands on her apron. 'You've brought darling Bella in to visit.' She held out her arms. 'May I?'

'Of course.' Maggie handed over three-month-old Bella. 'Gotta get a cuddle from Nana Shirley, don't we?' She headed towards the table. 'What have you guys been up to, then?'

'Look at that…' Joe pushed the ECG across the table to his wife. 'From a middle-aged man who had a GCS of less than eight when we arrived on scene.'

'Infarct? No…' Maggie frowned. 'It's too widespread. Pericarditis?' She caught Joe's gaze. 'Tell me more. What was he doing before he got sick?'

'Good question,' Tom said. 'He was climbing up a ladder to clean out the gutters on his house.'

'So he fell off the ladder. Traumatic brain injury?'

'Good guess.'

'But why did he fall? A cardiac event?'

'You could think so. But look at this.' Joe pushed the second ECG graph across the table. 'This was a couple of minutes after we did a rapid sequence intubation because he was so agitated.'

Maggie's eyes widened. 'That's normal.'

'Which is why we can be sure that the ECG changes were due to raised intracranial pressure and not a heart attack.'

Maggie sighed. 'I miss being here,' she said. 'As much as I love being home with Bella, I think I'm nearly ready to come back to work.'

'Did you hear that, Bella?' Shirley kissed Bella's curls as she came closer to the table. She grinned at Maggie. 'Maybe we should start a crèche here. I could look after Bella and Harley.'

Bella's squeak might have been agreement but Shirley clicked her tongue. 'Sick of my cuddles already, darling? Here…say hello to your Uncle Tom.'

Tom didn't have time to protest as he had to take the warm bundle of baby being pressed into his arms. He was aware of a surprised glance coming from Joe's direction and his friend moved, as if to rescue him from the situation, but Tom smiled to let him know it was fine.

Which it totally was.

'Hey, there,' he said to Bella. 'Did you come to see Daddy at work, huh?'

Bella's face crinkled into a toothless grin and Tom felt something melt inside. Not in a poignant, even painful way, as it might have done not so long ago. This felt warm and joyful—the way a baby's smile should always make you feel. As if you could believe for at least a few seconds that the world was a place brim full of hope and happiness.

Wow…he'd come quite a long way in the weeks since Bella had arrived in the world, hadn't he?

'We're on the way to see Laura and Harry,' Maggie said. 'Maybe for the last time in the ward. Fizz tells me that he's getting an ultrasound exam today and, depending on the result, they could be letting him go home tomorrow.'

'So I heard.' Tom was still smiling down at the baby. 'I popped up to the ward yesterday. I found a dinosaur colouring-in book in the gift shop and I knew Harry would love that.'

'I'll bet he did.'

Tom didn't say anything. He was busy making faces at Bella in the hope of eliciting another smile. One like the smile that had been on Harry's face when he'd seen the book and the big packet of felt tip pens that had been his gift?

'Did she tell you whether the pathology results from the surgery had come back yet?' Maggie sounded anxious. 'I didn't like to ask by text.'

'They did. And they couldn't be better.' Tom took Bella back towards her mother as she squeaked again. 'Totally clear margins and nothing abnormal in the gallbladder or the lymph nodes. I think he's going to be one of the lucky ones.'

'I'll bet Laura thinks she's one of the lucky ones,' Joe said quietly.

That was so true. For a moment, Tom cuddled Bella a little more tightly before he handed her over. Because he could remember that glow that Laura had had when she'd told him the news. He had felt her relief as if it was his own and he'd caught that flash of a renewed hope in the future that he could see in her eyes. The kind of hope you felt in exactly moments like this, when you were cradling a small baby in your arms.

'That is such good news.' Maggie took Bella from Tom. 'Okay, Button, come and give Daddy a kiss and then we'll go visiting. I can't wait to see how happy Laura must be.'

Joe was still smiling after he'd bestowed kisses on both Maggie and Bella but Tom could feel a curious gaze from Joe coming in his direction after their surprise visitors had gone. It happened again a while later, too, after Shirley had gone home, leaving enough fresh muffins for at least twenty-four hours, and it was so quiet that Joe and Tom were sprawled on the sofas, using the time to catch up on articles in emergency medical journals.

'What's so fascinating?' Tom finally had to ask as the intensity of the stare from Joe made him abandon his reading. 'Have I grown an extra ear or something?'

'There's something different about you,' Joe said. 'I'm trying to figure out what it is.'

'Maybe I need a haircut.'

'Nah…it's something bigger than that. It's your body language or something. You're more…relaxed.'

'I'm always relaxed.'

Joe gave a huff of laughter. 'You know, when we first started working together, I thought you were a bit uptight, to be honest.'

'Cheers…'

'You know what I mean. Reserved. Serious. You

didn't smile that much and you kind of stood back. Not clinically—you've always been outstanding in the way you work. It was more that you kind of kept your distance, you know? You had that ability to stay calm in any kind of emergency.'

Tom's grunt was agreement. Of course he knew. He still kept his distance when it came to being too emotionally involved with his patients. You had to, in order to do your best job. You had to be able to stand back and see the bigger picture.

'Anyway...' Joe was sitting up now, on the edge of the couch. Leaning forward, as if what he was saying was important. 'You seem different. You smile more and...'

'And...?'

Joe shrugged, as if he was a little embarrassed. 'You remember the day that Bella was born?'

'Of course. It wasn't that long ago.' And it had also been the day that Laura had brought Harry in to the emergency department and her world had begun to fall apart. It was the day when it had been impossible not to feel that connection with a parent who was possibly facing the end of the world as she knew it.

'I felt like I should have said something to Maggie. I hadn't told her about you losing your family because you said it wasn't something you ever talked about so I figured it was private.'

It had been. Very private. The only person Tom had ever talked to it about, apart from Joe, was Laura.

'I was worried that it might have seemed really insensitive when she asked if you wanted to hold Bella.'

Joe said. 'I thought that might have been why you rushed off.'

Tom still didn't say anything. Joe wasn't far off the truth, was he? It had been a flashback kind of moment and he had been grappling with some difficult emotions, like grief and the lingering, painful poignancy of enormous loss.

'But today,' Joe continued, 'you actually looked like you didn't mind at all when Shirley shoved Bella into your arms.'

'I didn't mind,' Tom assured him. 'She's got the best smile in the world, your daughter.'

'It's not just that,' Joe added. 'It's the way you've helped Laura so much since Harry got sick. Helping her shift into that new apartment. Making her your neighbour, even... She wouldn't have even known that apartment was available if you hadn't told her.'

'She's a friend,' Tom said. 'It's what friends do.'

They didn't usually start paying a good whack of their rent behind their backs, though, did they? Tom caught the quizzical look Joe was giving him and had the horrible thought that perhaps Joe somehow knew about that secret arrangement. Or worse, did he know about what had happened between himself and Laura that night he'd stayed so that she wasn't alone in her apartment without Harry? That was the sort of thing girlfriends talked about, wasn't it? If Laura had confided in Maggie, it wasn't hard to imagine that Joe might have found out. He swung his legs off the couch and sat up, rubbing the back of his neck.

'You're still staring at me,' he muttered.

Joe grunted his agreement. 'I was just thinking,' he explained. 'Remembering what you told me when I thought that Maggie and I were just friends. That I'd know if I was in love in with her or not. You said I'd know because it would be like the sun had been turned on in my personal universe. But you know what?'

'What?'

'You were wrong. Or kind of wrong. It was the opposite of that that made me realise how I felt about Maggie.'

'Not sure I follow.'

'You remember that accident she had on her motorbike.'

'Of course. When we arrived on scene and you realised who it was who'd had the accident, I think you looked worse than she did for a while.'

'That was because I knew how much I had to lose. The sun had always been there but I suddenly knew how dark my personal universe would be if I didn't have Maggie in my life any more.'

'Yeah…' Tom had to swallow hard. 'It breaks you, that's for sure.'

'Sorry, mate… I didn't mean to remind you of…'

'Her name was Jenny. And my little boy was called Sam. It's okay, Joe. Yes, it broke me at the time but I've put my life back together since then. Having said that, though, I'm not going there again and that's why my friendship with Laura is nothing like your friendship with Maggie. It's only ever going to be a friendship.'

Joe said nothing. He seemed to be carefully avoiding Tom's gaze at the same time and he could understand why his words might lack credibility, given that Joe's relationship with Maggie had grown from what they had both believed was nothing more than a friendship. For everybody's sake, he needed to make sure that Joe understood exactly where he was coming from. What if Joe got the wrong end of the stick and it got back to Laura via Maggie that maybe Tom was ready for something more in his life? That might have to be the end of their friendship and Tom didn't want that. He really didn't want that.

He blew out a long breath. 'Okay...maybe you're right. I am a bit different.' He found a smile to lighten this heavy atmosphere. 'Not so uptight.'

'You're more involved.' Joe nodded. 'Part of the gang now.' Maybe he wanted to finish a conversation that had become unexpectedly intense.

'That's precisely it. I guess I kept myself to myself for a very long time because, initially, I was too broken to cope with anything else and then it just became a way of life and it felt safe. I was in my own little bubble. And then I saw you and Maggie with Bella and Harry got sick and, somehow, that bubble got a bit bigger all by itself. Big enough to let friends in. But that's as far as it goes. And, hey...who wouldn't want to be part of a gang, when there's tacos involved sometimes?'

Joe grinned. 'True. Mmm... Tacos.'

'I'm getting hungry.'

'Me, too. Shall we check out those muffins Shirley made?'

Tom got to his feet. It felt good to move because it made it easier to stop thinking about how much his life might have been changing without him taking that much notice of it. He wanted to focus on making the most of one of his days at the rescue base and revel in whatever new challenges came his way. He wasn't about to enjoy one of Shirley's excellent muffins just yet, however. Right on cue, as the two men were within reach of the basket, their pagers sounded. They exchanged a glance and a resigned grin and then headed for the door.

Normal.

It was a word that could imply something very ordinary and not very interesting.

It was also a word that could be the best news ever when it came from the specialist who was interpreting the ultrasound results on the examination of Harry's liver.

'He said that everything's looking completely normal.'

'Oh, Laura, that's fantastic news.' Maggie had to swipe at her eyes and then she sniffed loudly. 'Sorry...' She looked down to where Bella was lying, sucking her fist, in her car seat. 'Ever since I became a mum, I seem to get emotional at the drop of a hat about anything to do with kids.'

'I know what you mean. I reckon when you have a

baby, your heart gets instantly bigger. And softer. You get used to it, but it's never quite the same.'

'Yeah…' Maggie was picking Bella up. 'You're hungry, aren't you? You don't need to eat your hand.' She adjusted her top and helped Bella latch onto her breast, softly stroking her baby's cheek as she settled. 'It's like falling in love, I think. The whole world just looks so different, especially in those amazing early days when you feel like you're floating.'

'Mmm…' Laura had to press her lips together.

She wanted so much to tell Maggie that she was having trouble keeping her feet firmly on the floor these days. That she could summon that floating sensation as simply as closing her eyes and letting her mind drift into thinking about Tom Chapman. She could usually stop that happening easily enough in the daytime but it was a lot harder when she was alone with her thoughts during the nights. She wanted to admit that she suspected she might be falling in love.

Worse, she wanted to confess what had happened that night when she'd been so strongly advised to take a short break from the tense atmosphere of the PICU. They were both the sort of things that you had to tell your best friend but maybe she didn't want to hear her own doubts out loud.

That Tom was never going to fall in love again because his heart still belonged to the family he'd so tragically lost so she needed to let go of that faint hope that things could change in the future. Or that she'd made a terrible mistake in practically begging him to make love to her that night because it had been when she'd been drifting off to sleep in his arms that she'd realised that her love for Tom and the power of her desire for him had coalesced into something huge. That this level of love for someone was way beyond any kind of acceptable emotional connection with a friend.

The only real question, here, was whether it was possible to stop that falling process once it had started. Or had it already gone so far she'd hit bottom with such a bump she was still a bit stunned? Maybe she needed a bit more time to think about that herself.

She had to look away before Maggie lifted her gaze from Bella and could instantly spot that Laura was keeping something hidden, but it was easy to make avoiding eye contact seem perfectly innocent. They were on a couch in the corner of the playroom and she needed to keep an eye on Harry and make sure he wasn't overdoing things, having been out of bed for most of today already. He and his friend Aroha were sitting at a low table on brightly coloured chairs. Aroha had big crayons and was drawing on a large piece of paper. Harry had the colouring-in book Tom had given him yesterday and he was carefully filling in the outline of a Triceratops. Because that had been the dinosaur that he and Tom had had a conversation about?

'Why has he got horns? So he could kill animals and eat them?'

'No...he was a vegetarian. I think he used his horns to protect himself, like when he got into an argument with a T Rex.'

Ooh…there it was again. That floaty sensation, sneaking back during daytime—just because she could actually hear Tom's voice in her head. Not only his words to Harry but the way he'd sounded when she'd shown him the pathology report she had been given.

'Intact liver capsule. Absence of vascular invasion. Negative resection margins… This is the best news ever…'

'I know, right? I don't think I've ever felt this happy.'

She'd come close, though, hadn't she? That night, when she'd taken that break from Harry's bedside, knowing that he was in safe hands and she would be back before he woke up. When she'd been falling into that desperately needed sleep, in the wake of a physical release she hadn't known she'd needed so much. When she'd felt Tom's arms around her and the steady beat of his heart and the way it felt as if her own heart could explode with the amount of love that was filling it. When, for a blissful, albeit short period of time, there had been nothing more that she could possibly need.

Except for those results that had come yesterday, of course. Knowing that Harry's surgery had been so successful. That life could very likely get completely back to normal in the foreseeable future. Or maybe not completely…

Falling in love—if the process couldn't be interrupted—presented a bit of a problem. Laura needed Tom in her life for Harry's sake as well as her own because every fatherless child needed a role model and she couldn't imagine anyone better than Tom, but there was only one way that was going to happen, which was to keep things the way they had been. A friendship and nothing more. She'd known that from the moment she'd woken up to find that Tom had slipped out of her bed while she had been so deeply asleep and he'd gone to sleep on the couch.

It hadn't been hard to pick up on how uncomfortable he was feeling as they sped through what needed to be done before heading back to the hospital. It was obvious that Tom thought he was going to have to spell out why they could never be anything more than friends and that perhaps they had made a bit of mess of things last night but he couldn't find a way to broach the subject. The tension had quietly notched up as they failed to find a way into the conversation that had to happen.

Laura had rescued him as they'd walked back to the Royal. She'd taken a deep breath and told him how it had been exactly what she'd needed but that she never expected it to happen again. That it was pretty much out of bounds for a normal friendship.

There it was again. That word.

Anyway, she'd also told him that nobody else needed to know so that meant she really couldn't tell Maggie because it would feel as if she was breaking a promise. If it got to the point where she couldn't cope with her secret, at least she knew she had friends she could turn to but it felt fine for now. She could do this.

She needed to focus on her son and make sure that

his recovery and the final chemotherapy he was going to need went as well as it possibly could. She could be friends with Tom and keep the knowledge of what it was like to be that much closer to him a memory that she could revisit when she needed an escape, perhaps. A bit of a fantasy about what life could have been like if things were different. When she wanted to feel special. Gorgeous, even...

'What is it?'

Laura hadn't felt her friend's gaze on her. She hadn't realised she was smiling.

'Oh, I'm just happy. Seeing Harry like this. Knowing that we're going to go home tomorrow.'

'Is there anything you need? I could do a grocery run or something for you.' Maggie eased a now drowsy Bella into an upright position on her shoulder and began rubbing her back. 'Or I could come and stay with Harry soon and give you a bit of a break.'

'Come and visit anytime,' Laura said, 'but I don't think I'll be needing a break. I'm going to enjoy every minute with Harry at home.'

Again, it was almost on the tip of her tongue to tell Maggie what had happened the last time she'd taken a break from watching her son. At least that couldn't happen with him at home again so maybe the memory would begin to fade soon. She could stamp on those errant thoughts that she might be wrong. That maybe Tom wanted it to happen again as much as she did. She wanted so badly to feel like it was safe to love this man, but it wasn't, was it? She could end up getting badly hurt.

She had to at least try to protect herself by keeping things real. Nothing was going to change in the future because Tom would never want that. If she started to think otherwise, she just needed to remind herself of that night when they'd almost, accidentally kissed and he couldn't get away fast enough afterwards. Or she could tap into that tension the morning after they'd made love. Yep…that was extremely effective. Laura could feel herself frowning now as she pushed away her own uncomfortable feelings.

'There's online shopping.' Maybe Maggie thought she was worrying about getting groceries. 'I've been using that since Bella arrived and it's great. You just order everything and it gets delivered to your door-step. I'm sure Tom would help carry it all inside.'

'Mmm…' No. Laura didn't want to think about Tom coming into her apartment with grocery bags in his hands—as if he was a part of her everyday life. So she said the first thing that came into her head to try and change the subject. 'Did you know that he eats microwave meals? How sad is that? I've told him I'm going to teach him how to cook a spa-ghetti bolognaise.'

Uh-oh… The way Maggie was looking at her sug-gested that there were cogs whirring in her friend's brain. That she was adding two and two together and coming up with a sum a lot greater than four.

Laura shook her head firmly. 'We're just friends.'

'Right…' Maggie's grin widened as Bella burped loudly. 'Now, where have I heard that before? Oh, yeah… That's exactly what Joe and I tried to convince ourselves we were. Before we realised that we'd already fallen in love.' She shifted her gaze to where Harry was still sitting, colouring in his picture. 'I guess the timing isn't right, though, is it? You're not going to go off and start dating anyone while Harry needs your undivided attention.'

She tucked her sleeping baby back into the car seat. 'I'd better get going. Joe texted to ask if Tom could come around for dinner tonight. For some reason, they've both got a hankering for tacos so I'll have to drop in to the supermarket. Didn't think to order taco shells online this week, that's for sure. I don't think we've had tacos since the day you moved apartments. Hey…maybe you could teach Tom how to make them, too. I'm sure he's going to love having a private cooking tutor.'

Laura was smiling now. 'Stop trying to start rumours. And don't you dare say anything to Tom or he'll regret ever suggesting that I become his neighbour.'

'My lips are sealed.' There was something rather serious in Maggie's gaze as she leaned in to give Laura a hug. 'You can tell me anything, you know. They'd still be sealed.'

Laura opened her mouth to tell her that there was nothing to tell but the words refused to come out. So she just hugged her friend instead.

CHAPTER NINE

THIS WAS GREAT.

A new normal.

It had taken a few weeks but Laura and Tom had found the space they could both be happy sharing. A solid friendship that meant they could stop and chat for a few minutes if they happened to be heading out or arriving home at the same time. They could work together, having lost none of their ability to communicate with each other so easily. Laura knew this because she'd had her first shift back in the emergency department since Harry had started back at school after his surgery and it had been a real joy. A sure sign that life was getting back to normal.

But maybe even better than the old normal because she still had Tom in her life and they had shored up the boundaries that meant that night together had been forgotten. Well, not forgotten as far as Laura was concerned, of course, but it was in a manageable place. She was coping so well, in fact, that she'd been totally relaxed in finally following up on that invitation to give Tom a cooking lesson.

So, here they were in her kitchen and the tempting aroma of frying onions and garlic was filling her kitchen.

'You can add the minced meat soon.'

'Okay.' Tom had the sleeves of his sweatshirt pushed up. 'It's beef, yeah?'

His hands brushed Laura's as he took the package of meat but she barely registered the tingle. Maybe because it was so much easier to control something like that when Harry was nearby. He was currently crawling around the floor of the living area, setting up the tracks for his model train set. Laura went back to the celery and carrots she was dicing.

'Beef and pork,' she told Tom. 'It's a lot better than beef on its own. I have a secret ingredient too that you won't find in most recipes and you certainly won't find it in a microwaveable version.'

'Oh?' Tom raised an eyebrow as he looked over his shoulder. 'I assume you're going to tell me what it is? Friends get to share secrets, don't they?'

'Sure…' But Laura had to drag her gaze away from Tom's. Oh, man… Did he not realise exactly what secret they shared that was going to pop instantly into her head? Maybe this wasn't quite as easy as she'd hoped it would be. She covered up her avoidance of his gaze by reaching for another package.

'It's bacon,' she said. 'Chop a couple of rashers up finely and put it in with the onion and garlic. Better if it goes in before the mince, actually.'

'No worries.' Tom still sounded completely relaxed so he clearly hadn't been reminded of anything that could become awkward. 'And then we put the veggies in?'

'Yes. And the tomatoes and stock and a bit of red wine. I'm not sure if we should use the bottle you brought, though. It looks like a very good wine.'

'I watched a cooking show once,' Tom said. 'And the chef said, if you wouldn't want to drink it, don't cook with it.'

'I don't usually put any in when it's just me and Harry.'

'Maybe we should just drink it, then?'

Tom's smile had a mischievous edge now and it made something melt deep inside Laura. Something very warm and…and safe, she realised. She could stop worrying about feeling things that might not be appropriate because surely they would fade eventually. They had to, because this friendship—and this feeling of safety—was too precious to lose.

She smiled back. 'I'll find the glasses. You keep cooking.'

By the time she had uncorked the bottle and poured them both a glass, Tom had added everything to the saucepan.

'It just needs to simmer for a while now. Sit down and enjoy your wine. I'll tidy up in here so that we'll be able to eat at the table. Or, if you've got anything you need to do at home, I can give you a yell when it's ready to eat?'

'Noo… I want Tom to come and play trains with me. He promised…'

Laura blinked. She'd had no idea that Harry had been listening in to their conversation. 'Did he?'

Tom took a sip from his glass. 'Well, I did say it looked like fun when I saw him emptying that box. But it is a long time since I played trains. I might have forgotten how.'

'It's all right,' Harry's tone was reassuring. 'I'll show you. It's not very hard. But we have to build a bridge first, okay?'

Tom looked at the fistful of train tracks Harry was holding up to show him. He looked at the wine glass in his hand and then he looked at Laura.

Her smile widened. 'Take it with you,' she advised. 'You might need it.'

Harry had been right. It wasn't hard to play trains at all. It was actually surprisingly enjoyable.

Maybe that was because it felt good to be here, instead of being alone in his own apartment, waiting for a frozen dinner to warm up. Not that he minded his own company, Tom reminded himself. Far from it—he'd learned to appreciate it over the last few years but it was nice to have a change sometimes and being with friends was something special. Like that taco dinner he'd had with Maggie and Joe just before Harry had been discharged from hospital. This evening, it was great to see Harry looking so much better and, he had to admit, the smell coming from Laura's kitchen was so much better than any boxed version of spaghetti bolognaise.

The wine he was able to snatch an occasional sip

from as he built a bridge, put curves into a straight line that was about to take the track into the kitchen where Laura was busy cleaning up the mess he'd made cooking, positioned a station and then started pushing engines and carriages around, was making the whole experience even more enjoyable. Tom was feeling a lot more relaxed than he had since…well, since the last time he'd been in this apartment with Laura, that was for sure. Even thinking about that awkward 'morning after' was enough to provoke a beat of…what was it, exactly? Wariness?

It was another good thing about this evening. To have the confirmation that Laura had been being completely honest when she'd said that night was just a one-off and that she'd never expect it to happen again. Ever since then, she hadn't given the slightest hint that she wanted more than a normal kind of friendship from him. Which was excellent, because it made a neighbourly evening like this possible.

'What's that, Harry?' Tom peered at the small black object Harry was slotting into an open train carriage.

'It's a seal.'

'What, a seal that goes in the sea and makes a noise like this?'

Tom flapped his bent arms like flippers and did his best to mimic the barking sound that seals make. Harry laughed out loud and copied Tom and from the corner of his eye Tom could see that the sound had brought Laura into the archway between the kitchen and living area. She was already smiling but clearly wanted to see what was causing so much amusement. The light behind her was stronger than in this room and it lit up that gorgeous auburn hair of hers in a glow that was an almost perfect match to that rust-coloured sweatshirt she was wearing again.

Which took him straight back to that evening when she'd come out of the shower and worse than that… much worse than that…it took him straight back to what had happened not long after that. He could re-member so clearly the softness and taste of Laura's lips and the perfect curves of her body. He could ac-tually feel the echoes of the touch of her hands on his skin that was so delicate, it was hard to believe they could ignite that kind of fire in their wake…

Oh, man… Tom was grateful for the noise of small plastic bricks cascading from the large box as Harry emptied his supplies onto the floor because the sound drowned thoughts that were escalating rapidly out of control.

'I've got a whole zoo,' he told Tom. 'Look, here's a lion…and a giraffe. What sort of noise does a gi-raffe make?'

'I'm not sure,' Tom admitted. 'But why don't you put them under the bridge? That way, the people in the train can see them as they go on their trip.'

'You'll have to be quick,' Laura said. 'Dinner's going to be ready soon.'

By the time dinner was ready, Tom was confident he had those disturbing reminders of that night with Laura under control. It was hardly likely that his body was going to let him forget that it had experienced the extraordinary release of sex for the first time in so long. After all, it had been a wake-up call to be as affected as he had been by that "almost kiss". Perhaps he'd been right in thinking that he needed to find someone to share a relationship like a "friends with benefits" kind of thing.

For one, crazy moment, Tom found himself wondering if Laura might be interested in a relationship like that and he must have had a strange expression on his face because her eyebrows shot up when she caught his glance.

'What's up?'

'That's not spaghetti.' He focused on the large bowl on the table. The pasta that had been mixed in with the sauce he'd made earlier was a lot flatter and thicker than spaghetti. 'I thought that's what bolognaise was all about.'

'It's tagliatelle. It's better than spaghetti because more of the sauce can stick to it. Plus, it's easier for small people to eat.' Laura was serving some into a bowl for Harry. 'Is that enough, sweetheart?' she asked. 'And do you want cheese on top?'

Tom watched her making sure that Harry had everything he needed before she served herself and the way she kept an eye on him throughout the meal. No…he'd known all along that Laura wasn't the type of woman that would be happy with casual sex as part of a friendship. She was such a loving person and such a wonderful mother. Someone to whom family was everything and that family was her precious son.

Her smile was amused but with a twist of resignation at the moment because Harry was using his fingers to try and wrap the pasta around his fork and he had such a fierce expression of concentration with his brow furrowed like that. When his fork was over-full, trying to eat it left sauce all over his face and hands. Now he looked worried because he knew he'd made a mess, but when he looked up at his mother he clearly knew he wasn't in trouble and his face lit up with a grin.

'I'll get a cloth,' Laura said. 'Don't move, monkey.'

It was Harry's grin that did it. The happiness of someone who knew they were loved unconditionally. Or maybe it was because he'd been thinking about the bond of family, and memories were never that far away if his guard was down. Faded memories that were almost dreamlike now and the emotions they stirred were more like longing than sadness. What-ever. It was Laura that had that bond, not him. And it was not something he ever wanted to have again himself. It was just as well that this meal was nearly finished. He could excuse himself and go home very soon. Tom used a piece of crusty bread to mop up the last of the sauce on his plate.

'That was absolutely delicious,' he told Laura. 'I can't believe I cooked most of it myself.'

She threw him a sideways glance as she went to-wards Harry with a damp cloth. 'Maggie reckons I should teach you to make tacos next time.'

Harry ducked his head to try and avoid having the sauce wiped off his face. 'I want tacos for my party,' he said. He peered under his mother's arm. 'Are you coming to my party, Tom?'

'Um... You're having a party? Is it your birthday?'

'Not yet,' Laura said. 'And the party's a wee way off, as well, but we're planning to celebrate the end of chemo. It's going to be in one of the cafés in the Royal so it might be just cake and not tacos but that makes it easy for Harry's friends from the ward to come, like Aroha. And Fizz—and maybe you—will be able to come for a while even if you're both working.'

'That's certainly something worth celebrating...' Although Tom wasn't sure it would be a good idea to attend the party, as if his inclusion in his neighbour's special occasions was automatic.

'Mummy says I can have a special present because I've been very, very brave.'

'That's true,' Tom agreed.

'He hasn't decided what he wants yet,' Laura put in. 'I think it's a toss-up between a bike and a new tablet to play computer games on.'

'No.' Harry's headshake was firm. 'I've decided now.'

'Oh?' Laura was still smiling as she began collecting empty plates. 'What's it going to be, then, this special present?'

'Tom.'

It felt like time stopped for an instant of confusion. Tom was halfway up from his chair. Laura froze with a stack of plates in mid-air. They were both staring at Harry.

'I want Tom,' he said. 'I want him to be my daddy.'

* * *

Oh...no... No, no, no...

The new normal had just been destroyed by a few innocent words from a six-year-old boy.

Laura had to fix this. And fast. If that was even possible. The look on Tom's face was...

Heartbreaking, that's what it was.

He'd been a daddy once. To a little boy who would be about the same age as Harry if he was still alive. Her son's words must have felt like he was having his heart ripped out and someone was stomping on it.

'Harry...' She tried to make it sound like this was all a joke. 'That's a funny thing to say.'

'Why?'

'Because...because you can't give someone a person for a present, can you?' Laura knew her laughter sounded forced. 'How would you wrap them up?'

'But...' Harry's lower lip was protruding—a sure sign that he was prepared to go into battle for what he wanted.

'Tom's our friend,' Laura added firmly. 'And that's special enough, isn't it?'

Harry was still scowling.

'How 'bout you go and tidy up those building bricks?' Laura said a little desperately. 'When you've done that, you can have some ice cream for dessert.'

Harry slid down from his chair and reluctantly took a couple of steps before looking back at Tom. 'Please will you help me?'

'Sorry, buddy.' Tom was out of his chair, as well.

'I need to help your mum with the dishes and then… ah…it's time for me to go home.'

He caught Laura's glance for no more than a split second. Just long enough for her to know that he was finding this as excruciatingly embarrassing as she was. This was far worse than the awkwardness of that morning after they'd slept together. Tom picked up the serving bowls from the table and turned towards the bench.

Harry wasn't giving up. 'Why?'

'Because I have lots of homework to do.' Tom put the leftovers down beside where Laura had deposited the plates.

'And because it's going to be your bedtime very soon.' Laura hoped her over-the-shoulder smile at Tom was both an apology and reassurance as she turned on the hot tap over the sink. 'I don't need any help with the dishes,' she told him. 'You did most of the cooking so you're excused.'

'You sure?'

'Absolutely…' She took a deep breath and lowered her voice. 'And…I'm sorry for that. He had fun playing with you, that's all. And he doesn't understand. He's just…'

'A kid. I know…' Tom was smiling back at her. 'It's okay, Laura. Forget it. But I do have quite a lot of work to be getting on with, if you're sure about the dishes. I've been meaning to write up a case report on some interesting ECG changes from raised intracranial pressure we captured a while back.'

'Go…' Laura's smile widened in relief at the normal tone of Tom's voice. 'And don't let Harry talk you into helping on your way past.'

She kept an eye on her son as Tom negotiated a path through the scattered bricks. She saw the way he leaned down to touch Harry's head in farewell. It would have been a hair ruffle but it would be quite a while before her boy's hair grew back enough to be ruffled.

The lump in her throat as she turned back to rinsing the plates was big enough to be painful. Hearing the sound of her front door closing behind Tom only seemed to make it worse. It wasn't the embarrassment of Harry having said something that unintentionally could have upset Tom that was the worst thing about how this cooking lesson and dinner had ended.

No. It was something far worse.

It was how Laura had felt when she'd heard Harry utter those words. The knowledge that it was what *she* wanted—probably a whole lot more than Harry did. There was no getting around the fact that she was completely in love with Tom but she'd known all along that the only way to keep him in her life was as a friend and she'd believed that could be enough. Now she knew that it wasn't enough. She would always long to have Tom in her life in the closest possible way. Not simply as a daddy for her son. She wanted him as her life partner. Someone she could love with her whole heart and soul for the rest of her life.

No…make that *would* love. Laura had another attempt to swallow that lump that was making it hard to breathe.

How she felt about Tom Chapman wasn't about to change.

Ever.

Writing up a case report hadn't actually been on Tom's agenda that evening but it had been a brainwave. A sure-fire way of clearing his head from what felt like a minor storm of unwelcome emotions that were still spinning around inside his skull even after he was safely alone in his own apartment.

Shock waves, that's what they were.

Partly because Harry's words had tapped into memories that he'd almost forgotten he had. Sam, as a toddler, saying 'Daddy' for the first time and the tears of joy in both his and Jenny's eyes as they'd heard him. That family hug...

That longing that he'd already been observing during that dinner had suddenly grown the sharp edges of reality because his memories of the family he'd once had were simply that. Memories that, more and more these days, had a dreamlike quality. Being with Laura and Harry was different. It was very, very real and there he'd been sitting at the table with them as he'd become so aware of that reality. He'd been playing with Harry and that train set only a short time ago.

Just like a father would.

He'd become far closer to both of them than he'd ever intended when he'd been drawn into helping with the crisis in their lives. When he'd had that apparently random thought of Laura being a "friend with benefits" this evening, it hadn't just been the idea of casual sex that had been appealing, had it?

Subconsciously, at least, it had been that whole concept of family. Of belonging. Of loving and being loved by others…? Certainly, if he let this go any further, Tom would be in danger of falling in love with both Laura and Harry and reaching to have that joy of family in his life again, and he knew what that meant. It meant having the other side of that coin. The risk of losing everything again. Of having your entire world destroyed.

Nobody thought it was going to happen to them but Tom knew that it *could* happen. He knew that it felt unsurvivable when it did. That putting the pieces of a life back together again to that extent was not something you could do more than once. The very thought of facing something like that again gave him a prickle down his spine that could only be caused by fear.

He'd learned how to protect himself so how the hell had his defences crumbled to such an extent?

More importantly, what was he going to do about strengthening them again?

CHAPTER TEN

IT WAS BECOMING a habit.

Sometimes with grocery bags at her feet, or Harry's schoolbag or just the two of them because they'd gone for a walk, there was always that moment when Laura was fishing for her keys in her handbag or her pocket and she'd know that Harry had turned around.

That he was staring at the front door of Tom's apartment. That the usual questions were about to be asked.

'Is Tom home, Mummy? Can I knock on the door?'

'I don't think so, hon.' Laura hated the pang it always gave her, trying to shelter Harry. It didn't matter if she was hurt by Tom's stepping back after that cooking lesson that had ended so disastrously but it was one thing for her to feel hurt and quite another that Harry was affected by it. 'It was really busy at work today and he has lots of sick people to look after.'

'He looked after me when I was sick.'

'Mmm…' Laura smiled as she fitted the key in the lock. 'He sure did.'

'I think I might be feeling sick again today.'

That beat of alarm was always going to be there. 'What kind of sick?'

'I think my tummy hurts.'

'You *think* it hurts?' Laura lifted Harry's cap off his head so that she could see his face clearly. He wasn't pale and he avoided her gaze by looking over his shoulder at Tom's door again, which was a good clue that he wasn't actually feeling sick—he just wanted an excuse to see Tom. Laura's suspicion was confirmed when he reached up and took his dinosaur cap out of her hands. 'Tom gave me my hat.'

'Mmm…' The sound was a little strangled.

That cap. No, all those caps. That had been the moment that falling in love process had started, even if she hadn't recognised it at the time—when she'd seen all those children coming out of school wearing the red dinosaur caps. Being part of "Harry's club".

Those feelings were never going to change but she couldn't blame Tom for having put his barriers up again. Not that he wasn't perfectly friendly still, but it reminded her of what he'd been like in the past. Before Harry had got sick. When he had kept his distance from people.

Becoming close enough to be considered a friend had been a privilege but, without realising it, Laura had let it go too far. She'd read too much into the connection she thought they had between them. He'd made it feel as if it was safe to love someone like this and what made it so much worse was that she hadn't protected Harry enough. He loved Tom, too.

Now she was following his lead and keeping things light and friendly because that had worked once before, hadn't it? After the awkwardness of having slept together, they'd managed to rescue their friendship and it had seemed even stronger than before but it appeared that it was going to take longer this time. Harry's notion that Tom could be his daddy had opened old wounds and it was no wonder that he needed to protect himself and that he needed some space. Maybe, one day, they could relax in each other's company again. If not, they could get used to that loss gradually, at least.

Harry was following her inside. 'I still like wearing it but I don't need it any more, do I, Mummy?'

'Not really. Your hair is growing back fast. It's great, isn't it?' Just a few weeks after his last chemotherapy session, Harry's scalp was covered with a fine, dark fuzz—so soft that it brought a lump to Laura's throat every time she stroked it.

She was the luckiest person on earth, she thought in those moments. All test results were coming back indicating that Harry had won this battle and, apart from regular check-ups, he was unlikely to need any further treatment. He was still a little underweight and got tired more easily than he used to but he was happy to be back at school and happy when he was at home—apart from those hopeful gazes at Tom's front door, as if he was going to see his hero appear while he watched.

Had he forgotten to shut the front door on purpose, perhaps, so that he would notice when Tom came home today? Having dropped his schoolbag in the middle of the living room floor, Harry had vanished into his bedroom so Laura went to shut the door but just before she closed it, she could hear two people coming in through the apartment building's main entrance. A woman was speaking clearly.

'...so it's only one-bedroom, but it does have a sunroom that opens into the garden and can be used as a second bedroom. I believe that's what the current tenant is using it for.'

Laura held the door just before pushing it shut. Were they talking about her apartment?

'And when are you planning to put it on the market?'

'Not immediately. We've only lost Mum recently and there's a bit to be decided in her estate but I knew you were looking for an investment. If you come upstairs, you can get a good view of the whole complex. I don't want to disturb my tenant yet and I would prefer to be able to tell her that it might only be the landlord that's going to change.'

They were going past Laura's door now, heading for the stairs.

'What's the rental return like, Carla?'

'Not bad at all. But that's another reason I don't want to approach my tenant yet. She's got a friend who's secretly paying half her rent.' The woman's voice was fading. 'Her little boy's got cancer...how sad is that?'

Very softly, Laura let the door click shut.

Her first thought was that her landlord was wrong. Harry didn't have cancer any more.

Her second thought, as she kicked off her shoes and sank down onto the edge of the couch, felt like a body blow. She had a friend who was paying half her rent? There was only one person who could possibly be doing that and it wasn't hard to summon a memory that should have made her suspicious all along.

'You're in a pretty exclusive part of town, Tom. I'd never be able to afford to live there.'

'You might be surprised. I think the rent is quite reasonable, actually.'

But why would he have done that?

Because he'd felt sorry for her?

Of course he had. That had been where their connection had come from in the first place. He had been through the agony of losing his own child and, at that time, he'd known that Laura could be facing the same, dreadful loss. And what else had he said? Oh, yeah... He'd offered to be a living donor for Harry because he hadn't been able to do something like that for his own son. Had he gone too far in helping them find a new place to live because of that same need to help another little boy who was facing a crisis?

Support was acceptable from friends. Welcome. But charity? It made Laura feel as if she had failed in some way. That someone thought that she wasn't capable of protecting her own child well enough.

And she felt...deceived. She had believed Tom when he'd told her what the rent was. She'd trusted him so why would the idea that he might be lying by omission have occurred to her?'

What else had he told her that she shouldn't have believed?

That she was super-smart? Gorgeous? They were just words. He didn't want to be anything more than her friend. He'd only made love to her because she'd begged him to…and because he'd felt so sorry for her?

How stupid had it been to think that a perfect apartment like this, in this part of town, would have been so affordable? About as stupid as moving in next door to Tom Chapman.

Oh…those echoes from the past were never that far away, were they?

You're so stupid…

Just get out of my way…

Laura pushed herself to her feet. She needed to get out of her own way right now and think of what needed to be done. Like a visit to the bank first thing tomorrow morning to organise a loan that would not only enable her to pay Tom back every cent he'd spent on her rent but give her enough time to find a more affordable place for her and Harry to live.

He'd probably be delighted to know that she would be living further away. It would make it a lot easier to avoid any awkward moments with either her or Harry. Oh, man…had she really believed that it was safe to open her heart to loving someone again? Tears weren't far away as Laura began to wonder if a fresh start might be the best plan despite how hard it would be to leave her friends behind. A new life in another city, perhaps?

It was partly that tears were blurring her vision that made it difficult to see the small, plastic bricks scattered over the living room carpet, but it was because she had kicked off her shoes that Laura suffered the pain of standing on one of the bricks that was out of all proportion to its size.

'*Ow…*' It was the last straw of too many upsetting thoughts and feelings. '*Harry*?' She hadn't sounded this cross with him in a very, very long time. 'Come out here right now, please, and tidy up these bricks.' Her voice was still rising as she marched towards the bathroom. 'Get them *all* in their box by the time I've had my shower and put the box in the hall cupboard. If I see a single one of those bricks again today, they're all going in the rubbish.'

As part of the Helicopter Emergency Medical Service, Tom was well used to the kind of drama that involved a lot of emergency vehicles, flashing lights and people in uniforms. Quite often, when they were arriving at an accident scene on the motorway, for example, it looked like they were landing in the middle of an action movie with numerous people and vehicles from the police, fire and ambulance service.

It was not something he was used to seeing, however, when he was arriving home in the evening after a hectic day in the emergency department of the Royal. Not that there were any ambulances or fire engines but there was a police car and a van with flashing lights looking even more dramatic due to the fading daylight, and there were people in uniforms, one of whom was blocking the gateway, which forced Tom to stop. Behind this officer he could see a handler with a police dog that seemed to be being used to search the grounds of his apartment building.

'What's going on?' Tom asked. 'Someone been burgled? Or attacked?'

'Do you live here, sir?'

'Yes, I do.'

'We've got a child missing.'

'Oh, my God…' Tom felt his heart miss a beat. '*Harry*?'

'You know him?'

'Yes. His mother's my neighbour. A good friend…' Not that he'd been a very good friend recently, had he? He hadn't even seen Harry in days. A week or more probably and that had only been a quick hi as they'd passed in the hallway. It had been so much easier to step back into safe territory and the longer they'd left it, the more uncomfortable it had seemed to become to address what was causing the growing distance between them.

'Where *is* Laura?'

'She's inside. She wants to be out searching but it's best if we do that. Especially as it doesn't look like he's on the grounds anymore.'

But Tom wasn't listening. He had pushed past the officer and was heading inside at a run. The front door of the building was open. So was Laura's door. Tom walked in without knocking. He walked past two police officers who were in the living area of Laura's apartment and straight into the kitchen where he could see Laura sitting at the table, with photographs spread out in front of her. She looked up as he reached the archway separating the kitchen and living area and by the time Tom had taken two more steps, she was on her feet.

And in his arms. They both spoke at the same time.

'I'm so sorry...' What for, Tom wasn't quite sure. For not being home earlier today so that he could have somehow prevented whatever had happened?

That Laura was facing yet another crisis in her life?

For the way he'd been keeping his distance from her? And from Harry?

'It's all my fault...' Laura was sobbing. 'I shouted at Harry for leaving his bricks on the floor. I was only in the shower for a few minutes but when I came out, he was gone...'

'He can't have gone far.' Tom tightened his hold on Laura. 'We'll find him.'

'I thought he'd just be hiding because I'd told him off. I was sure he'd be inside those bushes near the gate waiting for...waiting for you to get home. He wanted to knock on your door when we got home but I said he couldn't because you'd still be at work and...and...'

Something squeezed painfully in Tom's chest. He knew that there was a bigger reason that Laura wouldn't let Harry knock on his door. She didn't want him being a nuisance. Or upsetting him by saying something that might remind him that he'd lost his own son.

'And he said he felt sick.' Laura was still speaking quickly, as if she needed to tell Tom everything as quickly as possible. 'That his tummy was hurting and he remembered that you'd looked after him that first day when I brought him into ED…'

Tom could remember that, too. So clearly. That had been when he'd felt the first connection with Laura. When the urge to protect her had come from nowhere and had only grown stronger over the last few months. Right now, it was the strongest it had ever been and it wasn't only for Laura. He needed to be able to protect Harry, as well.

Somehow…

'What if he *is* sick?' Laura's voice was muffled, probably by a combination of tears and her face being pressed against his chest. 'And *where* is he? I looked everywhere I could think of and asked everyone I could find but nobody had seen him. Someone said I needed to call the police and that was when I got really scared and that's…' Laura gulped in a breath. '…hours ago now.'

'Just over an hour.' One of the police officers came into the kitchen. 'I know it feels like a lot longer.' She gestured towards the table. 'Have you found the most recent photograph of Harry?'

It felt like Laura was reluctant to move out of Tom's arms. He felt the same way. He didn't want to let her go. Ever. Could she see that when she looked up and held his gaze for a long moment? It felt like she could. For just a heartbeat, it felt as if any barriers between them had simply evaporated. But then Tom could see a flicker of something else. Wariness? Mistrust, even? He could feel the way she was gathering her strength from some inner resources as she pulled out of his arms and moved towards the table.

'This one's older.' Laura picked up a photograph. 'But this is his school uniform and that's what he's still wearing as far as I know.'

Tom was very familiar with that uniform of dark shorts and long socks and the blue polo shirt. He'd seen Harry wearing it dozens of times. He'd seen a whole school wearing it that day he'd taken the box of dinosaur caps there.

'And this one is the most recent, taken when he was in the oncology day unit having his last chemo session. But he's got more hair now. It's like a very short buzz cut.'

Really? It was great news that Harry's hair was already growing back but why hadn't he noticed that? Because he hadn't been looking, Tom reminded himself. He'd been avoiding a six-year-old boy who'd wanted to knock at his door. That squeeze in his chest ramped up a notch.

'He might be wearing a cap, though,' Laura told the police officer. 'I'll have a look to see if it's in his room.'

'What sort of cap is it?'

'A red one.' Tom answered for Laura. 'A red baseball cap and it's got a green dinosaur on the front. A T Rex.' He was following Laura into Harry's bedroom. It wasn't that he thought he could be helpful in searching for the cap, he just needed to stay close to her. Because the way she had just pulled away from him was so disturbing?

Harry's bedroom was untidy. The contents of his schoolbag were scattered over the floor amongst toys and books. The doors of a cupboard were open and the shelves full of clothes. Laura glanced over her shoulder as she completed a first, quick glance around the room.

'You don't need to stay. I can manage.'

'I know you can.' Laura's courage and ability to manage the worst of situations had been one of the first things he'd admired so much about her.

'Really?' There was a catch in Laura's voice as she dropped to her knees to peer under Harry's bed. 'Is that why you decided it would be a good idea to pay half my rent behind my back?'

Tom froze. How on earth had Laura found out about that? And why had it had to happen at the worst possible time?

'You lied to me, Tom.' Laura's voice was muffled but he could hear how much it had hurt her. She had trusted him and he'd let her down.

'I didn't *lie*, exactly…'

'You didn't tell me the whole truth and that's pretty much the same as lying.' Laura scrambled to her feet again. 'How can I trust anything you've ever said to me?'

'Because…because I'd never do anything to hurt you, Laura. You *or* Harry. Because…I love you.'

Laura gave her head a sharp shake, reaching into the shelves of the cupboard to pull at clothing in case the cap had been shoved between things.

'As a friend, sure. At a hint of anything more, you can't run away fast enough. I can't walk that kind of tightrope—especially right now.' She turned towards Tom and the pain in her eyes was shocking. 'I don't know where my son is, Tom. I'm *so* scared. And when you're this scared, you don't want to be with a friend you can't trust. Who can just push you out of their lives the way you can.'

Her words hit Tom like a physical blow. Hurting her had been the last thing he'd wanted to happen but it had. He *had* been trying to love her simply as a friend but he'd been lying about that, too, hadn't he? To himself as much as Laura.

They both seemed to be caught in one of those moments when time slowed and everything else became part of the background—even the terrible anxiety of not knowing where Harry was. Somehow, Tom had to let Laura know that she could trust him.

'I wanted to protect you,' he said quietly. 'I just didn't want to fall in love with you because I never wanted to risk loving and losing people I love that much again. But it happened when I wasn't watching... when I wasn't being careful enough...'

He couldn't tell if Laura was even absorbing what he was telling her. The words, even though they were coming straight from his heart, were astonishing to him and he was the one uttering them. Laura shook her head again, as if dismissing anything that wasn't relevant to what was happening right now, and after another rapid scan she left the room. 'It's not there,' she told the police officer.

Another officer came into the apartment. 'We haven't managed to pick up a useful trail with the dog yet. Have you thought any more about where he might think to go? Has he got any friends who live nearby?'

'The only person we really know around here is Tom,' Laura said. 'All his friends live up in the valley near his school.'

Tom swallowed hard. He'd been the one to persuade Laura to move into this apartment block. He'd made it easy for her by making sure she could afford it. He'd been so impressed with her attitude to life's difficulties—that you had to take the cards you were dealt and play the best possible game—but he'd been the one to put that card in her hand. He'd thought he was protecting her. Helping them both, but had he actually made life more difficult?

And Laura had been right—he had lied to her by omission. It was something else to add to the emotional storm he was currently experiencing.

'There's Aroha,' Laura added then, as if inspiration had struck. 'She's his friend from hospital and they just adore each other.'

'Could he have tried to go there? Does he know the way?' The police officer was reaching for the radio clipped to his shoulder. 'I'll get someone onto it.'

'We have walked there a few times but he's only six…he's scared to cross huge roads by himself. And besides, he knows that Aroha went home about the same time he did after his surgery. Ages ago… Oh, I've just thought of somewhere else his cap might be—in the hall cupboard.' Laura walked towards the front door of her apartment, opened the cupboard and bent down to search at floor level.

Again Tom found himself following her.

'I don't think it's here. It's a mess…' Laura shook her head. 'There's glitter everywhere and…some toys and…oh, I see what's happened.' She straightened up with the bag in her hands. 'My bag fell off the shelf here. Or maybe Harry moved it to find somewhere to put the brick box.' She peered inside the bag. 'Oh, *that's* where that big T Rex got to. It's always been one of Harry's favourites and it's been lost since that day he was in hospital for his pre-surgery MRI scan.'

Suddenly, Laura went very quiet.

'What is it?' Tom asked.

'The glitter…' Laura looked up to catch Tom's gaze and the look in her eyes was heartbreaking. 'There was a card in this bag. Harry had made it for you to say thank you for his dinosaur cap and I was supposed to put it on your desk for a surprise but…but that was the day that gang was in ED and…and it didn't get delivered but it's not in here any more, either.'

It was yet another reminder of how close Tom had become to Laura. That was the day he'd learned about her traumatic past with Harry's father. When that protective instinct had been almost overwhelming and he'd wanted to be the best friend he could be for her and to make sure that nothing awful ever happened to her again.

Well, he hadn't done a very good job of that, had he? Tom didn't like himself very much in this moment so it came as a surprise to see the way the expression in Laura's eyes changed. Any anger, or maybe it had been sadness, from the way he had deceived her seemed to have evaporated. The mistrust was gone—even the wariness. It looked like hope that she wanted to share. With him.

'I know where he's gone. He is trying to get to the Royal. Not to find Aroha. To find *you*… To give you his card.'

Laura handed the dinosaur toy to Tom and dashed back to the kitchen. She grabbed her phone from the table and then headed straight back to the door.

'You need to stay here,' one of the police officers called. 'In case he finds his way home. We've got plenty of people who can search between here and the hospital. We'll get hospital security onto it, too.'

'He'd hide from anyone like that,' Laura said. 'There's only one person he wants to see and that's Tom.'

He held out his hand as Laura reached him at the door and there was such a wash of relief to be found in the way her hand slipped into his and he could hold it firmly enough to make sure he didn't lose his grip. They were in this together, Tom realised. It felt like this mattered to him as much as it did to Laura.

He'd been an idiot to think that he could make something disappear by ignoring it. It was far too late to avoid the risk that would inevitably be there because of loving either Laura or Harry. The fear he was feeling right now told him exactly what had already happened. This was simply the push that had propelled him towards his own barriers hard enough to shatter them so he couldn't hide any longer. Laura and Harry were *his* people.

His family…

As they turned to head outside, Laura's phone rang. She had to pull her hand from Tom's to answer it but it was hard to make herself do that. The way he was holding on so tightly—the way he'd been looking at her ever since he'd stormed into her kitchen—had made it very clear that something had changed.

Something huge…

She hadn't trusted it. Part of what had caused this whole catastrophe had been what she'd overheard about Tom paying half her rent and the way he'd deceived her and the pain of realising that she'd fallen in love with someone she couldn't trust as much as she'd believed she could.

Had he actually said he was *in* love with her? She hadn't really been listening. She'd lashed out because she was so scared and all she could think about was Harry. But, right now, Laura could see that Tom was as scared as she was. He cared about Harry *that* much. He cared about *her* that much. The connection between them had never felt this powerful but Laura couldn't take the time to try and process what it could mean. There was still only one thing that she could focus on and that was, of course, her precious little boy.

The name on the screen of her phone was surprising.

'Fizz?' Frowning, Laura tilted the phone and Tom bent his head to listen.

'Where are you?' Her friend sounded worried enough to make Laura think she'd somehow heard about what was going on already.

'I'm at home.'

'Then what the heck is Harry doing here?'

Laura gasped. Her gaze flew up to catch Tom's and for a heartbeat they could share the ultimate relief that Harry was no longer missing. And it was in that moment that Laura could see the absolute truth. The love that was there for both her and Harry. She could hear the echo of his words.

I didn't want to fall in love with you...it happened when I wasn't watching...

A beat of joy morphed with that overwhelming relief but Laura had to push it aside. She would tell Tom exactly how she felt about him later. Much later—when Harry was tucked up safely in his own bed and fast asleep.

'Where's *here*?' she demanded.

'I'm still at work. It was Cooper who spotted Harry, out in the ambulance bay. He's not making much sense, though. He told Cooper you were cross and he doesn't know where Tom's gone and something about a sore tummy. He's upset.'

Again, Laura's gaze snagged Tom's and this time

she could see a reflection of her own anxiety that Harry had been telling the truth about feeling unwell. Abdominal pain could be an early sign of things Laura really didn't want to think about.

It was Tom who responded to Fizz this time.

'We're on our way.'

It might have been slightly quicker to get to the hospital on foot but the police officers needed to be sure their assistance was no longer necessary and they took both Laura and Tom in their car, parking in a designated slot at one side of the ambulance bay. Laura didn't let herself think about how Harry had managed to get across the main road to get here when it was already almost dark. She couldn't think of anything other than the need to hold her son in her arms and make sure that he was okay. Until then, she needed to hang onto Tom's hand as if she was drowning and he was keeping her head above water.

She was still holding Tom's hand as they went into the emergency department. Or rather Tom wasn't letting go of her hand and Fizz wasn't the only staff member to look astonished. Her smile, as she came to meet them, was both delighted and reassuring.

'Harry's fine,' was the first thing she said. 'He's with Cooper in the relatives' room.'

But Harry burst into tears the moment he saw his mother and Laura was in tears herself as she lifted him to hug him tightly. She heard Cooper saying that he'd leave them to it as Harry wrapped his arms around her neck and his legs around her waist, like a little monkey. She knew Tom hadn't left the room

with Cooper. She could feel him standing close behind her. So close it was easy to lean back and the
way his arm came around her shoulders made him
instantly part of this cuddle.

And it felt…

It felt like family…

She had to swallow very hard to try and stop her
tears. 'Is your tummy still sore?' she asked Harry.

'No…'

'So you won't need this fellow, then? To bite anybody?'

The sound of Tom's voice clearly startled Harry.
Had he not noticed him coming into the room with
her? She could feel the tension in his small body and
then he was wriggling to get down from her arms.

Tom must have put that green, plastic T Rex they
had found in the hall cupboard in his pocket. He was
holding it out now and his question had reminded her
of how he'd bonded with Harry from the first moment
he'd seen him in the emergency department that day.

Harry remembered, too. He was smiling as he
reached up for the toy.

'I made a card for you,' he said. With his other
hand, he was pulling a crumpled sheet of paper from
his pocket. Glitter sparkled as it rained down onto
the floor. 'I drawed T Rex. Mummy forgot to give
it to you.'

'I'm sorry about that,' Laura said. 'And I'm sorry
I was cross with you today. It wasn't your fault. I was
feeling a bit sad, that's all.'

Harry nodded as if he'd known all along. 'Because Tom wasn't at home,' he said, matter-of-factly.

Laura's breath came out in a surprised huff as her gaze flew to meet Tom's. In a way, Harry was right. She'd been devastated because of the increasing distance she could feel between herself and this man that she loved so much and she'd been wondering if he'd ever only been close because he felt sorry for her. He hadn't been "at home" for what felt like a long time.

But he was here now. Totally present. No barriers. He had Harry's card in his hands and there was a glint in his eyes that suggested an unshed tear or two.

'I'll be home from now on,' Tom said, his voice a little raw. 'As much as you want me to be.'

'I want to go home now,' Harry said. 'Will you come and play trains?'

Tom was still holding Laura's gaze. 'If that's okay with Mummy.'

'Mummy?' Harry tugged at Laura's hand. 'Can Tom come home with us now? Is that okay?'

Laura put her hand on the soft fuzz of Harry's new hair but her gaze never left Tom's. How could she look away from that question? That promise?

'It's more than okay,' she said softly. 'Let's go home.'

EPILOGUE

'I HAVE SOMETHING for you.'

'Ooh…' Laura Chapman turned from looking up at the inky night sky studded with stars to raise her eyebrows suggestively at the man who'd come to join her on the veranda of their home. 'Are the kids asleep already?'

Tom was grinning as he sat down on the double swinging chair beside her. 'That can wait.' He bent his head and placed a lingering, tender kiss on her lips. 'For a while, anyway. No…it's this…'

Laura took the small package from his hand. 'A gift? Is it a special occasion I've forgotten about? Oh, no… I don't have a present for you.'

'This is kind of a present for both of us.'

Laura opened the small box. For a moment, she stared at what was inside it, bewildered.

'A pack of cards? When do we ever play cards? Harry might like to learn but the twins are far too young…'

'Take them out,' Tom said. 'Look at the other side of the cards.'

Laura tipped them out of the box and turned them over. Instead of a normally patterned back, these cards had photographs on the other side.

'It's a kind of thank you,' Tom said softly.

'What for?'

'For changing my life.'

'But what's that got to do with cards? Oh...' Laura pressed her hand to her mouth. 'It's about that time when Harry was first sick, isn't it? When I came into your office and rambled on about the cards that you get dealt in the game of life and having to play the best game you can.' She shook her head. 'How cheesy was that? I was really embarrassed when I thought about it later.'

She picked up one of the cards. The photograph on the back was one of Harry in the oncology day unit. Totally bald but smiling proudly as he pushed his IV pole ahead of him. Laura's smile was poignant. Harry's hair had grown back thicker than ever in the end and it was black and tousled looking. So like Tom's, in fact, that anyone meeting them for the first time would have trouble believing they weren't biological father and son. Or that Harry had ever been sick. Every check-up he'd had since had been clear and they had every reason to hope that they always would be.

'Cheesy enough for me to think about it later myself,' Tom said. 'It made me wonder if I really was playing the best game I could and when I thought about you and the way you were fighting for Harry— loving him that much—it felt like I was awake for the

first time in years. Emotionally, anyway. And I felt...
lonely. I had no one to fight for. Or to fight for me.'

The photograph Laura was holding now had been
taken at their wedding—well over a year ago now.
It had been such a joyous celebration that had taken
place in a garden and had included all the most important people in their lives. This particular photograph was of Bella, who had only just learned to walk
but was being a flower girl. She had sat down on the
grass at this point, however, and Harry was trying to
persuade her to hand over the basket so that he could
scatter the petals before Harley's fat little fist could
remove any more of them.

'I thought you never would want to have people
that close again,' Laura said. 'And I totally understood why.' The chair swung gently as she tilted her
head to kiss Tom. 'I'm so glad you changed your
mind, though.'

'There's a photo of Jenny and Sam on one of the
cards. I hope that's okay.'

'Why on earth wouldn't it be? You loved them.
They're part of your story so they're part of ours, too.
Part of our family.'

Laura breath came out in a huff of laughter as she
turned over another card. 'That's the night you pro-
posed to me.'

'And we asked Harry if he remembered what he'd
asked for as his special present for being so brave.'

'And he said that he wanted his present wrapped up.'

'And you found all the old paper you had in the
cupboard and let him try.'

Laura's smile was misty. She touched the picture with her finger. Tom was lying on the floor with crumpled wrapping paper all over him and Harry had never looked so pleased with himself. She could remember how wonderful that evening had been with so much love between them all.

It was still there. Getting bigger.

She turned over another card.

'There's our house. And me looking the size of a house. How on earth did we think it was a good idea to move when I was six months pregnant with twins?'

'Your apartment was about to burst at the seams. And we'd finally found the perfect house.'

Her apartment. The one Tom had found for her. The one he'd been secretly paying half the rent on. She'd asked him why he'd done that, that night that Harry had run away to find him. That terrifying, amazing night when they had both known they were in love with each other.

'I wanted to protect you,' he'd told her. *'I just didn't want to fall in love with you...but it happened when I wasn't watching...'*

Laura gathered the cards up and snuggled more deeply into Tom's arms. 'You're so right,' she said softly. 'This is a gift for both of us. For all of us.

'And it's a reminder.' Tom pressed a kiss to Laura's hair. 'To play the best game you can. To take risks. If you're not prepared to live with the risk of losing something, that means that you don't have that something. And when it's this good...' He touched Laura's cheek with a soft stroke of his finger that finished on her lips. 'This close to perfect…'

Laura's lips parted, ready for the kiss she knew was coming. 'It's as perfect as it gets, I reckon,' she whispered. 'And we both know that loving anyone is never without risk. But life without love isn't what it should be. I love you so much, Tom.'

'Snap.' Tom's lips were touching hers now. 'It's a card game, you know…'

* * * * *

A FAMILY TO
HEAL HIS HEART

TINA BECKETT

MILLS & BOON

To my children,
who put up with my crazy schedule
and who love me in spite of it.

CHAPTER ONE

Lindy Franklin's pulse hammered, and she swiped at the alarm clock to silence it, just as she had every morning for the last two years, before falling back onto the bed in relief. Six o'clock. Just like always. Only now there was no reason to leap up and try to rush to Daisy before she woke up and started to cry. No reason to make omelets and toast for her husband. But she still needed to get up, or her mom would arrive, and she'd be late for her new job.

An actual paying job this time.

Moving back to Savannah had been the right thing to do. Even if admitting she'd been wrong was one of the hardest things she'd ever done. So had realizing that most of her old friends had moved on with their lives. And who could blame them?

Climbing out of bed and sliding her feet into a pair of fuzzy slippers, she went into the bathroom, where the words taped to her mirror caught her eye.

"New beginnings, Lindy. New beginnings." She recited the phrase just as she had every morning.

Ever since the judge had told her she was free to leave Fresno—and her old life—behind.

Today really was a new beginning for her. For the first time since the move to California she'd be able to practice medicine again. Her marriage had closed the door to a lot of things. Her release from it was slowly opening them back up again.

Mouthing her mantra one more time, she hurriedly showered and got dressed and fixed Daisy's breakfast.

The doorbell rang, and she froze for a pained second. Then she laughed. It was just her mom coming to pick up Daisy.

She swung it open and there stood Rachel Anderson, as tall and elegant as ever.

"You're early. I was just about to get her up."

"I know. I wanted to make sure I was here in plenty of time."

"You always are." She grinned and drew her mom into the house. "I don't think you've been late a day in your life."

Unlike Lindy, who tended to run just a few minutes behind no matter how hard she pushed herself. It had been one of those "failings" that had been used as a hammer.

New beginnings.

"I'm not sure that's true, sweetheart."

She was pretty sure it was. But her mom's sweet southern drawl spelled home the way nothing else ever had. She wrapped her in a tight hug.

"What was that for?"

"Just for being you."

Her mother had been a huge help in making sure she got back on her feet, first by watching Daisy while Lindy had volunteered at the women's crisis center. And now by insisting she apply for the nursing position at Mid Savannah Medical Center.

Lindy drew a deep breath. "I'll get Daisy. And I've just put breakfast on the table. Do you want something?"

"No, and I told you I could fix Daisy breakfast at the house."

"I know you did. But I want to try to keep things as normal as possible for her, since I'll be away from home a lot longer than I was before."

Normal. What a beautiful word. She'd only recently realized just how beautiful it was.

"And you will." Rachel peered into her daughter's face. "How are you holding up?"

"Good, Mom. Good. It's just been crazy, trying to get settled in the new house. I didn't expect to get an answer on the job so soon."

Her husband had left her one good thing: a life insurance policy that had helped her coast along. It had made her squirm to take the money, but that money had also paid for therapy and sundry other things.

Mid Savannah Medical Center had asked about the three-year lapse since her last position in Georgia, but she'd covered by saying she'd taken some time off to be home with her daughter. Not exactly a lie. She'd gotten a surprise phone call the next day telling her she had her dream job as a surgical nurse in the pediatric ward. Her parents had cosigned for the loan on her little starter home—since she hadn't had a job at the time. She'd vowed to herself that she'd make them proud.

"I told you it wouldn't take long. Maybe you should have waited a little while longer before getting back out there. I'm sorry if I rushed you into applying."

She gave her mom's hand a squeeze. "You didn't. I needed to do something, and this was the perfect opportunity."

Her mom was a music professor at one of the local colleges. She'd been alarmed when Lindy had told her she wasn't going back to work after getting married. She'd been right to be concerned, because Luke had wanted to pack up and move to Fresno almost immediately, effectively isolating her from everyone and everything she'd known.

But that was all water under the bridge. She was back, and she intended to stay back. Nothing or no one would ever change that again.

"Why don't you let me get Daisy ready? I promise I'll lock the doors behind me when I leave."

She hesitated. Locking the doors herself had become her own personal ritual. One she wasn't sure she was ready to give up. But she'd have to sometime. And the last thing she wanted was to give her mom more cause to worry. "Are you sure you don't mind?"

"No. It'll give me and my granddaughter some time to bond before heading out."

Lindy's chest ached. Living on the other side of the country meant that her mom hadn't seen Daisy until she'd moved back home. Not for lack of trying.

Luke had thought of every reason under the sun why her parents couldn't come to see them, though: the house was too small; the trip would be too hard on them; he couldn't spare the time away from work.

Those days were behind her now. And her parents had already spent the last two years getting to know Daisy. And Daisy—maybe because of how young she was—had adapted to her new life quickly. Her daughter hadn't asked once about her father, for which Lindy was truly grateful.

"I think you bonded the moment she saw you and Daddy. But thank you." She glanced at her phone. She still had twenty-five minutes to get to work, but Savannah traffic could be unpredictable. "Maybe I can be on time for once in my life. Hopefully they'll like me."

"Just be yourself, honey. They're all going to love you. How could they not?"

And with those words ringing in her ears, she scooped up her keys, gave her mom a kiss on the cheek and hurried out the door.

Zeke Bruen was not loving the new surgical nurse. She'd done nothing wrong and was on top of every request almost before he asked, but he'd seen her eyes repeatedly stray toward the big clock on the wall. Counting down the hours until she was with her husband? Boyfriend?

Gritting his teeth, he ignored those thoughts. Some people did have a life outside the hospital. He certainly didn't expect everyone on his team to be like he was. But when they were here, he expected them to be present. Especially when it was a certain person's first day on the job.

Things had been so rushed getting into the surgical suite that he hadn't had a chance to introduce himself, although he'd been told the new nurse's name as he'd scrubbed in: Lindolynn Franklin. So maybe someone had told her his as well. Well, it wouldn't hurt to have a little chat with her after they were done here.

And do what, Zeke? Confront her about looking at the clock?

He looked too, but it was to keep track of whether things were going as expected.

Maybe Nurse Franklin was doing the same thing. Somehow he didn't think so. Those glances had seemed furtive and once, when she'd caught his eye afterward, color had flooded into the portion of her face visible above her surgical mask. The sight had turned his stomach inside out. That certainly hadn't helped.

Returning his attention to his patient with an irritated shrug, he busied himself with reconnecting the pulmonary artery, making sure each tiny stitch he placed was secure. The last thing he needed was to close this little girl's chest and have the repair leak.

A half-hour later he was done, giving a nod to each of his team with murmured thanks. Then he left the room and stripped off his gloves, relief washing through him. He'd done this particular surgery dozens of times, but each time he cracked open a child's chest, a moment of doubt threatened to paralyze him.

He'd always gotten over it, his muscle memory taking over until he could get his mind back in the game. Maybe that's what had happened with the new nurse. The only thing to do was feel her out.

He propped a shoulder against the wall outside the double doors as the surgical team slowly filed out, many of them congratulating him. That wasn't what he was waiting for, however. He was searching for an unfamiliar face.

There. Her eyes connected with his for an instant before she attempted to veer off in the other direction. Good try. He fell into step beside her. "Sorry. I didn't get a chance to introduce myself before we got started."

He held out a hand. "Ezekiel Bruen."

"Oh, um, I'm Lindy Franklin. I'm new here."

Lindy. That fit. As did the rest of her face, now that her mask was gone. Delicate bones and the subtle curve of her cheeks gave her a breakable air that made him uneasy, and he had no idea why.

"So I've heard." He thought for a second she was going to ignore his outstretched hand, but then she stopped walking and placed hers in it, the light squeeze reaffirming his musings and making him hesitate. Maybe he shouldn't say anything.

And if it had been another member of his team?

He stiffened his resolve, determined to keep things professional. "I noticed you were in a rush to get out of surgery. Not happy with where the administration placed you?"

"What? Oh…no. I mean yes." That vibrant color

he'd seen in the operating room reappeared, only this time he was actually able to watch as it flowed up her cheeks before receding like an ocean wave. "Why would you think I was in a hurry to get out of there?"

He ignored the quick tightening of his gut. "You were watching that clock pretty closely."

The pink returned, darker this time, and white teeth sank into a full lower lip. "I was just..." She paused as if trying to figure out how to explain herself. "I didn't realize I was. And I'm perfectly happy with where I've been placed."

So she wasn't going to let him in on whatever had kept her mind so occupied.

Well, if that's the way she wanted to play it... "As long as you're up to the demands of working with the surgical staff."

Her back stiffened, and her chin angled up. Light brown eyes rimmed with dark lashes met his head on. "I am quite up to the demands. Thank you for your concern, though."

That show of strength made him smile.

It wasn't a true thank you, and they both knew it. But he'd gotten his message across. Time to revert to his normal, friendly self. If it even existed anymore.

"Have you been in town long?"

"I was born and raised here in Savannah." The slightest flicker of her eyelids said there was something more to that story.

"So was I." He studied her for a second. "Did you transfer here from one of the other hospitals?"

"No."

So much for being friendly. He guessed it was none of his business where she'd come from. She could have just graduated from nursing school for all he knew. But the way she'd handled those instruments said she knew her way around an operating room. That kind of self-assurance only came with experience. But if she hadn't transferred from one of the local hospitals, where had she gained that experience? Unless she actually did have something to hide. Some kind of mistake that hadn't shown up on her résumé? He didn't want to go digging through her past or call her previous place of employment, but maybe he should. Just so he'd be aware of any issues before they cropped up and became a problem here. Or maybe he should just ask her outright.

"Where did you practice before this, then?" He could have asked Human Resources, but he wanted to see if she would balk about answering.

She named a place in the heart of Savannah.

"I thought you said you didn't transfer."

"I didn't." She gave a quick shrug. "I took a few years off and then decided I couldn't live without nursing."

She'd taken a few years off…

It hit him all of a sudden. His glance went to her ring finger. It was empty, but he was pretty sure there was an indentation there where a ring had once been. So she'd been married, but wasn't any longer? She could have taken some time off during that relationship, but he had a feeling he knew what had caused her inordinate interest in that clock. "I take it you have a child."

Her mouth popped open and then closed again, the color that had seeped into her face disappearing completely. "How did you know?"

"Just a hunch. The clock-watching had to be for a reason. And you took 'a few years off.' I wasn't trying to pry."

"It's okay. She's three. It's my first time leaving her with anyone for this length of time."

Including the child's father? Something about that made the hair on the back of his neck stand up, although it was ridiculous. Maybe the man had traveled so much that there'd never been time to leave her with him or with anyone else. Or maybe the mark on her finger was a figment of his imagination.

It was also none of his business.

She gave a quick shake of her head as if reading his thoughts before meeting his gaze again. "Well, it was nice working with you, Dr. Bruen—"

"Call me Zeke. Everyone does."

"Okay…" She drew the word out like it made her uncomfortable. Did she think he was hitting on her? Damn. Nothing could be further from the truth, despite that quick jerk to his senses after seeing her without her surgical mask for the first time. He hadn't felt that since… Well, in quite a while.

Time to put her mind at ease, if that were the case.

"We're pretty informal here at Mid Savannah."

"I guess I'm not used to that. You can call me Lindy, then."

"What's your daughter's name?" He had no idea why he asked that, and the last thing he should be doing was talking about baby girls with anyone. He never encouraged his colleagues to talk about their children, and most of the old-timers knew why. Maybe it was because of how reticent she'd been to talk to him. About anything.

"Her name is Daisy."

Daisy. He liked that. His own daughter's name had been Marina.

A shaft of pain arced through him and then was gone.

"Nice name."

"Thank you."

His glance went past her to see Nancy, one of the OR nurses, coming up the corridor, heading for them. She touched Lindy on the shoulder, only to have her give a squeak and nearly jump out of her skin. She whirled to the side, face white, eyes wide. She seemed to go slack when she saw who it was.

Her fellow nurse frowned. "Sorry. I didn't mean to scare you." She held up a phone. "Is this yours? It was left on the desk."

"Oh! Yes, it is. Thank you." She suddenly grinned, her nose crinkling on either side. That smile made her face light up in a way that made his gut jerk even harder. He kicked the sensation away, irritated with himself.

"And you didn't scare me."

He wasn't sure he believed her, but he'd already shown far too much interest in her life—and her—

than he should have. The last thing he needed was to have the new nurse get any wrong ideas.

Because there weren't any to have.

And if he was going to get out of here, now was the time to do it without feeling like he'd abandoned her. "Well, I have a few other patients to see, so if you two will excuse me."

"Of course." Nancy sent him a smile, while Lindy seemed to take her time looking at him, her phone now in her hand, her expression wary once again.

"I'll try to do a little less clock watching the next time we work together." As if she couldn't help herself, her lips soon turned up at the edges and those tiny lines beside her nose reappeared.

He swallowed. "Not a problem. If you have any questions about the hospital or how we do things, I'm sure Nancy, myself or any of the other staff members can steer you in the right direction."

"I appreciate that."

With that he gave the pair a quick wave, before turning around and heading in the opposite direction. Part of him wanted to solve the mystery of the newest staff member and part of him wanted nothing to do with those kinds of guessing games. Especially if it involved someone who'd recently broken up with their spouse or significant other.

Or who had a young daughter.

Better just to do his job and pretend not to notice what Lindy Franklin did or didn't do. As long as she did her job, he had no complaints.

And even if he did, he was going to keep them to himself.

For his own good. And maybe for hers too.

CHAPTER TWO

LINDY WASN'T TOO sure about bringing her mom and Daisy to the hospital for lunch. Especially not after what had happened with Dr....Zeke. Would he think she was distracted again?

She was off duty, so it was really none of his business.

Besides, she hadn't been distracted per se. She'd been well aware of what she was doing and what she was supposed to be doing. And none of that involved the hunky surgeon.

Hunky? Really, Lindy? She gave an internal roll of her eyes.

Besides, her mom wanted to see the hospital, and she could think of no good reason to tell her no. And Daisy had seemed excited about eating somewhere other than at her or Mimi's house.

"It's hospital food, so don't get your hopes up."

Her mom laughed. "I don't have to cook, so I'm sure it'll be great."

"Poor Dad. Is he fending for himself today?"

"No. He's headed to the lodge to see his buddies.

Which leaves me with time to spend with my favorite daughter."

"I'm your only daughter, Mom." She flashed a quick smile. "But I'll take whatever time with you I can get."

Especially since she hadn't seen her parents for the duration of her marriage, something that should have sent up a red flag. Luke had supposedly landed a fabulous job across the country almost as soon as the ceremony was over. But, looking back, she wondered if quitting his job in Savannah had been the plan all along. There'd actually been quite a few flags that she'd missed along the way. All because she'd "fallen in love" and hadn't taken precautions. Then, when she'd realized she was pregnant, she'd been too quick to say yes when he'd asked her to marry him.

But no more. If she ever found herself in a relationship again, she was going to make sure she let her mind do most of the work, rather than putting her heart in charge.

She had no desire to jump into that particular lake again. Maybe she'd wait until Daisy was grown up before dating. When she thought about what could have happened the last night she and Luke had been together...

She swallowed, her hand going to her throat as a phantom ache threatened to interfere with her breathing.

Stop it, Lindy. Daisy is fine. You're fine.

Leading the way through the door to the cafeteria, she frowned when she spied the doctor she'd thought of as "hunky" just a few minutes ago. Great. Just what she needed.

She hadn't had to work with him for the last several days, thank God. But she hadn't really expected to see him here either.

Why not? The man had to eat, just like everyone else.

Just as she was ready to shepherd her mom and daughter back the way they'd come with a manufactured excuse, Zeke's eyes met hers, narrowing slightly before moving from her to her mom and then to Daisy.

Then he frowned, deep furrows giving his face an ominous look that made her shiver.

Her chin went up. She wasn't cowering ever again. She had as much of a right to be in here as anyone. She changed her mind about leaving and ushered her mom and Daisy over to the line and got behind them, swinging Daisy up into her arms. "What do you want to eat, honey?"

"Sheeshburger."

"A cheeseburger? How many of those have you had recently?"

Her mom shook her head. "Hey, don't look at me. We had plenty of fruits and vegetables to go with yesterday's burger."

Lindy's dad loved to cook out on the grill, and his meals were always delicious. "I was teasing."

Against her volition, her gaze slid back to Zeke, who she found was still watching her from the coffee bar. The frown was gone, and in its place... Another shiver went through her, this time for a completely different reason. When he snapped the lid onto whatever he'd just poured in his cup, he didn't move away from them like she'd hoped. Instead, he headed their way.

The shivery awareness died a quick death. She had no desire for her daughter to meet any of her male colleagues. Especially not Zeke.

She wanted her daughter to have a good long stretch of stability to hopefully counteract anything she might have seen sensed or heard during her mother's disastrous marriage.

Then Zeke was in line with them. "Hi. You must be off today."

This time it was her brows that came together, until she realized she wasn't dressed in scrubs. Although there were people who did bring their street clothes to work and changed into them after their shift. "I am. I thought I'd show my mom and Daisy around."

"Good idea."

There was an awkward pause, which her mom was quick to fill. "I'm Rachel Anderson. I take it you and my daughter know each other?" She shot Lindy a glance filled with curiosity.

Oh, no, Mom. Not you too.

"He's one of the pediatric surgeons here at the hospital." The words came out a little gruffer than she'd meant for them to.

Zeke held out his hand and introduced himself, making her realize that she should have at least told her mom his name. But the momentary awareness she'd felt a few minutes ago had left her flustered, and Lindy didn't like it. She'd been flustered by Luke as well and look how that had turned out.

"Why don't you join us?" her mom said as Lindy just stood there, staring at him. Damn. Soon Zeke was going to think he'd been right when he'd said she seemed distracted. She was. And this time it wasn't by thoughts of her daughter.

It was by the surgeon himself.

"That's up to Lindy."

What? Why was it up to her? She did not want to cast the deciding vote. "It's fine with me." She shifted Daisy a little higher on her hip, keeping her close. But thankfully Zeke hadn't shown much interest in her daughter. And Lindy would rather keep it that way.

They somehow made it through the line, although she no longer felt like eating. And it wasn't due to the quality of the food on offer in front of them. She tried to take one of the two trays her mom was wrestling with, only to have Zeke take it instead. "I'm not eating much, so I'll put mine on your tray, if that's okay."

Great. She guessed it didn't matter since she'd already said he could join them. "It's fine. No surgeries this afternoon?"

"I had one in the middle of the night and ended up staying. As soon as I eat, I'm heading home to crash."

A surgery in the middle of the night was never a good thing. "Was it bad?"

He nodded, a muscle in his jaw tight. "Very bad. A teenager hung herself."

"Oh, God." Her mom was thankfully ahead of them, since her lungs had suddenly seized as remembered sensations washed over her. The cramping of muscles starved of oxygen. The blackening of her vision. The realization that if she passed out, it was all over.

Somehow she got hold of herself and swallowed several times to rid herself of the memories. She cleared her throat, somehow needing to ask the question. "Did she make it?"

"Yes. Her trachea suffered a partial separation, and we had to do a tracheotomy and then go in and repair the damage. But she'll be fine physically. And hopefully she'll get the emotional help for whatever caused her to do this."

"How terrible." Lindy had been fortunate that there'd been no permanent damage to her throat. Nothing to repair. Except her heart. And she was still dealing with some of the fallout from that. Like when Nancy had tapped her on the shoulder. Even after two years of freedom, she was sometimes easily startled. And she tended to walk on eggshells around people, afraid of making someone angry, even though she knew that fear was irrational. But, like her therapist had said, it would take time.

Lindy picked out an egg salad sandwich and a small cup of fruit, while her mom put Daisy's picks on her own tray. And, yes, there was a cheeseburger. That made her smile.

She still had her daughter. There'd been no custody battles. No lengthy court cases. There'd been no need for anything, other than a coffin, in the end.

Daisy would never know her father. But she couldn't help but think that was for the best.

A minute or two later they were seated at one of the small tables. Zeke yawned and downed a healthy portion of his coffee.

"Sorry. I'll try not to fall asleep on you."

A pang of compassion went through her. Anyone who saw medicine as a glamorous profession hadn't seen the toll it took on those in the field. Zeke had probably been uprooted from his bed to come in and do the surgery. And then he'd probably gone on rounds this morning and dealt with his own caseload of patients. "Were you scheduled for today?"

"Yes. But I wasn't slated to come in until seven."

"And your surgery was when?"

"Two."

"You have to be exhausted. Are you off tomorrow?" She wasn't sure why she cared. Plenty of healthcare professionals went through the same thing on a daily basis. But she could see the tired lines bracketing his mouth and eyes. Maybe that's what had made his earlier frown seem so fierce.

"Yes."

Her mom laid Daisy's food out on a napkin and put a straw in her cup of juice. "I remember the days when you pulled those kinds of hours before you got…" Her voice faded away.

Thankful her mother had caught herself. Lindy nodded and forced herself to smile. "I'm sure you pulled your share of all-nighters when I was a kid."

"Of course. But that's different from what you and Dr. Bruen do. And you were a pretty healthy child."

As was Daisy, thank goodness.

"Call me Zeke, please."

Lindy's brows went up. So it wasn't just the staff who were allowed to call him by his given name. That privilege evidently extended to their immediate relatives.

He took another gulp of his coffee, bloodshot eyes glancing at her for a second before moving over to Daisy. Then they closed, and he pinched the bridge of his nose as if suddenly sporting a massive headache.

"You don't have to stay here and keep us company. Why don't you go home and get some sleep?" This time her smile wasn't as difficult to find. "Besides, if you drink too much of that stuff you won't be able to do anything but stare at the ceiling."

"Said as if you've done exactly that."

"I have. And it wasn't fun." It also wasn't for the reasons he thought. It had been when her marriage had been at its lowest point, and she'd been worrying about Daisy's future and the hard decision ahead of her. That choice had been taken out of her hands a day later.

At least Daisy would never have to decide whether or not she wanted to see her father in the future.

Zeke pushed his cup away. "I'll take your word for it. And sleep sounds like heaven right now." He stood. "I think I'll try to do just that. Thanks for letting me join you."

"You're welcome."

Daisy lifted her cheeseburger and waved it at him. "Bye-bye."

He looked like he wasn't sure what to do for a second, then he gave a half-smile. "Goodbye to you too. And nice meeting you, Mrs. Anderson."

"Call me Rachel, since I'm calling you Zeke."

"Okay. It was nice meeting you…Rachel."

"You as well."

Once he was gone, her mother looked at her. "The doctors here are a lot cuter than at your last hospital."

"Mom!" It wasn't like she hadn't noticed how good looking Zeke was. The word *hunk*—of all things— wasn't something she threw around every day. But the last thing she needed was to fantasize about the man.

Oh, Lord, no. You are not having fantasies. About anyone!

"Don't you 'Mom' me. You can't let one bad experience turn you off love forever."

"It was a little more than a bad experience, don't you think?" She worded it carefully. Even though Daisy didn't know exactly what had happened, she might be able to understand more than Lindy thought.

"I know, but not all men are like Luke. Take your father, for example."

"I know, but I'm not ready to date. I honestly don't know if I'll ever want to again." Even Mr. Hunk himself would have a hard time moving her off that mark. Even if he wanted to. Which he didn't.

Her mom reached over to squeeze her hand. "I understand. Really, I do. When the time is right, you'll change your mind."

This time Lindy let it go. There was no use arguing over her decisions about dating. And as much as her mom said she understood, how could she possibly know what it had been like to live with someone like Luke? A good chunk of his life insurance policy had gone to pay off credit cards he had taken out in her name. Her discovery of those cards had been what had set him off that last time. It was no wonder she was now leery of relationships. And Daisy had to come first at this point in her life.

"*If* I change my mind, you'll be one of the first to know."

Rachel gave her daughter's hand one last squeeze and then withdrew. "That's my cue to change the subject. Are you getting used to living on your own?"

Lindy's quaint little cottage wasn't all that far from the hospital. It was within walking distance, which was nice. And it overlooked a nearby park, which was even nicer. She and Daisy had strolled through it on more than one occasion already. "I am. Thank you so much for helping me find the house. We're making it a home, little by little, aren't we, Daisy? She loves the princess stickers you got for her wall. We've already put them up."

"Princess!" Daisy said the word in a loud voice.

"I saw them. She is my little princess, aren't you?" Her mom tweaked Daisy's nose.

The tyke repeated the word like a battle cry, stretching her arms out as if showing her grandmother just how much of a princess she was.

They laughed and suddenly Lindy was fiercely

glad she'd decided to return to Savannah when she had. She was back among familiar landmarks and people she loved. It made the odd little pangs in her chest bearable.

She couldn't change the past, but she could make the future something her daughter could look forward to without fear. And if she'd never met Luke, Daisy might not be here at all. Didn't that make it worth it?

Worth it? Lindy hadn't deserved what she'd gotten, but she did love her daughter more than life itself. And, yes, she was glad that at least something good had come out of their marriage.

"I guess I know what she might want to be for Halloween."

Lindy's chest swelled with love. Her mom hadn't showered her with recriminations or accusations. She'd been truly glad that her daughter had come back. If she'd known how the marriage would turn out, she'd kept that declaration to herself. Both of her parents had. They loved Daisy like she did, unconditionally, insisting that they be the ones to provide childcare rather than Lindy finding a daycare center. And Daisy was thriving. Finally. She hadn't noticed the pale fear in her baby's eyes while she'd been in the situation, but now that they were out? Oh, yes, she could see nuances she'd never known were there. It made the guilt that much worse. She'd thought she'd protected Daisy from the worst parts of her marriage, and she had. But, even as an infant, had she been able to pick up on the subtle emotions Lindy thought she'd hidden?

She'd probably never know.

New beginnings.

No more staring in the rearview mirror. There was nothing back there she needed to see. She was supposed to be looking to the future.

And if her glance strayed to places it shouldn't?

Like Zeke Bruen?

Yes. She could acknowledge that he'd caught her eye. But if she was smart, Lindy would make sure that was all he caught: her glance. Because a glance was temporary. A gaze, however…well, that carried a lot more permanence. And that was going to be reserved for Daisy and Daisy only.

No matter how difficult that might prove to be.

Zeke could see Lindy standing by the nurses' station, staring at the patient board.

Lunch the other day had been a blur of exhaustion and depleted emotions. Suicide attempts were always difficult, but this was one life they'd saved.

For how long, though?

The kicker was that these teens thought they wanted to die. Zeke's daughter, on the other hand, had wanted to live. Only she hadn't gotten to choose.

He glanced at the board. Two of those up there were his patients. Lindy would be one of the surgical nurses. He'd asked for her and wasn't sure why. He suspected some of it had to do with seeing the object of her clock-watching up close and personal. Small and full of smiles, Lindy's daughter was a miniature version of her. Only Lindy's smile seemed much more elusive than her child's. And something Rachel had said stayed with him over the last couple of days. And he couldn't even remember exactly what it had been. It was more her tone of voice.

He should turn around and walk away before he found himself caught up in something he wanted no part of. But to do so might make her think it was because of her. And she'd be right.

Better that he go over and talk to her as if she were any other member of the team. "Off to an early start?"

She whirled around, a hand pressed to her chest, face draining of all color. When she focused on him, she gave a nervous laugh and leaned back against the counter. "Oh, God, sorry. You startled me."

Startled? That was the second time he'd seen her react like that.

"I didn't mean to. Did you think I was the hospital administrator or something?"

"No." She shook her head. "I was just lost in thought. Didn't anyone ever tell you not to sneak up on people?"

"They did. I just wasn't aware that I was sneaking."

"No, of course you weren't." She sucked down a deep breath and blew it out. "Sorry. Anyway, did you catch up on your sleep?"

He couldn't remember the last time he'd scared someone like that, and he was pretty sure that time it had been on purpose. But her explanation was reasonable.

"I did, thanks. Just checking in about the surgeries I have scheduled. You'll be scrubbing in on both of them?" Since he'd put her name in as someone he wanted on those cases, the question was more rhetorical than anything.

Her glance went back to the board. "Ledbetter and Brewster? Yes. Anything I should know?"

"Ledbetter has had a reaction to anesthesia before, so they're tweaking the ratios. Just wanted you to be aware in case we have to make a sudden shift in care."

"Okay, got it. And Brewster?"

"We're doing her first. Pneumothorax. Routine."

Lindy gave a visible swallow and looked back up at the board. "She's only five? Since when is a collapsed lung in a child that age considered routine?"

"When that child has been kicked by her father. And I worded that badly. It's never routine." Just saying the words made a jet of anger spurt through Zeke's chest. What kind of monster hurt his own child? Or any child?

"That's horrible." Her voice came out as a whisper.

The boards listed names and ages and team members, but nothing more.

"I know. I thought maybe you'd looked at the charts."

She reached behind her and gripped the edge of the desk. "I just got here. I was going to look at them once I figured out which cases I'd be working on."

The hospital had code numbers for staffing the surgical suites, with the surgeons sometimes handpicking their crews, and other times it was the luck of the draw, depending on scheduling.

Zeke had asked for her, telling himself he wanted

to see her in action now that he knew a little more about her. There were a few surgical nurses that he preferred not to work with, either because they were difficult or because they were slow to hand over instruments. Every surgeon had their own style and not everyone meshed with his. He knew he could sometimes be demanding.

Like confronting Lindy about being distracted that first time working together?

It had nothing to do with idle interest and everything to do with watching her work. She definitely had compassion, judging from her reaction to the patient with the collapsed lung.

"These kinds of cases are always difficult."

"Yes. Yes, they are."

The thread of resignation in her voice gave him pause. Maybe her other hospital saw more cases involving domestic violence than Mid Savannah did, although even one case was too many.

"We'll get her patched up, and hopefully the system will do what it's supposed to do and keep her out of that home. I think the dad is in jail right now."

"As well he should be. And her mother?"

"She said she was at work when the incident happened."

"The incident. That's one way to put it." Her tight voice spoke volumes. Then she sighed. "Sorry. I didn't mean to snap. The wheels of justice just never seem to turn fast enough."

"I didn't think you were, and you're right, they

don't. But those wheels can't move on their own. There has to be that initial push."

First she'd jumped when he'd come up behind her, now this. Was she just out of sorts today or was something else going on?

"Those situations are just so hard. I actually volunteered at a center helping victims of domestic violence, so it's just straying a bit too close to home."

"That's interesting. I sat in on a meeting of department heads a couple of weeks ago. The hospital has discussed putting together a center for victims of domestic violence or abuse. They already have a grant from a private donor, but they need someone to jump start things. So far no one has stepped up to volunteer."

Lindy's head came up. "Really? I would love to be involved."

"Are you still volunteering somewhere?"

"Not at the moment. I took a leave of absence so I could focus on this job. I thought once I got established I could go back at some point."

An alarm sounded in one of the rooms and a light flashed in the panel of monitors behind her. She glanced back.

"Go," he said. "I'll see you in surgery as soon as our patient is prepped. If you're serious about helping out with the center, let the administrator know. I'm sure they could use someone who already knows the ropes."

"Thanks. I might just do that." With that, she walked away, headed for the nearby room, leaving

Zeke with more questions than answers. He was usually pretty adept at figuring people out after talking with them a time or two. But she was proving to be an enigma.

There was part of him, though, that wondered if he wasn't missing something obvious.

Like what?

He had no idea. And he was definitely not going to start asking her a bunch of questions. He barely knew her. Maybe he should drop in on the hospital administrator himself and let the cat out of the bag about her experience. Not everyone could stomach what went on behind closed doors. The fact that she could...

How did one decide to volunteer for something like that? Especially if you had no first-hand knowledge?

Something kicked up in the back of his head. Lindy had never mentioned a husband.

So? That meant nothing.

Or did it?

Back at the cafeteria it had been Daisy and her mother with no mention of anyone else being involved in her life.

Again, it might not be significant.

And if it was?

Then helping with the program might be the best thing that Lindy could do. Not only for the hospital's sake. But if the weird feelings he had going on were true, then it might do Lindy some good as well.

CHAPTER THREE

FIVE DAYS AFTER helping to re-inflate a little girl's damaged lung, Lindy went and talked to the administrator about the program and offered to help. In doing so, she told him about her past, including the truth behind Luke's death. As she did so, a weight lifted off her chest. He asked if she'd be willing to speak at an informal Q&A about the program that was already in the works. If there was interest, they would move forward. If not, they wouldn't. He would leave it up to her as far as how much she shared.

Could she do it? Well, it was too late now, since she'd already agreed. She just had to figure out what she was going to say.

By concealing her past from her colleagues, she'd wondered if she wasn't contributing to a culture that encouraged people to hide behind a mask of normalcy.

In fact, she'd almost told Zeke in front of the schedule board as they'd talked about the little girl's injuries but had chickened out. If he was at the meeting, he would probably soon know, anyway. And that scared her to death. Would he look at her differently? Feel pity for her?

She didn't know why it mattered, but it did.

As painful as it was to look back at what had happened, Zeke's words about the wheels needing a push to start them turning made a lot of sense. In fact, they'd played over and over in her head all weekend long, and they were still going strong today. Even if it was just manning a phone on a helpline for an hour or two a week after her shift, she could help to be that push that changed someone's life for the better. And it fit right in with her "new beginnings" motto.

She might not be a trained psychologist, but she was a medical professional. She also had first-hand knowledge of the excuses that kept someone from leaving a deplorable relationship. She'd used those same excuses. Luke's gambling problems—which she hadn't known about when they'd dated—had been spiraling out of control for years.

That was probably part of the reason for the job change right after their marriage, although she didn't know that for sure. He'd gone to great lengths to hide the truth, his behavior becoming more and more erratic and threatening. Once she'd found out about the credit cards he'd taken out in her name, it was all over. Lindy had almost lost her life. But in the end, it was Luke who'd paid the ultimate price.

She still had nightmares about the last day they'd been together. In fact, the night before Zeke had startled her, she'd woken up in a cold sweat and had lain awake for hours. So when Zeke's voice had come out of nowhere at the desk that day, her hands had curled into fists out of instinct.

There'd been no danger, though. Not from him.

But it also made her aware of how she'd changed in the years since the police had come to arrest her husband. She'd dropped her guard in some ways, but in other ways those walls were just as tall and as thick as they'd ever been. Time did dull the fear, but it hadn't obliterated it completely.

And maybe that was a good thing. It kept her wary of what could happen if she didn't stay vigilant. She'd made a vow to herself never to put her daughter in a situation like that again.

Would Zeke be interested in volunteering, if the hospital program did get underway?

What had even brought that to mind?

Maybe the memory of the way he'd operated on five-year-old Meredith Brewster. That man had been a study in compassion that brought tears to her eyes. He'd been worried about an injury to her spleen. Something that was insidious, often having few symptoms as the organ slowly filled with blood. But if it ruptured, the effects could be catastrophic. Luckily everything had come back normal, aside from the collapsed lung and a fractured rib.

Normal?

Nothing about it had been normal.

But she could be the change that started that wheel turning. And maybe asking Zeke to help could be part of that initial push.

Besides, she was curious about what his response would be.

She was sure her parents wouldn't mind watching Daisy for an hour while she talked to the group. Even if it meant exposing scars that weren't completely healed?

If not now, then when?

That was the question and one she had no answer to. So it was time to jump in and make sure that terrible period in her life did some good. Even if it meant she and Zeke might be seeing a lot more of each other.

She wasn't watching the clock. It appeared Lindy had been able to settle into her role of surgical nurse without worrying about her daughter.

Not much of her face was visible with the mask and surgical cap. But those light brown eyes were there. And they were still wreaking havoc with his insides. They came up unexpectedly and caught him looking. Damn. He needed to pay more attention to what he was about to do and less attention to the way she was affecting him.

This might be a routine 'scope, but the child deserved every ounce of his attention. He jerked his glance to the anesthesiologist, who was standing at her head. "She's ready for the procedure," the man said.

The twilight sedation would allow his patient to swallow and follow instructions, but she would have little or no memory of doing so when they were done with the procedure.

Zeke pulled the loupes down over his eyes. "Okay, Tessa, open your mouth."

It always amazed him that part of the brain was still aware and could obey simple commands even while the patient's conscious self was wandering through a gray haze. He slid the endoscope into place. "Big swallow."

Tessa complied, gagging slightly as the scope was introduced. Then it was all business.

"Suction."

Lindy was right there, clearing excess moisture from the child's mouth.

He relayed his observations, knowing the microphone that hung overhead would pick up his words, which he could transcribe later. "Pink mucosa with no abnormalities. Advancing to the sphincter."

He then slid past it, moving into the main part of Tessa's stomach. This was where he needed to take his time. "How's the patient doing, Steve?"

"Everything looks good."

He adjusted the focus of the 'scope and went over the surface of the stomach. "Normal appearance of the fundus and the lesser curvature." But when he turned the 'scope to face the other direction he pulled up short. There was a large eroded section of the lining and a mass about the size of a golf ball. "I'm seeing a nodule with irregular borders in the middle of the greater curvature. There is a moderate amount of erosion of the surrounding tissue. Going to attempt a biopsy of the mass."

He moved in closer and changed the setting, snapping several pictures, and then grabbed a piece of the tissue with the pincers. He cut and cauterized in one fluid motion. "I've got it. Bleeding is negligible."

He surveyed the rest of the stomach but didn't see anything else abnormal, so he eased the 'scope out, his chest tight. He had only seen one other growth similar to this one and the outcome hadn't been good. He could only hope the pathology findings were different in this case and would allow the child to go on with her life.

This time it was Lindy's eyes who were on him, the narrow furrow between her brows saying that she'd had the same suspicion. But now wasn't the time to dwell on that. He needed to finish the procedure and make sure Tessa was okay. Then they could worry about the other stuff.

Fifteen minutes later, she was waking up, lids fluttering as her awareness returned. "Am I okay?" Her voice was raspy, which was normal.

"You did just fine." It wasn't exactly what she'd asked, but close enough. He forced a smile, pulling down his mask so she could see his face. "That wasn't so bad, was it?"

But what was coming might very well prove to be.

"No, I didn't feel anything."

"That's what I like to hear. Dr. Black is pretty good at his job." He glanced at Steve, whose face was as solemn as everyone else's.

"I do my best." The other doctor laid his hand on her head, ignoring the surgical cap. "You did a good job too, kiddo."

Yes, she had. And she'd been stoic every time he'd met with her parents, although they described her pain levels as varying between moderate and debilitating. And now he had to go out and talk to them. The procedure itself had gone like clockwork. Everything else? Well, they would know that soon enough.

"I'm going to go see your mom and dad and let them know you're awake, okay? They'll be able to see you once we get you into your room."

He motioned for Lindy to follow him out. "You said you wanted to talk to me?" She'd mentioned wanting to meet with him after the procedure.

"It can wait."

He frowned at her. Maybe it could, but with the way his day had been he might not have many opportunities to come find her later on. "Follow me down to the waiting room. We can discuss whatever it is afterward."

"Seriously, it's nothing important. Not like…" Her voice trailed away, but he knew what she meant.

"Maybe not, but I think I need something else to think about once this is over."

"It's a hard case."

"Yes, it is." She had no idea how hard. And he hadn't been joking when he'd said he needed something else to think about. Cases like Tessa's brought back memories that were still raw and painful, even after five years. He remembered all too well the pain of that diagnosis, of the symptoms he felt he should have seen. Of the fear that had followed him all the way down to the bitter end.

Did Lindy ever wonder about Daisy when she went into that operating room? Did she think about what it would be like to…lose her? He swallowed hard to control his emotions, forcing himself back to the here and now.

Heading toward the waiting room, Lindy took out her phone and trailed behind a few steps. Texting to see how her daughter was? If it had been him, that's exactly what he would have been doing. Instead, he was pushing through the door to the waiting room to address two people who still had their daughter.

For now, at least.

"Mr. and Mrs. Williams?" He turned his thoughts to his patient's care. The family deserved that.

Tessa's mom and dad separated themselves from a group of people who had been huddled in the back. Zeke was glad he'd stripped his surgical gown and cap off, although he wasn't sure why. He normally left them on, choosing to notify the family as soon as possible. But he'd wanted to face them as a human being first and a doctor second.

Mr. Williams clasped his wife's hands in his. "How is she?"

"The procedure went very well. Tessa is already awake and will be anxious to see you, although her throat will be sore, and she may still be a little bit groggy." He paused. "Can we sit for a minute?"

He motioned to a bank of chairs that were a little removed from the group, sensing they would rather hear the details in private. He glanced at Lindy and gave a slight nod to indicate that she was welcome to join them. He hoped she did, in fact. "This is Lindy Franklin, she's a surgical nurse who assisted me."

"Tessa is a very sweet girl," Lindy said.

Mrs. Williams already had tears streaming down her face, maybe sensing what was to come. "Do either of you have children?"

Zeke froze, the way he did every time he was asked that question. What did he say? Yes, he had a child? Because saying he'd had a daughter who had died of an insidious disease would do nothing to help reassure the two people in front of him.

Lindy saved him from having to say anything. "I have a little girl. She's three. Her name is Daisy."

Tessa's mom nodded and then turned her gaze to him. "It's bad, isn't it?"

"We did find a mass in her stomach. We biopsied it but won't know exactly what we're dealing with until the pathology results come back."

Mr. Williams put his arm around his wife's shoulders. "What do you *think* it is?"

"I don't really want to speculate. It could be benign." He leaned forward, planting his elbows on his knees. "Let's just take this one step at a time, shall we?"

Tessa's father dragged a hand through his hair, his eyes closing for a second. Then he looked at Zeke with a steady gaze. Steadier than Zeke's had been when he'd heard a piece of devastating news. "How long before the results are back?"

"I'm thinking they should be in by Monday. I'll call you as soon as we hear anything."

Mr. Williams drew his wife closer as tears silently tracked down her face. "Thank you for everything." He glanced at Lindy. "And you as well."

"I was happy to be there." The sincerity in her voice was unmistakable. A zip of pride went through him at the great team they had at Mid Savannah. And that included Lindy. Two weeks ago he hadn't even been sure he was going to like her, and now he was sitting here glad she'd come with him to notify the parents. Glad that she'd worked beside him in that operating room. There was something about her that...

Maybe it was the fact that she had a child almost the same age as his would have been. His eyes skimmed down her profile as she quietly talked to Mrs. Williams about the joys of having a daughter.

He'd once known that same joy.

But there were joys in the memories, weren't there?

Yes, but not enough to want to go on that particular journey again. He'd seen enough in his days as a doctor to make him realize how very tenuous life was and all the things that could go wrong. He saw it day in and day out. Even sitting here talking to Tessa's parents. He had no idea what they were facing.

And Zeke wasn't sure he could face those kinds of odds again in his own life.

As glad as he was to have Lindy here for moral support, he'd better make sure it stayed on a professional footing. Having lunch with her mom and daughter last week had been harder than he'd thought it would be. He dealt with kids every day, but for the most part he was able to compartmentalize that. But interacting on a social level was something else entirely. By the end of the meal, he'd found himself avoiding the child's glance in order to make it through until the end. Hopefully he'd hidden it well enough that they hadn't guessed.

They finished up their conversation and the parents looked at him as if waiting for him to make another statement. "You're welcome to go see her now. And as soon as the discharge papers are ready, you can take her home." He forced a smile. "I'm sure she's more than ready. You'll be hearing from us early next week."

They thanked him again and headed over to be with their family. Tessa's mom was immediately caught up in the embrace of an older woman. Her mother, maybe? He was glad this family could support each other through the good times and the not so good—something he hadn't had.

Lindy met him outside the doors. "Are you okay?" she asked.

"Fine." He leaned against the wall and faced her. Had she seen something in his expression back there? Hell, he hoped not. "Now, what was it you wanted to say to me?"

He hadn't meant it to sound brusque, but when her eyes flickered and glanced away he realized the rough edge hadn't gone unnoticed. Dammit, why did he always do this? He'd done it with Janice too, pushing her away when they should have been clinging to each other.

Turning toward her, he let his fingers trail over

hers in apology. The warmth of her skin, even with that brief contact, awoke an answering warmth within him that quickly spread. Big mistake. Big honking mistake.

"Sorry, Lindy. It's been a long, hard day."

"I know, and I don't mean to add to it. Like I said, it can wait."

The warmth evaporated, a sudden chill sending prickles over his scalp. A thought hit him, and his gut lurched sideways. "Are you quitting?"

"What? No." She wore scrubs adorned in balloons today, the multicolored bunches that danced across her red top looking almost obscenely cheerful after the procedure they'd just taken part in. Worse was the fact that his touch hadn't seemed to hijack her senses the way it had his. Except, when he looked closer, her pupils were large and bottomless, handing back his reflection in a way that made him wonder.

She bit her lip. And, dammit, that act sent his thoughts careening in a completely different direction.

"You don't *want* me to quit, do you?" she asked.

He forced his eyes back up. No. He didn't. And he wasn't sure how he felt about that.

"No, of course not. You handled things with Tessa's parents admirably. Better than I did, actually."

She grinned, looking relieved. "Doctors don't always have the best reputation as far as that goes."

Thankful for the lighter tone, he feigned offense. "We don't?"

This time she laughed. "You know you don't."

"Well, on that note, let's change the subject to something a bit more positive."

"Okay, so I did something." She reached into the pocket of her scrubs and pulled out a sheet of printer paper with something typed on it. "I took your advice and went to see the hospital administrator."

He focused on her words, not quite sure what they meant for a second. Then his gaze shifted to the sheet, more notably the hand holding it. It was shaking.

So much for a lighter tone. He started to ask about it, but a group of residents walked by, laughing about something one of them had done earlier today.

"Let's go back to my office. We can talk there."

They arrived, and Lindy dropped into one of the leather chairs.

He rounded the desk and sat as well. "You talked to the hospital administrator about…" Their earlier conversation came flooding back. "About the women's crisis center?"

"Yes."

"What did he say?"

"Well, I remembered what you said about a wheel needing a push to get it turning—"

"I said that?"

She leaned forward in her chair, seeming more at ease now. "You did, actually. And so I went in and gave a little push. I volunteered to help with it."

That shocked him. He hadn't really expected her to go in, even though he'd been the one to suggest it. Or that his words had been what had spurred her to action. He wasn't sure whether to feel guilty or glad.

"And?"

"He's planning on having an informal Q&A on Friday. And he wants me to do one of the presentations."

Lindy? He knew she'd volunteered for a period of time, but it almost sounded like she'd done more than that. "Wow. That's great. What are you presenting?"

"About why the community needs something like this so much."

"It does, of course." He still wasn't quite sure what was happening. "The hard part seems to be getting women in those situations to leave…to get away from the person or situation."

"I know." She shook her head before he had a chance to say anything else. "No, Zeke. I *really* know."

The emphasis on that word made him stare. "Oh, hell, Lindy. You?"

"Yes, unfortunately. That's what Neil wants me to talk about. I was one of the ones who stayed. Until I realized it wasn't just about me anymore. It was also about my daughter."

His jaw tightened until it sent a warning. He would never understand it. What kind of man hurt the people he was supposed to love?

Well, he might as well point that finger back at himself. Hadn't he hurt Janice by refusing to acknowledge her requests to talk? By not budging when she asked him to redirect his professional life to something that didn't involve kids? But he'd never in a million years raised a hand to her or any other woman.

It didn't make any sense to him. And what kind of person stayed?

Lindy had, evidently. An ache settled in his chest.

"And if Daisy hadn't come along?" The thought of her cowering in a corner while some piece of scum stood over her, glorying in what he'd made her do, made Zeke want to do some serious damage to the man.

"I think I eventually would have left. At least I hope I would have."

The ache spread to the backs of his eyes.

"Is he in prison?"

"No."

Shock roiled through him. Had she not pressed charges?

"He's still out there? They didn't prosecute?"

"He's not out there."

"But I thought you said—"

"I did." She shut her eyes for a second before fixing him with a look that made his blood run cold. "He's dead. And before you ask, no, I didn't pull the trigger. The police did."

He hadn't expected that. Then again, he hadn't expected Lindy to just admit that she'd once been one of those that Mid Savannah hoped to help.

"God. I'm sorry."

"Don't be. The only people I'm sorry for is his family. His parents had no idea what was going on. And I said nothing. I know exactly what it's like to cake on makeup and present a smiling face to hide the damage."

"How long were you with him?"

"A year. I left him two years ago."

Daisy would have been, what, one at the time? Hopefully too young to remember anything.

"I'll say it again… I'm sorry. Not that he's dead, but that you went through any of it."

"I wish I'd left sooner. But there came a point when I didn't have a choice. When I realized that if I didn't get out right then, I probably wasn't going to live to see another day."

She'd almost died? Hell, what had the man done to her?

He reached across and put his hand over the one holding the flyer. "I'm glad."

"You're glad…?"

"That you left."

"So am I. The kicker is that he died before I could get a divorce. So according to legal documents I'm a widow, not a divorcee."

The irony wasn't lost on him.

"At least he's out of your life."

"Not entirely, I'm afraid. Luke had a gambling problem. Some of the debts he incurred affected my credit, even though I paid them off."

This was one of the things that people didn't think of: the financial ramifications of leaving and how to navigate those waters. No wonder Neil wanted her to speak.

"Did you see an attorney?"

"Yep. He helped me negotiate with the credit bureaus to wipe out some of the ones Luke defaulted on. But I couldn't prove that all of them were his."

"Do you need help?"

"What?" Her eyes widened, then flashed with anger. "No. I can manage just fine on my own."

Realizing he'd offended her, he rephrased slightly. "I didn't mean to imply that you couldn't. Sorry if it sounded that way."

"It's okay." She smiled. "Maybe I haven't come as far as I thought I had. I still get defensive from time to time. And having people come up behind me can still make me jumpy."

He'd witnessed that a couple of times. He let go of her hand and came around the front of the desk, sitting on the edge of it. "That's why you took a few years off. It wasn't just because of Daisy."

Another thing that was none of his business. But he was curious.

"Yes. He didn't want me to work…wanted me there when he got home. At first I convinced myself that it was sweet, and that I would be perfectly happy as a housewife and mother. Lots of women are, and I think that's their path. But I have always enjoyed my job. I'm glad to be back in the thick of it."

"Well, we're happy to have you."

This made her laugh. "Are you? That's quite a turnaround from my first day on the job."

An extra little cleft appeared in her left cheek when she smiled. Not a dimple exactly but more of a line caused by her smile pulling more to one side than the other. Whatever it was, it was damned attractive. As was that glossy head of dark hair.

Easy, Bruen. You don't need to be noticing things like that. Especially not on someone who's suffered so much hurt at the hands of another man.

Maybe his reaction was just a misplaced sense of needing to protect someone.

Whatever it was, he was glad she'd landed at Mid Savannah Medical Center.

"I guess it is a little bit of a turnaround." And he wasn't exactly sure what had made the difference. Maybe it was that smile. Or maybe it had nothing to do with the ridiculous way he seemed to be noticing everything about her. Much better to attribute it to the dedication he saw in her after that first wobbly start.

And he couldn't fault her for worrying or staring at the clock that day.

Weren't there days when his lungs still slammed shut in grief over a loss he might have been able to prevent had he recognized the signs? Yes, there were. More of them than he cared to admit.

It was strange how death could be at opposite ends of the spectrum. To one person, it meant freedom from abuse. To another, it meant the loss of something irretrievable and precious. Like his daughter. And the trust of his ex-wife.

"So this is my cue to ask you that question I mentioned."

"Question? I thought you wanted to tell me that you went to the hospital administrator."

"Yes, that, but I also wanted to see if you'd be interested in volunteering."

His eyes widened. "You want *me* to volunteer? In the program? I thought that's what I was asking you to do?"

"You did. And I am. But you're the head of pediatric surgery. You can bring another side to this. There are a lot of women who were in the same position I was. Women with children. Women who stay, in spite of those children." He watched her take a deep breath. "Remember Meredith Brewster?"

"The pneumothorax case?"

"Yes. There are thousands of Meredith Brewsters out there, who get hurt because women stayed in terrible relationships. You could speak about that. Tell hurting women what you've seen over the years. Maybe you can change someone's mind."

He frowned. "I'm not sure about that. Would I have changed your mind?"

The answer was suddenly very important to him. Especially in light of what he'd just learned about her.

Her eyes met his, staring at him for a long second. "Yes. I think you might have." Her index finger wrapped around his. "This feels right, Zeke. I'm glad I'm here."

Glad she was at Mid Savannah? Or glad she was in his office, practically holding his hand?

Because hell if he wasn't glad of both of those things.

The swirling in his head started again, maybe in reaction to her words. Or the light scent that her movements sent his way. Whatever it was, it was making him want to do something crazy. Something more than what they were currently doing.

"I'm glad you are too." He turned his palm and caught her hand, drawing her to her feet. "And it does feel right. Very, very right."

Her eyes held his, a growing warmth in their depths he hadn't noticed when this conversation had started.

He tightened his grip slightly and the muscles in his biceps tightened as he drew her hand closer. Except it wasn't just her hand that answered the request. Her whole body did, taking a step toward him.

Sliding off his desk, he found himself standing within inches of her. He willed himself to let go of her, and he succeeded in uncurling his fingers. Except his hand seemed to have a mind of its own, lifting to cup her face.

"Yes. I think you could have talked me into almost anything."

As soon as she said the words he was lost, his mouth coming down to meet hers and finding her lips so much softer than he expected. And when she kissed him back, his world exploded—a million fragments flying in all directions. And for once in his life he didn't care which pieces he found. Or which ones were lost forever.

CHAPTER FOUR

SHE'D THOUGHT SHE'D never enjoy another kiss.

But, God, when Zeke asked if he could have made her change her mind, she'd melted inside. He acted like it mattered. Said that her being here did feel right.

And so did this.

The heady warmth of his mouth filled her senses, and she couldn't get enough of the taste of him, of the smooth slide of skin against skin. It all melded together into a luscious blend she would never get out of her head. The second he'd come around that desk, she'd started wondering what it would be like if he touched her.

It was so much better than she imagined.

Maybe that was what had made her curl her finger around his. Curiosity. What she hadn't expected was the jolt of need that rocked her world and nearly made her gasp aloud. Had she ever experienced that before? She didn't think so.

Then he'd done the unthinkable and wrapped his whole hand around hers. Her senses had been swamped. A tsunami striking shore and wiping out every rational thought in its path.

She was still caught in its grip.

A tiny sound came out of her throat, and she inched closer, his hard chest brushing her breasts. Her nipples tightened instantly.

She wanted him with everything that she had.

The hands that had been cupping her face moved to her hips, and she thought he was going to haul her against him completely, but he didn't. His grip was tight, but it was as if he were holding her in place, keeping her still. Was he trying to torture her?

Something warred inside her, telling her to take another step and test that theory...see just how strong his resolve was, and just how much this kiss was affecting him.

Surely he'd been swept along by the same wave.

I dare you, Lindy. Do it.

She opened her mouth, dumbfounded by the fact that it was something she'd never done before. Would never have thought of doing.

Ever.

The thought awoke some rational part of her brain, and she froze.

What was she doing here? Wasn't this exactly what she'd warned herself about: impulsively jumping into something she should avoid?

Maybe. But for now...

She closed her eyes, realizing this was about to end. Just one more second. Then she would move away.

As if he'd read her thoughts, the pressure on her

hips increased. Only instead of easing her closer, he propelled her a step backward, removing all points of contact—right before his head lifted.

There was a glazed look in his eyes, that said stopping hadn't been easy.

Well, join the club, mister.

Only in the end he'd been stronger than she had, and that bothered her on a level she didn't want to explore.

He spoke up first. "Damn." He pulled in an audible breath and let it hiss back out. "I'm sorry, Lindy. I have no idea where that came from."

She did, but she wasn't about to shoulder the blame by herself. At least not out loud. Inside, it was a whole different matter. She was the one who'd started down this road, but she wasn't quite sure why. Maybe the realization that she wasn't afraid of him, at least not physically.

Emotionally?

Lord. This man could destroy her, if she let him.

She needed to make sure something like this didn't happen again. She'd been so proud of her resolve, telling herself she would turn down any and all offers to date if they came about, which they hadn't.

Would I have changed your mind?

His earlier words whispered through her head, and suddenly she wasn't sure she could have been as strong as she'd thought. If he'd asked her out, could she have refused?

Hadn't that kiss answered that question? It had.

And that scared her on a completely different level.

She went with the first thing that came to mind. "Domestic violence is an emotional subject. You didn't know about my past—and, honestly, I had no intention of saying anything until the Q&A. The last thing I need is anyone's pity."

Oh, God, was that why he'd kissed her? Because he felt sorry for her?

"You think that came out of pity?"

This time he took hold of her hips and tugged her against him, making her very aware of where things stood between them. "This has nothing to do with pity."

Then he was gone, this time back behind the refuge of his desk, leaving her standing there...her breathing not completely normal yet. Neither was the rest of her. Little charges of electricity were still zapping between neurons, hoping to be reignited.

Not a chance.

She needed to get out of there. Before she did something she'd regret.

"I should go."

He pushed the flyer across the desk to her. "If you still want me to be there on Friday, I will. How long does my part of the presentation have to be?"

She was tempted to tell him to stay away. But surely by the end of the week she'd be able to put out the rest of today's embers.

And if she couldn't?

Then she was in big trouble.

"Around ten minutes. Do you want me to put you down?"

His thumb tapped out a rhythm on the surface of his desk, and she held her breath. As scary as this was, she really did think he could make a difference in the program.

And if he ended up making a difference in her instead?

Well, she would have to deal with that when and if it came up.

"Yes. Put me down."

"Okay, I will. And thank you."

She didn't say what she was thanking him for. Instead, she just turned around and hightailed it out of there, all the while praying that tomorrow would find her strong enough to put this all behind her.

Because the last thing she needed was to get involved with someone, especially someone she worked with. Because if things went south...

Lindy, they've already gone so far south they've jumped off the bottom of the globe.

Ha! Well, then, it was up to her to reel them back in until her feet were standing on firm ground.

No more talk of tsunamis. Or electrical charges.

And, most of all, no more kissing of hunky surgeons.

Who was she kidding? The truth was she would probably be reliving that kiss in her dreams. Tonight. Tomorrow night. And any number of unnamed nights in the future.

And although Friday might seem like quite a way off right now, it would come long before she was ready for it to.

So all she could do was regroup, and hope she could pretend she'd recovered from their encounter. Even if it was a complete and utter lie.

Tessa's results were in. Zeke counted to five before opening the digital file. Either her parents would be referred to an oncologist, or he would schedule her for surgery to remove a benign tumor. He certainly knew what he hoped for. But what he hoped for didn't always come to pass.

He clicked on the folder, his glance skipping through everything but the meat of the report: ...*atypical cells... noninvasive*...

He almost went slack with relief. It wasn't quite benign, but it wasn't cancerous either and more than likely confined to the area in which it was found. That was good news. Great news, in fact.

The tumor would still have to be removed, and Zeke would need to get clean margins so that the growth didn't come back, but there would be no need for radiation or chemo treatments.

His fingers went to his cellphone to tell Lindy the good news, then he stopped. He didn't usually call his surgical team individually and relay test results. They normally found out, but that was because of follow-up surgery or treatment.

The truth was he just wanted to hear her voice. Maybe to make sure she was okay.

His oath as a doctor was to do no harm. And he wasn't quite sure he'd lived up to that in this case.

He still wasn't sure what had caused that kiss the

other day, even though he had repeatedly micro-analyzed everything that had led up to it. To the point that it kept him awake at night and had ended with him standing under a cold blast of water on one occasion.

Not that he was any closer to an answer now than he had been the day it happened. It had changed the way he scheduled his surgeries, though. Whereas where he might have requested her as part of his team before, he was now loath to attach her name to anything connected with him. She'd probably noticed, but if she was smart, she'd be relieved by it.

Of course, there was the little matter of her wanting him to help with the Q&A on Friday and with the program itself, but surely that wouldn't require a lot of time together.

He picked up the phone again. But this time it was because he remembered her asking to be kept in the loop regarding Tessa's results. But maybe he would simply text her rather than call.

He punched in the words as quickly as he could, as if it would limit his contact with her. Tessa's results are in. Atypical cells, but no malignancy. Will follow up with surgery at a later date. He then hit "send" and set the phone down again, forcing himself to go back to work, rather than worry about whether or not she would get the message and/or respond. He'd almost succeeded when a little *ding* told him he had an incoming message.

From Lindy?

Just leave it.

Too late. His glance was already on the screen. It was from Lindy, but the message was short and succinct. So glad!

And that was that.

The next thing he knew, the phone was ringing. He swallowed when he saw it was from the same person.

This time his subconscious didn't argue with him. He picked it up and punched the button. "Bruen here."

As if she wouldn't know who was on the line.

"Hi, um…I was just checking to see if you know when surgery will be."

"I haven't scheduled it yet. I just got the report."

"Oh, okay." She hesitated, then said, "I'd like to be on the surgical team, if I could."

"Of course." He wasn't sure why she felt she had to ask. His heart clenched. Maybe because he'd avoided putting her on the schedule. It had probably made something that wasn't really a big deal into something more than it was. Except to him it had been a very big deal. He'd never kissed a woman in his office before. And certainly not someone he worked with.

"I was already planning on it."

"It just seemed as if…"

He could almost hear the shrug on the other end of the line. Not willing to confirm that he was avoiding her, he countered by finishing her sentence in a completely different way. "It just seemed as if the schedules have changed? They have. I feel like I've been overtaxing some of the nurses and am trying to make things a little more equitable. Spread the load out among more people."

It wasn't exactly the truth, but it was better than saying he didn't want to work with her anymore. Because he did. He just wasn't sure it was a good idea.

"Okay. I just didn't want what happened to change our working relationship."

He assumed she was speaking somewhere where she couldn't be overheard. Maybe she wasn't even at the hospital today. "It won't as long as neither of us lets it."

Hadn't he already done that?

"Thank you. I, um…I promise I wasn't throwing myself at you."

That was the last thing he would expect from her. "I know. I promise I wasn't throwing myself at you either." He couldn't stop the smile that formed at those words. "Like you said, Lindy, it was an emotional subject. I think it just caught us both off guard. I'm glad you told me, though. I do think you'll be a great asset to the new program."

"I think you will be as well. You still want to come, don't you?"

Hmm…that was probably going to be a yes on more than one level. But he wasn't going there.

"I do. And like I said, you're the perfect person to talk about what it's like to survive domestic violence. Not everyone there has been through what you have."

"I'm very glad of that." He thought he heard a sigh. "I'd appreciate it if you'd keep this between the two of us."

Was she talking about the kiss or her background? It didn't matter. He'd never been one for indulging in workplace gossip—or workplace romances, for that matter—and he wasn't about to start now. "Don't worry about it. I've told no one. It's no one's business but yours."

"Thank you. I know I'm talking about it at the meeting, but I'd rather control how much is shared."

"Completely understandable." He picked up a pencil and wiggled it between his fingers, surprised by how comfortable he felt talking to her, even after what had happened. What he'd expected had been awkward silences on both ends of the line. It was nice. As was hearing her voice again.

A little too nice.

"Well, I'll let you go."

The pencil went still. "Okay. I'll let you know when Tessa's surgery is."

They said their goodbyes and then she was gone, leaving him to wonder if the next face-to-face meeting would prove to be just as easy as that phone conversation had been.

Somehow, he doubted it. But if they could do it once, they could do it again. At least he hoped so. Because it would make work—and his life—that much easier.

Why had he thought this would be easy? He scheduled Lindy on his next surgical day and the second he saw her brown eyes peering at him from above that mask, he knew he should have waited a few more days. Because his glance had slid over her and remembered exactly what her lips looked like. What they felt like.

How they tasted.

Damn. But the only thing he could do was stick to the plan of getting past that memory. It would get easier with time.

Lindy, on the other hand, seemed fine. Her eyes twinkled when she saw him, and he knew she was smiling beneath the mask, her nose crinkling in that adorable way that went straight to his gut. "This looks like an interesting case."

It was going to be interesting all right. And that wasn't including the case.

"The infection hasn't responded to antibiotics, like we'd hoped." These pulmonary cases actually were interesting, but they were also nerve-racking. There was always the possibility of spreading the bacteria to other parts of the lung. This time, though, the pocket of infection was encapsulated and hopefully it could be removed and the lung re-sectioned, barring any complications.

That wasn't the only reason they were nerve-racking. They also brought up a lot of unwanted memories. His ex-wife had wanted him to change specialties for just this reason. Pulmonary cases almost always sent him home in a stupor that had nothing to do with drugs or alcohol.

That first year had been the worst. He would spend weeks either not speaking or lashing out in anger if Janice tried to talk to him. Not physically, but he'd made it clear he didn't want to interact. In failing his daughter, he'd also failed his wife. She'd needed him. And he hadn't been there. She'd rightfully filed for divorce on the anniversary of Marina's death.

"Zeke?"

Lindy had asked him a question.

"Sorry, what?"

"How many of these have you done?"

He told the truth. "Too many." He'd saved a lot of lives, but he'd also lost the one he'd needed to save the most.

His daughter had died of childhood interstitial lung disease, only he hadn't recognized it for what it was. Not at first. Not until it had been far too late.

The guilt of that had almost killed him. He was a surgeon, supposedly one of the top in his field, and still he'd missed it.

He could remember the times when Marina's cough had turned into something worse, the recurrent bouts of bronchitis and pneumonia visiting their neck of the woods time and time again.

By the time they realized what they were dealing with, they'd been unable to stop it. The fluid in her lungs that last time had been virulent and aggressive, and her tired body could no longer fight the ravages of her disease. Marina had died, obliterating his heart with one swift blow. And his marriage had imploded a year later, when he'd refused to leave his field of medicine.

His wife had protested his decision, saying, "It won't bring Marina back."

It hadn't. But what it had done was destroy any possibility of saving his marriage.

At the time, he'd felt he had no choice. As if his penance was in trying to save other people's children. Even if doing so carved out another little piece of his heart.

Lindy shifted beside him, reminding him that he had a job to do.

So he took a deep breath. "Ready, people? Let's get to work."

And work they did. The patch of infection was the size of a baseball, bigger than he'd originally thought, and it required cutting away more tissue than he'd anticipated. But he wanted to get it all, otherwise it might come back, and none of them wanted that.

Lindy was right beside him, having instruments at hand almost before he asked for them. It was what separated a good surgical nurse from a great one. And she was definitely one of the great ones. Even after having been out of the game for…what had she said? A little over three years?

"Looks like we've gotten it all. We'll ship the tissue off to Pathology and have another culture done."

"It looks good. Really good." Lindy murmured the words over his shoulder.

Her praise sent a burst of warmth through him that had nothing to do with a job well done and everything to do with the stuff that had led to that crazy kiss.

He'd better put a stop to those thoughts right now.

Soon they'd closed the wound, and Zeke breathed a sigh of relief. Part of the patient's aftercare would be IV antibiotics, and the culture would help determine what this particular strain would respond to, although they'd tried most of the broad-spectrum ones already. The ball of infection had lain there unchanged by anything they'd thrown at it. Hopefully manually removing it would make any microbe that remained lose its hold on her.

One of the other nurses took the specimen cup and marked it with their patient's number and date of birth and hand-carried it down to the pathology lab. She called up saying the lab was going to put a rush on the results. "Tell them I said thanks. They can ping my cell when they get it."

"I'll let them know."

Zeke waited until his patient came round, while other members of the team worked on getting their instruments packed away for sterilization.

When they were done, he turned to Lindy. "I could use a coffee. How about you?"

At her slight frown he realized, given the circumstances, he probably shouldn't have asked, but he'd done it out of habit. How many times had he invited whoever happened to be standing around if they wanted to go for coffee? It didn't mean anything, but she evidently thought differently. And maybe it did. But he wasn't going to attempt any big explanations. If she wanted to say no, that was fine.

"Sounds good."

He blinked in surprise but couldn't say he was disappointed by her answer. He liked having company after a difficult surgery. No one had ever taken those invitations to mean anything other than what they were. The camaraderie of teamwork. Sometimes there were seven staff members seated around that table in the hospital cafeteria. And sometimes there were two. He looked around, but the room had basically emptied now that the patient had been wheeled to Recovery, so there was no one else to invite.

He could do this. They were both grown-ups, both capable of getting past one little mistake. Little? Hmm, not according to the dreams that still plagued him at night.

Saying that, he'd rather not have a bunch of people see him having coffee with the new nurse, especially in light of what had happened. So, yes, he'd been stupid to ask. But maybe if they went somewhere else, there would be less cause for tongues to wag.

"I know a coffee shop just down the road from the hospital. It'll get us out in the fresh air for a bit, if you can spare the time."

"I'm due for a half-hour break, so it's fine." But she didn't sound quite as sure as she had a moment ago. Did she think he was asking her out on a date? He didn't want to set her straight and embarrass her, although he had a feeling she had no such illusions.

"Are you up for walking?"

She glanced down at her shoes, which looked comfortable. "I'm good."

Soon they were out the door. "Is it Mulroney's just down the street?"

"Yes. I forgot you're from the area."

He stuffed his hands in his pockets as the full force of the Savannah heat hit him.

"I might need to worry more about melting than what kind of footwear I have on." She laughed as she said it, though.

"I take it you'd rather not have your coffee on the shop's patio?"

"I'd prefer my air to be conditioned, if you don't mind. The cooler the better."

This time he was the one who laughed. "I admit I didn't think this out as well as I might have."

Thankfully, it didn't take long to reach their destination, and the interior of the shop was indeed blessedly cool.

He found a table in a secluded corner of the coffee bar and motioned her to take a seat. A minute later, one of the servers came over and asked for their order. "Go ahead," he said.

"I'd actually like an iced coffee, please, with extra sugar."

His brows went up, but he said nothing, instead ordering his own coffee black and waiting until the server moved away to another customer.

"Would you have ordered that at the hospital cafeteria?"

She smiled. "Have you actually had the coffee there?"

"Have you?"

"No." Her teeth came down on her lip. "I just assumed it was the same as most hospital cafeteria meals. I've come here the last two times I've had a break. I even brought Daisy here once and ordered her a hot chocolate."

"Your husband never…?"

She didn't ask what he was talking about. "No, never."

There was a tight set to her lips that warned him not to push his luck, so he moved on to a less volatile subject. "Did Mulroney's chocolate get Daisy's stamp of approval?"

"She loved it. My mom actually brought her to meet me that day. She's been great about watching Daisy for me. She insists, actually. I don't blame her. She missed out on a lot."

So had his mom.

His mom had loved Marina, had loved every second of the time they'd spent together. And then after her diagnosis everything had changed.

They'd no longer had entire days to simply let her visit with her grandparents. By that time Marina had been sick more often than not. Their lives had been taken up with fighting an enemy that refused to let go. In the end that enemy had won, and Zeke had lost everything.

His parents had been devastated when they lost not only their granddaughter but also their daughter-in-law. Janice had told them she was sorry, but it hurt too much to stay in contact with them, so she'd dropped out of their lives completely, moving out west.

His mom never said anything directly, but every once in a while she hinted about him remarrying one day. Her ultimate dream was probably another grandchild, especially since she was now alone, his father having died a year ago. She was still grieving his passing.

As for marriage, Zeke didn't see that happening.

After the way he'd shut Janice out during his grief, he'd been wary of relationships. He hadn't liked who he'd become after Marina's death. He'd been selfish and unsupportive, basically crawling into a dark emotional tunnel that only had room for one occupant: him. His wife had been out of luck.

It had been ugly and wrong, and he didn't trust himself to do things differently if faced with a similar crisis. So he didn't try. He wasn't willing to risk someone else's happiness.

And that kiss with Lindy?

It had been a momentary surge of lust. Nothing more. Nothing less. He'd already nipped that in the bud.

"What about you?" Lindy said. "It seems we're always discussing my personal life. What do you do when you're not at the hospital? You're not married… right?"

She was fishing. It made him smile.

"Don't worry, Lindy. You didn't break up a marriage with that kiss. I did that all by myself quite a while ago."

"So you were married?"

"Yep." He already knew what was coming and braced himself for it, although he was surprised she hadn't already heard. There were still some people at the hospital who'd been there at the time of his daughter's illness.

"Any kids?" Her eyes were curious, but there was still no hint that she knew anything about Marina.

What did he tell her? The truth. After all, look at what she'd shared with him.

"I did have. She died five years ago."

"Oh, Zeke, I'm sorry. What happened, if you don't mind my asking?"

"Not at all. She had an incurable lung disease. She died when she was three and a half."

Her hand touched his, but this time it wasn't out of anything other than sympathy. "I didn't know."

"It's not something that comes up in most casual conversations." Was he saying this wasn't that type of conversation? Maybe. Either he was slipping in his old age, or she had a knack for inviting confidences.

Before he could say anything else, their coffees came, and the discussion soon turned to work, and Tessa's case. "Any idea yet when surgery will be?"

"Soon. The hospital is trying to sync their schedules with our open time slots. I imagine it will be sometime this next week after the open house on the women's crisis center."

"She's a sweet little girl."

"Yes. She reminds me of Marina a little bit."

And just like that, he'd circled back around to the subject of his daughter.

"Tell me about her. What was she like?"

"She was a sweet baby. Janice—my wife—and I knew each other in high school and fell in love. Then came med school and all the pressures that came with it. By the time I was done with that and we were ready to have children, nothing seemed to work. We finally went in for fertility treatments and along came Marina. Everything seemed good. At first."

"You said she had a lung condition. Was it asthma?"

"No, an interstitial lung disease. ChILD, to be exact. She had a type called cryptogenic organizing pneumonia, which is just what it sounds like. She had repeated bouts of lung infections until she couldn't fight them off any longer."

"Did you and your wife split over that?"

"About a year after Marina's death. I wasn't a very nice person during that time."

Lindy's head cocked to the side. "What do you mean?"

He could almost see the wheels in her head turning. "I found out too late that I don't react well to crises. I shut down. Not a trait most women want in a life partner."

"There are worse things."

Looking at it from her point of view, he guessed there were. "Maybe, but in our case it meant the end of our marriage."

"Does it hurt? Treating other people's children, I mean?"

Today's case had been hard. "Sometimes. Especially when the patients are the same age or have a similar illness."

"I can imagine. I'm surprised you still opt to treat those patients."

He shrugged. "How fair would it be of me to refuse to treat a patient simply because it made me sad? Or uncomfortable?"

"I get it." She paused as if thinking. "I get it, but it can't make it any easier."

"No, it doesn't."

They sat in silence for a minute or two, then Lindy sighed and closed her eyes. "They do have great coffee here."

No more confessions? Maybe she was right. There'd been enough soul-baring for one coffee session. And it was probably time to get back.

"I'm not sure about calling a drink with ice 'coffee.'" He smiled to show it wasn't meant as a true criticism.

"Hey, it's made from the same bean that yours is. Like iced tea or hot tea."

He couldn't really argue with that.

The door opened and two nurses from the hospital came in. Lindy recognized them and waved. It served to officially mark the end of personal conversations. And thank God she'd taken her hand off his when their drinks had come. That was all he needed…for the hospital gossip chain to decide to do a little matchmaking based on mistaken assumptions. It was why he hadn't wanted to go to the hospital cafeteria.

Talking about Marina had brought back memories he'd rather have left buried. And to get involved with someone who had a child that was almost the same age as his when she'd died, well, he couldn't imagine it would be good. Or that he wouldn't wonder, year after year, what Marina would have been like at each of those year markers.

Hadn't he already wondered that? His daughter would have been almost nine years old by now. He'd actually looked up a program that could "age" the subject of a photograph. He'd done it with his daughter's picture last year to see what she might have looked like at different stages of her life. He'd printed the images off as a keepsake, but it had been a mistake. The passage of time on those faces had haunted him for months afterward, and he preferred to remember the flesh and blood child, rather than some hazy possibility that would never come to pass. He'd finally had to bury those prints deep inside one of his desk drawers at home. He probably should throw them away, except the thought of doing so felt wrong, like he was throwing away everything that could have been. So he'd kept them. He hadn't thought about those photos for months.

He'd be better off not thinking about them now either.

"My mom is planning to come to the Q&A, even though I told her it was no big deal."

"I don't blame her. She must be proud of how far you've come."

Lindy shrugged. "I'm only mentioning it because she'll want to bring Daisy. Are you planning to show anything graphic?"

"I haven't actually thought about what I'll say, but no. No graphic shots of wounds or anything upsetting."

Although the fact that they even had to have a center like this should be upsetting.

"The hospital has a daycare center for employees. I wasn't sure if you were aware of it. I imagine it will be operating for the Q&A as well, if she wants to drop her off there."

"That's a great idea. It might free up time for my mom, if they take kids on a part-time basis as well. Thanks. And speaking of people in the medical field, I'd probably better get going, I imagine my break is just about up."

"And I need to check on today's surgery patient, so I'd better head back as well." He picked up their trash and tossed it into a nearby waste bin. "And I'll let you know as soon as Tessa's surgery date is set."

"Thanks." She smiled, settling the strap to her purse on her shoulder. "And thanks for suggesting coffee. It was good to get away from the hospital, if only for a few minutes."

"Yes, it was."

And with that, they headed back toward the big white building and the reality that came with it.

CHAPTER FIVE

JUST AS SHE'D SUSPECTED, Lindy's mom had insisted on coming to the Q&A, promising she'd whisk Daisy to the daycare center as soon as the actual meeting started, just in case the conversations became too much for little ears.

Lindy wasn't planning on sharing the worst of the worst, but still it made her nervous to have her mom there.

"Just pretend I'm not here."

"Oh, sure." She smoothed her skirt down over her legs. If she knew her mom, she'd be waving from the audience, which would make it almost impossible to pretend anything.

"And if you want to go out with friends afterward, I can always keep Daisy for the night."

Friends? Was her mom serious?

She barely knew any of these people.

Um…hadn't she kissed one of them?

That didn't count. Besides, she didn't know Zeke any more than she knew anyone else.

Didn't she? She'd told him things that no one else

knew, except her parents, and Zeke had shared things about his daughter that he said didn't get thrown around in casual conversations.

Well, after today everyone in the room would know the basics of what had happened to her, but she certainly wasn't going to get it tattooed across her forehead.

She glanced at the clock and saw there were only ten minutes until she was on.

"Okay, Mom, I should probably go."

"Love you. I'll take our girl out in a few minutes." Rachel kissed her on the cheek and settled into a chair with Daisy on her lap.

By the time Lindy got to the front, Zeke was already beside the podium, talking to a group of people. So was Neil, the hospital administrator. He waved her over.

Taking a deep breath, she smiled and joined them. Were they already volunteers, or were they new to the program like she was?

Dressed in tan khakis and a snug black polo that hugged his biceps, Zeke looked confident and unruffled. A world away from the nervous slosh of stomach acid she was currently dealing with.

"You look nice," he murmured.

A rush of warmth flooded her face. Great. Just what she needed.

"So do you."

And her mom, right on cue, was holding Daisy up

and using her hand to move her granddaughter's in the semblance of a wave.

Ugh. So much for presenting a professional appearance.

She pulled herself up short. This wasn't about professionalism. This was about helping women. Women like she'd once been.

Neil nodded at the podium. "Once people take their seats, I'll open with some introductions and then you're on, okay?"

"That's fine." She was as ready as she'd ever be.

"Princess!" Daisy's voice rang out across the gathering, causing a quick burst of laughter.

Oh, brother. Why had she ever thought having her mom here was a good idea? Oh, wait. She hadn't thought that. Not once.

If that wasn't bad enough, her mom was suddenly up front, mingling with the other hospital employees. "Look, Daisy, there's the man you ate lunch with." Rachel turned to Lindy and whispered, "Isn't his name Zeke, or something like that?"

"Yes, but—"

Zeke had moved a short distance away to talk to someone else.

"Let's go say hi. You can tell him about your new princess castle."

"Princess!"

Lindy broke into her daughter's mounting excitement before it got out of hand. "I don't think that's a good idea. I'm sure he's busy."

"Nonsense. I'm sure he'll be happy to see Daisy

again." And before Lindy could say anything else, the pair sauntered off, leaving her to groan out loud.

"Mothers."

"Ain't it the truth?" A voice to her side made her look. Nancy, a glass of some type of cola in her hand, smiled at the consternation on her face. "They drive you crazy, but you wouldn't trade them for the world."

"I don't know. Today might be the day…"

They both laughed, and Lindy glanced at her. Maybe the thing about not having made any friends wasn't entirely true. She and Nancy had shared a few moments of chitchat here and there. "Are you interested in volunteering if the center opens?"

"Yep. I have a vested interest, since my baby sister is in a bad relationship and won't leave."

"I'm so sorry." Lindy bit her lip. Not to stop herself from sharing her story but out of embarrassment. She'd once been like that baby sister. And Nancy was going to hear her talk about it soon enough.

"I'm hoping one day she'll realize."

"I do too."

She glanced up to see Zeke staring at her and realized he was holding Daisy. Oh, no. She'd never seen a man look any more uncomfortable than he did right now.

Then it hit her. He no longer had a daughter to hold. And to have Daisy thrust at him like a sack of potatoes…

Her mom had no idea, though, because her mouth was moving a mile a minute just as Daisy threw her arms around Zeke's neck and squeezed.

That was her cue.

"Will you excuse me? I think I have to rescue Dr. Bruen before he passes out."

Nancy giggled. "He does look a little odd. His face is beet red."

"Yes, it is." She made her way through the small groups of people who were conversing, hoping she could get up there before Zeke made some kind of "no-kids" rule for any future meetings, not that he made those kinds of decisions.

She arrived and held her arms out. "Sorry, Zeke. I'll take her."

"It's okay. Your mom was just telling me about your new place. It sounds charming."

She turned toward her mom and gave her a hard look. "It is. But I'm sure you must have other things to do than chat about my living conditions."

"On the contrary. I'm way down on the program so I have plenty of time to kill. Besides, Rachel and Daisy are keeping me from becoming too nervous."

That was the funniest thing she'd heard all day. He was a well-respected surgeon who commanded the operating room the way a ship's captain commanded his vessel. There was no way he would be scared to face a group and talk about what he did on a daily basis.

"I have my doubts about that."

He smiled. "Now, Daisy, on the other hand, wants me to dress up as a princess with her. That does make me nervous."

Oh, Lord. She should have known. How many

times had she had to dress in one of her best party dresses in order to have tea with her pint-sized daughter?

"I'm sure. Although that could be an interesting look." She smiled at Zeke, letting her nerves settle. Maybe the look he'd thrown her hadn't been one of horror after all. She'd offered to take Daisy and he hadn't taken her up on it. Although he was right. Lindy was the first one to present.

Lindy's mom chimed in. "We'll have to have you over for dinner sometime. I'm sure both Daisy and Lindy would love that."

It seemed that with every word she uttered her mom was digging her daughter into a hole and had no idea she was throwing another shovelful of dirt on the growing pile.

"I'm sure Daisy would. I'm not so sure about Lindy," was all Zeke said, throwing a quick smile in her direction.

"Well, I guess this princess had better find her way to the daycare center." Her mom held out her arms. "I'll have Lindy get with you about a date for dinner."

"Do that."

Oh, Lord, why did her mom have to have that ingrained Southern hospitality? And she was so gently insistent that it was the rare person who got offended by it. It was just the way she was. Lindy had learned to appreciate it, for the most part, even if she hadn't quite embraced the trait.

By the time her mom moved away, Neil was asking everyone to find a seat. He presented the basics about what the hospital hoped to do, going over the funding that had already been secured, then went over the list of presenters, which included herself, two of the hospital's resident psychiatrists and Zeke. Once they'd finished, the floor would be open to questions.

Her mom slid back in the room and took a seat in the back just as Neil was finishing up.

"A sign-up sheet will be in the back for anyone interested in giving a few hours of their time. The ultimate fate of the program rests in your hands. And on that note, I'll turn the floor over to Lindy Franklin, who is new to Mid Savannah but certainly not new to working in this type of program." He nodded at her. "Lindy?"

The nerves that had been settled suddenly rose to her throat and threatened to choke her. Then she caught sight of Zeke. Maybe he saw the hint of panic in her face because he edged forward until he was standing just behind her elbow. But far enough away that those around them would simply think he was waiting for his turn.

Just knowing he was there helped her get through the rough patch and she cleared her throat. "Hello, everyone."

A spatter of returned greetings made her smile, and then she was fine. "As Neil said, my name is Lindy Franklin and I am indeed new here. But what he didn't tell you is that I was once the victim of domestic violence."

She watched people shift in their seats as they took in her words. Nancy looked shocked, as did some of the other nurses she worked with. "Most of you didn't know that about me, and that's at the heart of the problem. Most victims will never speak out about what is happening. They rarely seek help. But if they know help is there, it becomes a safety net. One that people like I was desperately need."

She talked about some of the things she wished she'd known when she'd been with Luke and ways to get the word out to others.

Lindy ended by saying, "We want Savannah to know that help is available. It's free. It's confidential. And we can help you get out. Thank you."

Applause went up and Nancy gave her a thumbs-up sign, while her mom was dabbing at her eyes with a tissue.

Both of the hospital's psychiatrists came up and took her place, discussing between them the psychology of abuse, referencing several things she'd said and using them as illustrations.

"Good job, Lind." Zeke's low voice filtered through, carrying with it a note of admiration. "If what I saw out there is any indication, this program is really going to take off. I'd be surprised if we didn't get fifty volunteers right off the bat."

She'd spoken from her heart, but surely it hadn't made that much of a difference.

You just need to give that wheel a push to get it moving.

Then it was Zeke's turn. And wow. Just wow. He told the story of Meredith Brewster's injuries, being careful to keep any identifying elements out of his

speech. But listening to him, she remembered the horror she'd felt on learning a five-year-old child had had
to deal with a horrific injury at the hands of a parent.
She looked around the room. No one was shifting or
looking around. Even her mom was totally caught up
in what he was saying. True to his word, he didn't
give any of the gory details, but he still got his point
across. At the end of his speech, the applause was
almost deafening.

Neil moved forward, shaking Zeke's hand and
murmuring something to him before turning to the
audience. "Thank you to our staff for taking time
out of their busy schedules to talk to us. And thank
you for being here. We'd like to hear any questions
or comments you might have. If you like what you've
heard, there are packets stacked at the door that have
a list of helpful numbers. And as I mentioned earlier,
there's also a sign-up sheet, if you'd like to help this
program get off the ground." He glanced at Lindy.
"Let me say one more thing. If you feel someone's
life is in immediate danger, I would urge you not to
wait but to call 911."

The presenters fielded questions between them,
with Lindy getting more than her share. She answered
as best she could, grateful that everyone was respect-
ful about not asking specifics about her own situation.
Twenty minutes later there were no more lifted hands.

"Any other questions?" Neil asked, scanning the
group for hands. She kept hers firmly down, even as
his eyes slid over her and kept going. "Well, I guess
that's it. There are refreshments at the back. Help

yourselves and thanks again for letting us take up your time. If you're due back on the floor, please make your way there."

And then it was over. Zeke bumped her shoulder and gave her a smile. "Thanks for asking me to come. I think the hospital is going to do some great things with the program."

"I do too." The casual nudge had made her feel warm and tingly inside. It felt like they were finding their way back to where they'd started. Before that kiss had derailed things.

She spotted her mom, who'd evidently already picked Daisy up from daycare, coming through the door. She glanced back, to see that Zeke was just behind her. "I wanted to say bye to your mom and Daisy."

She smiled. "I'm sure they'll like that."

Rachel spoke up when they got there. "I was just about to suggest Lindy and Daisy come to the house for popcorn and a movie later tonight. You're invited as well."

Well, since she hadn't even given Lindy a chance to say yes or no to her own invitation, it was a bit forward of her to start inviting other people.

"I can't tonight, I'm sorry. I have other plans, but I'd like a raincheck on that dinner invitation you talked about earlier."

"Of course. That's a given. Well, I guess we'll have to watch *The Princess Bride* without you."

"Princess, huh? Looks like I'm missing out. By the way, a little girl gave me a packet of princess stickers that I think Daisy will probably get more use out of than I will."

"Princess!"

"I'll be kind of glad when we move into the martial arts stage," Lindy muttered.

He tilted his head. "Martial arts?"

Lindy laughed. "Basically anything other than princesses. But I'm sure she would love the stickers, thanks for thinking of her."

"I don't have anyone else to entrust them to." A brief shadow went through his dark eyes before it was gone. Remembering his own daughter?

A shard of pain went through her chest. She didn't know what she would do if she ever lost Daisy…didn't even want to think of that possibility. But she wasn't immune from tragedy, she'd already proven that. But surely she had been through the worst that life had to throw at her. Hadn't she?

She knew no one could guarantee that they'd be exempt from tragedy, but she was pretty sure most parents would trade places in a second if they could take away the pain from their child. She imagined Zeke had made all kinds of promises to God, asking Him to spare his daughter. He'd probably even offered his own life up instead.

Except Lindy couldn't imagine a world where Zeke didn't exist, even though she'd only known him a matter of weeks.

Did he still have contact with his ex-wife? Had they divided Marina's things or pictures to remember her by? How heartbreaking would that be during a divorce? Had they squabbled about what things the other could have and what they wanted to keep for themselves?

Lindy hadn't had to go through that. Even if Luke had lived, he'd have been in prison. And the courts would have made sure he had no contact with his daughter ever again.

"Anyway, she'll love them, thank you. I'll get a sticker book for her to put them in."

"I forgot they had books. I'd like to pick one up if I could."

A dangerous prickling started behind her eyes. She blinked it away, but when she found her voice she was horrified to hear a slight waver in it. "You don't have to do that." She didn't want to be the cause of stirring up painful memories. Her parents had tiptoed around the subject of Luke since she'd been home. They knew kind of what had happened, but she'd never told them about the choking incident.

The only people who knew were the police, actually. And the medical professionals that had checked her trachea for damage and swelling. And the bruising… She'd waited for it to subside before she'd packed her things and headed home. For her parents to see that would have been too much. Her dad would have blamed himself for not coming after her. But she might not have left any earlier than she had, and it could have put him in danger as well.

"I'd like to, unless you'd rather I didn't."

"Of course not." She tried to tell him with her eyes that it wasn't necessary, but he simply smiled her concern away. And then her mom kissed Daisy on the cheek and with a quick glance at both of them said she wanted to stop at the store and get some popcorn for their movie night.

"Mom, I can do that."

"No, I'm sure you need to finalize things here." She looked at Zeke. "If you change your mind about coming, have Lindy give you the address. If you've never seen *The Princess Bride* you're missing out. It's quite funny, even for adults."

"I'll keep that in mind. And thank you again for the invitation."

No mention this time of having plans. Had that all been a crock?

"I'll see you in about an hour, Lindy."

Knowing it would do no good to argue with her mother, she nodded.

Once they were out of earshot, Lindy looked at him with what she hoped was a rueful expression. "I am so sorry about that. She doesn't get that not everyone is all about watching movies with her granddaughter."

"She's proud of her, as she should be."

He was right, of course. "Well, I am sorry she pressured you into coming over to the house. She won't be offended if you don't come, especially since you have plans." It was meant as a gentle reminder of what he'd said earlier.

"I did have something planned, but I think I've changed my mind about doing it."

He gave no more explanation than that, so she

didn't know if the plans had involved someone else. A date, maybe?

That thought made her heart cramp as a million images marched past her mind's eye, each worse than the one before it. Zeke kissing other women, trailing his fingers over their bodies. Moving over them as he...

Stop it! Of course the man dated. He'd be crazy not to.

Hmm....*she* didn't date. Did that make her crazy?

That was different.

Before she could respond, Zeke went on, "If the offer is still open, I think I might like to see this famed movie."

"Y-you do?" She'd gotten the impression he wasn't eager to spend time with her outside work, so what had changed? And did she even want it to change? But she couldn't very well retract the offer without having some kind of explanation available, and right now those were in short supply. "Um, okay, Daisy will be ecstatic. If she can even stay awake. She tends to nod off halfway through."

He gave her a quick look. "Are you okay with it? I don't want to intrude. These meetings are always hard to get through. The reality of what people go through..." He stopped as if realizing who he was talking to. "I'm glad you got away."

"Thank you. I am too. I'm swearing off relationships, though, for a long time."

"I've sworn them off too, so we're even. So, are we good? A movie as colleagues and friends?"

Friends? Wow. A warm mushy feeling crept up from somewhere deep inside her. She'd just been thinking about the fact that she didn't have many friends here yet…that she hadn't had time to develop any, and now Zeke and Nancy had both stepped a little closer. And as much as she didn't want to, she found that she liked it. A little too much.

CHAPTER SIX

ZEKE KNEW EXACTLY why he'd accepted Rachel's invitation. His plans for that evening had revolved around a resolution he'd made as he held Daisy before the open house. He'd originally been pretty horrified when Lindy's mom had thrust the little girl into his arms, but nothing had prepared him for the feeling that erupted when Daisy threw her arms around his neck.

Since Lindy said she'd walked to work that day, they drove to buy popcorn together. The plan was for Zeke to drop her and Daisy off at her house when they were done with the movie. It was on his way home anyway. And Lindy had said if an emergency came up and he needed to leave, she'd just stay with her folks and have them take her home the next day.

"Daisy's in the kitchen with her Mimi" said the man who'd opened the door.

Lindy made quick introductions and her dad, Harold, shook his hand.

"Nice to meet you."

Letting Lindy lead the way, he entered a home.

Not just a house, like his and Janice's had been on too many occasions, even after Marina was born, but a genuine home, filled with warmth and pictures and memorabilia of Lindy's time as a child.

It was much like the home he'd grown up in.

Why had he and Janice done so little of that? He wasn't sure, but it made him wonder if there hadn't been a crack in the foundation of their relationship even before Marina had come along. Her death had just split it wide open and exposed it for what it was.

Looking back, he wondered if he should have taken his ex-wife's advice and kept some of his daughter's belongings. Instead, he had little more than a few ragged photos and several age progression images. Which was what his so-called plans had originally involved this evening. He'd been going to search for them until he found them, and then he was going to shred them.

And that made him a coward. Because the only reason he'd come here was to avoid doing something he probably should have done long ago. Because thinking of all the might-have-beens had eaten at him for the last five years.

And yet here he was, spending time with a family that highlighted everything he'd lost. Wasn't that adding torture to torture?

He didn't know, but it was too late to back out now. He could feign an emergency at the hospital, but he'd already committed to staying for the movie and he wasn't willing to throw the invitation back in

Rachel's face after she'd seemed so happy that he'd changed his mind.

He felt a little ludicrous sitting on a couch with a family he didn't really know, watching a film and eating popcorn. But it was ludicrous in a good kind of way. He ate a bite, and then another, and watched the crazy antics of the characters on the screen. In the end it was a movie about falling in love, just like a million other movies he'd watched over his lifetime. But this time it was different somehow.

Daisy stretched out and pushed her socked feet against the arm of the sofa, forcing Lindy over until her leg was pressed against his. "Sorry," she whispered, trying to pull away.

Except she couldn't. And he was against his side of the couch with nowhere else to go. The temptation to slide his arm around her came and went without incident. But not without a trickle of awareness that went almost unnoticed at first. Almost. But not entirely.

She might be sorry, but he wasn't. At least not yet. Right now he was enjoying that low steady hum. The one that lingered just below the surface of his mind, waiting for permission to grow and become bolder. Zeke had no intention of granting that permission, but it was nice to imagine what might happen if he did.

The banter between two of the characters made Daisy chortle loudly. Lindy gave a choked giggle in return. "Sorry," she whispered again. "She loves this movie, especially the sword fight."

"Sword fight, huh?"

He couldn't hold back a smile. And suddenly the

hum grew in intensity, egged on by her whispered words and how they were meant for his ears and his alone. Despite being in the middle of her parents' living room, it was as if they were cocooned in their own little bubble of a world. He could see her folks sitting in their chairs, facing away from them as they watched the movie, but they were like so much background noise. As was Daisy, despite her laugh.

Was he the only one who felt it? Or did Lindy sense it as well?

He hoped so, because he was going to feel incredibly stupid if he was the only one who was getting an emotional buzz out of her proximity.

Then a slight sonorous noise came from beside him. He glanced at Lindy, wondering how she could have fallen asleep. But it wasn't her. It was Daisy. She was lying half across her mother's lap, mouth open, making tiny gargling sounds. He chuckled. A second ago, the child had been wide awake.

"Told you," Lindy whispered again, and his innards ratcheted another notch tighter.

"Yes, you did." He kept his own voice just as quiet, not wanting her parents to turn around and see them with their heads close, talking in quiet whispers. Heaven only knew what kind of ideas they would get from that.

Heaven only knew what kind of ideas *he* was going to get.

And that continued pressure of her thigh against his wasn't helping matters. If he wasn't careful, he was going to give them some concrete evidence that he'd rather they not see. The physical attraction was there without a doubt, but Zeke had no intention of letting it go any further than that. Because juxtaposed against the sweet, sweet press of her leg was the reality of Daisy and how it made him ache for Marina. And would likely continue to make him ache with the passing of years.

Someday he was going to have to face throwing away those age progression pictures he'd made. But today was evidently not the day.

"How long is this movie?" he asked.

"We're about halfway through. Everything okay?" She again tried to shift her leg away, but Daisy's feet were still firmly planted against the arm. It looked like she wouldn't budge.

"Fine. And don't worry about moving her."

"I thought you might be getting claustrophobic."

He was getting something, but it definitely wasn't claustrophobia."

"No." On the other side of the attraction issue was the sense that it felt right having her against him, and Zeke didn't want that at all. Because it wasn't "right." None of it was. It was an illusion that would go up in a puff of smoke as soon as they were back in their respective homes.

At least that's what he told himself. It was the only thing currently keeping him sane.

Time to concentrate on the movie. Then he realized that Harold's head had canted sideways, and a sound louder than Daisy's assailed his ears. He glanced at Lindy and she nodded. "Yep. He always falls asleep. I think that's where Daisy gets it from."

And that did it. Zeke put his arm around her, and Lindy melted against him as if she'd been waiting for that all evening.

Had she?

All too soon, the couple got their weird, but happy, ending and he unhooked his arm, pulling it back to his side before they got caught and had to give some kind of explanation. As it was, no one noticed.

Rachel was too busy shaking Harold awake. He grumbled and acted like he'd been watching the film all along. Lindy giggled. "Something else that happens all the time."

Okay. And that was his sign to get up.

In a minute. His right leg had fallen asleep from the way they'd been sitting, but he hadn't wanted to make her move. He still didn't.

Lindy's mom stretched. "Why don't you all stay the night?"

His gut seized. What was she saying? She wanted him to spend the night with Lindy and the rest of the brood?

As in the same room?

"Mom, Zeke has his own house." Lindy smiled to take the sting out of it. "And so do I."

"Yes, I'll take Daisy and Lindy home and then head back to my place."

"Are you sure?" Rachel insisted.

Lindy saved him from answering. "Yes, we are, aren't we, Zeke?"

Well, she didn't save him entirely.

"Lindy's right on my way so yes. Thank you for the hospitality, though. And the popcorn." He held up his mostly empty bowl. "Where do you want me to put this?"

"I'll take it." Rachel held her hand out. "And thank you for coming. We're really glad you changed your mind."

Zeke stood, pushing his khakis down over his legs.

Harold nodded and shook his hand, grip firm, even after falling asleep. "Come back any time."

"Thank you, sir. I will."

Lindy was still sitting on the sofa, pinned beneath Daisy's slight frame. Rachel moved forward as if to help, but Zeke got there first. "Here, let me take her."

He hefted the child into his arms, surprised that someone so small could feel so solid. It was good. Felt right.

There were those words again. Words he needed to banish from his vocabulary.

Lindy stood, stretching her back. "I think my whole right side is asleep."

The same thing he'd thought about his leg. It made him smile. "This little thing cut off your circulation?"

"You try holding her for a two-hour movie and see how you feel afterward. Although I wouldn't trade it for the world."

He remembered those days. In fact, the memories of those days had helped him get through the worst of his grief.

"Are you sure about driving us home? I'm sure one of my parents could."

"Like I said, it's on my way. And it'll save your mom a trip there and back."

Lindy switched the car seat from Rachel's car and installed it in his while he held Daisy. "I'll give it back to her tomorrow when she picks us up."

He lowered Daisy into her car seat and carefully buckled her in. Despite the passing of years, he still remembered how to secure a child in their seat.

They were soon on their way, getting onto the highway.

"Thanks again, Zeke. I hope we weren't too boring for you. I'm sure your Friday nights are normally much more exciting."

"Not really. My plans weren't with friends, just myself. I had some things I wanted to catch up on. But that can happen another time. The movie was cute."

"It's a classic. Kind of slapstick humor, but it grows on you."

Kind of like having her beside him had grown on him. A little too much actually.

She leaned back and stretched, the act making her breasts jut out. "I have about a thousand kinks in my spine."

He swallowed, hoping he wasn't about to get a kink in something else. Having her plastered against him had been the best kind of torture. His nerve endings hadn't completely recovered. Maybe they wouldn't until she was out of the car.

"You've been on your feet most of the day, then

had the question and answer session and then movie night. It's no wonder."

"Hmm…and your day has been so much lighter?" The words came with a smile and raised brows.

"Okay, we've both had a full day."

"At least I'm off tomorrow. You?"

"I am as well. I try not to work Sundays if I don't have to."

She turned to look at him. "You go to church?"

"Sometimes. My taking off Sundays isn't for religious reasons, though. It's more personal."

When she tilted her head, he knew he was going to tell her, although he wasn't exactly sure why. Maybe it was the time spent at her parents'. Maybe it was the arm he'd draped around her shoulders. But right now he felt connected to her in a way that made him trust her.

"Marina died on a Sunday. It's been long enough ago that I could probably work now, but it's just become a habit. So I've continued it."

A sense of relief whooshed over him when she didn't react in a way that made him feel ridiculous. Instead she covered his hand with hers as it lay on the gear shift. "I think that's a great idea. We all need rest. And it kind of makes her day sacred and ensures she's remembered. I think Marina would like it."

"Thanks." A lump formed in his throat that had nothing to do with his daughter's death. Lindy had endured her own tragedy and yet she was able to see past it to other people's suffering. Maybe he should try being a little more like her.

She glanced behind her to the back seat. "I can't believe she's still asleep. I hope this doesn't mean she'll be up at the crack of dawn. I wouldn't mind sleeping in for once."

An image of Lindy waking up slid into his mind. Brown eyes blinking open, a slow smile on her face as she peered up sleepily…

At him.

And there it was. The stupidity that he couldn't seem to shake. With each instance it seemed to embed itself deeper into his brain, making it harder and harder to shake.

Hell, he was a surgeon. Shouldn't he be able to cut it out, the same way he was going to dissect the mass in Tessa's stomach?

That was evidently beyond his purview. He could operate on real people, but not on himself.

He suddenly realized Lindy was looking at him— waiting for an answer to her statement.

"Daisy's had a pretty big day. We all have."

They arrived at her house a few minutes later. When he started to get out of the car, she said, "I can get her."

"I'm sure you can, but it'll be easier if I help. Plus we have the car seat."

"Oh, that's right."

Exiting the vehicle, he opened the passenger door and undid the straps of Daisy's car seat. "Do you want me to get her or the seat?"

She hesitated. "You decide."

"How about if you unlock the door and I'll carry her in and then come back out and get the car seat?"

"Are you sure?"

He was already lifting the sleeping child out of the seat. Lindy watched for a second, then suddenly spun around and headed up the walk, digging in her purse for something. Probably her keys.

By the time he got to the door, it was standing open, with Lindy beckoning him inside. "It's this way."

He followed her into the house and down a hallway. She turned on lights as they went. Then she opened a door and pressed a switch, but the lights must have been on a dimmer switch because the room didn't erupt in a blast of light. Instead it was soft and muted. He saw a toddler bed over to the right and headed there as Lindy pulled down the covers.

He padded over to the bed and carefully laid Daisy down. If this had been Marina, he would have kissed her goodnight. But it wasn't, and it wasn't for him to tuck her in. He took a step back and let Lindy do the honors. And just as he would have expected, she leaned down and kissed her daughter on the forehead before tucking the light covers around her. She put a finger to her lips.

Ha! He wasn't about to say anything, so no worries there.

She tiptoed out of the room and shut the door behind her.

"Is she a light sleeper?"

She smiled. "No. That girl could sleep through a hurricane, I believe."

"That makes it nice for you."

"Yes. She's always been a good sleeper, even as a baby."

Then she shut her eyes. "Sorry. You don't need to hear about that."

"About what?"

"Nothing. Can I get you some coffee? A glass of wine?"

"No wine. A beer would be nice, if you have one."

"I do, actually, although it's light. Is that okay?"

"That's actually perfect, since I'm driving home." Light beer had a lower alcohol content than the regular version. Those calories had to be cut from somewhere, didn't they?

"Why don't you sit in the living room while I get them? I could use a glass of wine to unwind."

Instead of going into the other room like she'd suggested, he followed her into the kitchen while she popped open the refrigerator and emerged with a long-necked bottle and some wine.

"Do you want yours in a glass?"

"Nope. I'll drink it straight up."

He waited for her to get a wine glass down from a tall glass-fronted cupboard and then took the bottle opener she handed him. He popped the top on his beer and the contents of the bottle made a satisfying hiss as the carbonation was released. He took a long pull and followed her into the other room.

"I haven't finished furnishing the place."

She was right. The living room consisted of a sofa, a coffee table and a television set.

Which meant he was going to have to sit next to her. Again. But at least he wouldn't have a child shoving them against each other.

He'd already been desensitized to her proximity during the movie. Right?

Somehow he didn't think so. But rather than looking like a coward for standing while she sat, he eased himself down onto the sofa, grabbing a coaster and setting his drink on it.

"Nice place."

"My parents helped me find it." Her lips twisted, and she took a sip of her wine, kicking her shoes off and tucking her feet under her. She turned toward him. "Actually, they helped me in a lot of ways. They offered to let me keep living with them until I could get back on my feet, but their house is small, and I thought I'd be in the way with Daisy. They love her dearly, but I felt they needed to be able to have some semblance of privacy, although she still takes up a lot of their lives. It's worked out, though."

He picked up his beer and took another slug, the brew tasting good as it went down. "So you like your job at the hospital?"

"I love it more than you can know."

"Oh, I think I already know. If it's anything like the way I feel about surgery, then it's irreplaceable. It has its drawbacks and heartbreaks, but for the most part I couldn't ask for a better life."

There was a photo of her and Daisy on top of the

television. Lindy was in a hospital gown and she was holding Daisy in her arms. There was no sign of her ex. Maybe he was the one who'd taken the shot, although he couldn't imagine Lindy wanting to keep the picture if that was the case.

He could remember his ex holding Marina when life had been simple and still filled with happiness. But in the end they just hadn't been able to cope with the loss as a couple.

A thought came to mind. "I got a text during the open house about Tessa's surgery. It's scheduled for Tuesday. Do you still want to be on the roster?"

"Yes. Please." She wrapped her hand around her bare feet and tugged them in closer.

Her toes were tipped in some kind of silvery glitter polish that he hadn't noticed when she'd first taken her shoes off. It was not a color choice he would have expected her to wear, and he found himself fascinated by the way the flecks of color caught the light. "Interesting choice in nail polish."

She glanced down and smiled. "Sometimes I like to be a little wild and crazy. Just because I can."

He'd almost forgotten. There'd evidently been a time when she couldn't express herself without fear of recriminations. But over something as simple as nail polish? "Did he control that too?"

"No, not really. But there were times he'd ridicule my decisions if they didn't fit in with who he thought I should be."

"And who did he think you should be?"

"I was never quite sure. Maybe the perfect little

wife. But I was the wrong person to choose, then, because I'm so far from perfect that it's not even funny."

"Oh, I don't know. I don't think you're that far off the mark."

He hadn't meant to say that. As her eyes came up and met his, he saw a flurry of emotions go by in quick succession. Then she smiled. "You obviously don't know me very well if you can say that. And I remember when you were worried that I couldn't keep up with the surgical department."

"Like you said, I obviously didn't know you back then. Because you keep up just fine."

"You didn't know me back then, but you do now?"

A strange expectancy hung in the air between them, and he wasn't sure what she wanted him to say. Or if she wanted him to say anything at all.

He was torn. He did feel like he'd gotten to know her over the last weeks. And that was part of the problem. Part of what made him keep circling back toward her, even when he wanted nothing more than to fly far away.

"I think maybe I'm coming to."

"I think maybe I'm coming to know you too. You're not quite the ogre I thought you were in the beginning."

His brows went up. "You thought I was an ogre?"

"Well…maybe ogre is too strong a word. But I was a little intimidated by you."

In the same way her husband had intimidated her? He didn't like that. He propped his arm on the back of the couch. "I don't normally have that effect on people. At least I hope I don't."

Even when he'd been at his worst, Janice hadn't been afraid of him.

"It was me. You've been great, and I appreciate it." She leaned a little closer and the heat from her body slid in and made his muscles loosen and then slowly tighten again.

He thought for a minute she might lay her head on his shoulder. He swallowed, suddenly wanting her to do exactly that. He wanted her pressed tight against him like she'd been at her parents' house. Only this time there'd be no one to see them.

Maybe that was his cue to leave.

Except she chose that very moment to tip her head back and look into his eyes. What he saw there made him stay exactly where he was, his breath stalling in his lungs long enough to make him feel woozy. Then it pumped in a full load of oxygen, sending it throughout his body in a rush of endorphins that made him want to do the unthinkable.

Time to break the spell. "Tell me it's time to go."

The fingers behind her on the sofa went to her shoulder and cupped it.

"Do you want to go?"

That was a loaded question if ever he'd heard one. He tipped his beer from side to side. "My bottle's empty."

She licked her lips. "So is my glass. Do you want another one?"

"No. I don't."

"Then what *do* you want?"

That was a tricky question, because what he wanted didn't come in a bottle. Or a glass. He should repeat that he wanted to leave, but somehow he couldn't force the words out.

He touched a finger to the polish on one of her toes. "I want to be like this nail polish."

"I don't understand."

"I want to be wild and crazy. Just because I can. Isn't that what you said?"

"Yes," she whispered. "It is."

"So if I did something wild and crazy…what would you do?"

"It depends what it is."

His brain told him to stop right here, even as something else told him to keep on going. "'It' would be kissing you."

She gave him a slow smile. "Then I might have to do something a little wild and crazy too. Like kiss you back."

"Honey, that is what I was hoping you'd say."

And with that, he did something he'd been wanting to do ever since that day in his office. And again on her parents' sofa. He drew her close and planted his mouth on hers.

CHAPTER SEVEN

SHE'D THOUGHT THEIR first kiss had been out of this world?

Well, nothing could have prepared her for the sudden overload of sensations—the heady extravagance—of finding his lips on hers again. Why had she ever thought avoiding this was the smart thing to do?

Even as he drew her closer, her arms snaked around his neck and she gave herself fully to the kiss. It was what she wanted. What she needed. And just like her nail polish it was wild and crazy and just for her. She deserved a night of wanton sex. Sex that was offered with open arms and freely accepted.

She moaned when his tongue slid inside her mouth, the sweet friction sending goosebumps dancing across her body. A body that could rapidly grow used to his touch. His tongue eased back, and she was suddenly afraid he was going to take that away from her. Her hand went to the back of his head as if to hold him there. He surged forward again, and the burst of pleasure it brought was almost too much to bear.

Zeke was all she wanted right now.

Her fingers twined in the hair at his nape, and what she'd thought of as slightly long before became the perfect length. She tightened her fingers and felt him smile against her mouth.

When he pulled back, her eyes opened in a rush, afraid he was going to leave after all.

Instead, his thumb rubbed across her lower lip, the lip that was now hyper-sensitized to his touch. "Are you wild and crazy enough to let me stay? Just for tonight?"

"Yes."

He scooped her up in his arms and stood, his mouth descending for another swift kiss before saying, "Where?"

"I don't care. You choose."

"I would say right here, but I want complete privacy. I don't want some small visitor wandering in."

He was right. She didn't want that either. "My bedroom is the last door on the left."

That was all he needed evidently. He strode down the hallway, his steps light but sure, quick but not rushed. Was that what his lovemaking would be like?

She gulped. She wasn't sure she could wait.

And then they were inside. He pushed the door shut with his foot and turned them to face it. "Lock it, Lind."

She did, although her fingers trembled slightly as she turned the latch.

He walked to the bed and dropped her on it without warning. She bounced a time or two, making her laugh. The laughter died when he leaned over her, hands landing on either side of her on the bed.

God.

A quick flash of muscle memory made her freeze, before her heart and mind set her straight.

She wasn't trapped. If she asked him to stand up, he would. She blinked, and Zeke's face was all she saw. He was sexy, strong and so very intense. But he was also kind and gentle. He'd asked permission every step of the way, had taken nothing for granted.

He was what she needed. What she wanted.

Her bare feet went to the backs of his knees, the fabric from his khaki slacks smooth and cool against her soles. Then his arms folded until he was down on his elbows, and he kissed her again, making all those heady sensations from the living room come roaring back to life. But only for a second, then he was up and off her again.

When she started to protest he held up a finger and then reached down to haul his shirt over his head.

The man was taut and tanned and altogether too gorgeous for his own good, and she had no idea why he'd decided she was the one he wanted to spend the night with, but she was damned glad he had.

She sat up, not wanting this to be one-sided. She wanted tonight to be about give-and-take. She unbuttoned the first two buttons of her blouse then fumbled with the third for half a second, before he came to the rescue, slowly undoing one after the other, then tugging the bottom of it out of her skirt. He peeled it off her torso, and then he swallowed with a jerky movement of his Adam's apple. "You're beautiful, Lind. So very beautiful."

The sudden prick of tears behind her eyes was altogether unexpected.

He leaned down with a frown, one of his thumbs brushing at an area of moisture and carrying it away. "What's wrong?"

"Nothing. Nothing's wrong. I promise." She reached up and cupped his face, breathing in his scent and letting it sift down to the part of her brain where her long-term memories were stored. She dropped it there, never wanting to forget tonight. Then she shrugged out of her shirt and threw it toward the footboard. "Take me to bed, Zeke."

It was kind of a ridiculous statement since they were already in bed, but she trusted him to know what she meant.

He did, because his fingers went to his belt and pulled the tab through the buckle, the metal clink of the tongue making her shiver with anticipation. He pulled his wallet out of his pocket and drew out protection, tossing it onto the bed beside her.

She hadn't had to ask. He'd just taken care of the obvious.

God. She needed to tread with care, because it wouldn't take much for her to fall for this man. And that's the last thing she needed in her life right now, just when she was starting to find herself. But for tonight she could soak in his presence and luxuriate in what he was going to do for her. Without guilt. Without recriminations.

Then he was shedding his trousers, kicking them away from him and standing there in snug black briefs that did nothing to hide what she was making him feel. What he was making *her* feel.

Her hands went to his lean hips, letting herself explore the skin above his waistband, a ripple of muscles under her touch making her smile. "Tickle?"

"Mmm, yes, but in the best kind of way." His voice was low with a hint of gravel that made her mouth water. She did that to him. And she wanted it all. Wanted to explore and taste and take everything he had to offer.

She tunneled her fingers beneath the elastic waistband and around to his butt, giving it a squeeze. A low groan from him told her he liked what she was doing.

Pushing the undergarment down, easing it over the tense flesh and letting it spring free, she couldn't help but stare. She was drunk. But it wasn't from the wine she'd had. Zeke intoxicated her, made her feel wild and free.

Her hands went back to his hips and then she leaned forward, her mouth sliding over him in a rush, his quick epithet following soon after. But it did nothing to stop her. Instead, it drove her forward, wanting to please him in a way that went to the very heart of who she was. And yet there was a hint of greed, wanting to make him need her in a way he'd never needed anyone else.

"Lindy..." Her name was groaned in a long stream that made her heart leap in her chest.

She leaned back and licked her lips with a slow smile.

Then he was pushing her backward, undoing her slacks and tugging them off in a quick motion that left no doubt as to what his intentions were. Her bra and lacy briefs followed in quick succession until he was leaning over her, kissing her mouth then letting his lips trail down the side of her jaw, nipping at her ear, suckling at her throat and then finally reaching one of her nipples and pulling hard. She arched off the bed, a storm tearing across her nerve endings as every part of her vied for his attention all at once. It was incredible. And she was quickly moving toward the point of no return. And when that happened, she wanted him inside her.

"Zeke." She breathed his name, her hand patting the area near her hip where he'd dropped the condom. He beat her to it, ripping open the packaging and rolling it down his length in one smooth movement. Seeing his hand on himself was heady and if they'd had the time she would have tried to explore that avenue a little bit more, but for now...

He parted her knees then reached beneath her hips to drag her toward the end of the bed. He lifted her toward him but then hovered there as if thinking.

She didn't want him thinking. She wanted him doing. Wrapping her legs around his ass, she let him know in no uncertain terms what she wanted. What she expected from him.

And then he was there, thrusting inside her with a quick move that took her breath away. He lowered her hips, following her down, and took her mouth even as he started to move. Her eyes fluttered closed, reveling in each and every sensation as it washed over her. He hadn't fully touched her, and yet she knew he wasn't going to need to. The friction of their bodies coming together was all the stimulation she needed as she pushed up, begging for more of the same.

When he changed the angle slightly, she gasped, eyes flicking back open to find him staring down at her. "Oh, God, Zeke, I've never…"

The heat in his gaze burned her alive. "Say my name again." He pushed hard inside her. "Say it."

"Zeke. Zeke… Zeke…"

He quickened his pace as she continued to whisper his name, hitting something with each thrust that made her nerve-endings burst into flame. Suddenly she was consumed in a rush that sent his name screaming from her lips, her body contracting around his. And then he was driving into her at a pace that seemed impossible before straining hard, every muscle in his face tense. Then he collapsed on top of her, his body rocking hers as tiny explosions continued to burst inside her.

Then it was over. His cheek slid against hers, and he rolled over, taking her with him. He kissed her. "What just happened here?"

The question took her aback, before she realized he wasn't really looking for an answer. He was just voicing the exact thing that she'd just thought.

And it was a good thing. Because she had no response to give him.

But the question repeated in her head. What just happened here?

And like his name during the height of passion, the question started getting louder and louder, until it was all she could hear.

She had to go to work and face this man the day after tomorrow, and she suddenly wasn't sure she could. Not without him seeing the truth on her face. She'd meant this to be a one-time thing. A way to get him out of her head and off her mind. That plan had backfired, because right now he was all she could think about. Her new normal no longer felt so normal. She was jittery and unsure and starting to wonder if this had been such a good idea after all. She had no idea how to explain any of it to herself, much less to him.

"About Monday…" She couldn't find a single word that would get her meaning across. Especially not when she was lying on top of him, still enjoying the feeling of being connected to him.

He frowned. "What about it?"

And she heard it. A wariness in his voice that matched her thoughts and had her up and off him in an instant. He made no effort to get up and cover himself, but she sure as hell did, going into her bathroom and sliding into her robe.

When she went back into the bedroom he was sitting up, his hair sticking up in odd directions that gave him a boyish appearance that stopped at his eyes. They were old and weary, and held a resignation she'd never seen in him before.

Before she could try to assuage his fears and assure him that she didn't want things to change between them at work, he said, "I know this wasn't planned, on either of our parts, but it happened. As much as I enjoyed it, it can't change what happens in the operating room. Because if it does…if it interferes with our patients…" He took a long careful breath. "Then I don't want you there anymore."

He didn't want her there? Doing surgery with him? Or at the hospital itself.

"I'm not sure I understand."

He reached for her hand, catching it before she could pull away. "People put their lives in our hands. They trust us to have our minds fully on what needs to be done. If this changes that for either of us then we can't work together anymore."

A slice of pain went through her. Where she had just been going to say that she wanted things to be business as usual, he was saying he might not want to be associated with her at all now.

"Do…" Her voice caught, and she had to stop. Then fear was replaced with a bubble of anger. She had been about to ask him if he wanted her to quit, but that was something the old Lindy would have done when backed into a corner. The new Lindy had to grow a backbone or she would regret it. She changed the question to a statement. "I'm not quitting, if that's what you mean."

He stared at her for a second. "Hell, no. Where did you get that idea?"

"I just thought… You said we might not be able to work together anymore."

"I wasn't talking about the hospital in general." He dragged a hand through his hair and then got up. "Hold that thought for a minute."

He went into the bathroom with his briefs and when he re-emerged he was wearing them. "I don't know where you came up with that idea, but I would never ask you to quit. I just don't want what happened tonight to affect our patients. I feel I can put this into a compartment and keep it there during surgery. I hope you can too."

"Absolutely." He'd actually said what she'd been thinking much better than she could have. Relief washed over her. "It's not something that will happen again, so I vote that we just put it behind us."

"I concur." He looked a whole lot surer than she felt, but if he could adopt that certainty, she could too.

She really should thank him. It was much better to have had her first post-marriage sexual experience with someone that she instinctively trusted. Someone like Zeke.

Just thinking his name made her shiver. It had been exciting to know he liked hearing his name on her lips. And she liked hearing him call her Lind. Not many people called her that. Certainly never Luke, who'd never ever used a pet name for her. She'd liked it a little too much, and she needed to be careful not to infer anything from it.

Because what she'd said was true. She could fall for this man. Only he obviously had other ideas. Ideas that did not involve him and her together forever.

They were not a couple, and they were unlikely to ever become a couple, so she needed to get that thought right out of her head. They both needed to be on the same page about this. She didn't need to be mooning after him and wondering whether or not he felt the same. He didn't. He'd just said he could shove what had happened between them into a box and seal it up, probably for all eternity.

Lindy only hoped she was strong enough to do the same. She wasn't stupid. She knew that the feelings he'd generated in her tonight would easily turn into a form of infatuation if she wasn't careful. One that was based on nothing more than pleasurable sensations.

Pleasurable sensations? That was such a weak way of expressing how she'd felt. Which was part of the problem. She shouldn't be looking for stronger words.

She shook herself from her mental ramblings to see him standing there with his hands on his hips. Her heart skipped a beat. He was one of the most attractive men she'd ever laid eyes on. She needed him to get dressed before she did something stupid. Like peel those briefs off and haul him back to bed. If that happened, it would be a whole lot harder for her to let him go, or compartmentalize what had happened, like he wanted her to do.

"I'm glad we're in agreement on where to go from here." She wasn't sure they were, but that was all she could think of to say to get him out of her bedroom and out of her house.

As if reading her mind, he reached for his slacks and pulled them on, one leg at a time, buckling them around his waist. Realizing she was staring, she turned away and tidied her bed and gathered her own clothes before sitting on the edge of it. Except that reminded her of the way she'd pulled him toward her and slid her mouth…

Lord! She wasn't sure there was a compartment big enough to pack all of this away. But she'd better find one, even if it meant building it with her own two hands.

But at least he now had his clothes on, and that wallet was tucked back in his pocket. No fear of repeating what had happened. At least not tonight, and hopefully not any other night. He'd already warned her. If she wanted any possibility of continuing to work with him, she'd better get her act together.

So she smiled and saw him to the door, and kept smiling as he walked toward his car and got in, leaving her with one of the worst cases of doubt she'd ever had.

Because as easy as it might be for Zeke to erase this from his memory, Lindy wasn't at all sure that she was going to be able to follow his example. But if she couldn't then she needed to pretend. And she'd better do a damned good job of it, or he was going to see right through it and straight into her heart.

CHAPTER EIGHT

ZEKE WAS GLAD to see Lindy already gowned and inside that operating room on Monday morning.

Even though she'd said she wanted to scrub in on Tessa's case, he hadn't been entirely sure she'd be there. Especially since he'd been so damned pompous about doing what was best for their patients. As if Lindy didn't feel the same way. He wouldn't have blamed her if she'd turned around and refused to work with him, and not because of what had happened the night before last. But because he'd acted like her boss and not her coworker.

Yes, she was a nurse, but that didn't mean he was higher than she was on the hiring chart. Yes, he might command the OR, but he didn't have the power to tell nurses where they could and couldn't work. Not without a good reason.

And he wasn't about to tell anyone what had happened between them.

He only hoped she could be just as tight-lipped. Not because he felt embarrassed or ashamed. He wasn't. But the workplace wasn't the best place to let these kinds of things play out. Things got twisted out of shape, and heaven forbid something went really wrong...

There it was again. That attitude that he was the only one who knew how to keep this contained. Lindy had just as much at stake as he did, if not more. She was new to the hospital. There was no way she'd want everyone to know that she'd slept with him. And he had no desire to hurt her career, or his own for that matter. So they would just do as he'd said and keep this between the two of them. Surely he was capable of that.

He gave her a smile that was a lot warmer than it should have been, but he was truly glad to see her. "Everything okay?"

"Yes, thank you." Her response was stilted and formal, but he could understand that. He hadn't meant to make her feel her job was in jeopardy, hadn't realized until afterward how she'd taken his words. He hoped he'd cleared that up, but maybe he hadn't entirely. But he wasn't sure at this point how to make his meaning any clearer.

Did he really think she couldn't keep her personal life and her professional life separate? No. The reality was that as he'd been lying on her bed, looking up at her, he had suddenly felt unsure whether or not *he* was going to be able to keep them separate. And that had terrified him.

There had been a sense of eager exploration on her part that had shocked him. As if the world before her was new and bright, waiting for her to go out and conquer it. It had hit him right between the eyes and moved him in a way that was alien to him.

He and his ex-wife had had a sexual relationship when they'd both been new to the game, but this had been different and new. Not that he had anything to compare it to. She was the first woman he'd been with since his divorce.

Maybe her reaction had stemmed from her abuse. The fact that she trusted Zeke to *not* be that person touched him. It humbled him, but also made him realize that he was not the best person for her. He couldn't promise to be there when she needed him. After all, he'd proven once before that he wasn't trustworthy when it came to that. Instead of working through issues, he withdrew, resisting all efforts to reach him.

But he needed to get over that and be the professional he'd claimed he could be. So he took a deep breath.

"Ready, people?" He glanced around at the individuals in the room with him and saw the nods of those who had devoted themselves to the same cause that he had: saving lives and helping children live those lives in a way that gave them the best chance at happiness and wellness.

Unlike last time, when they'd used twilight sedation, Tessa was now under general anesthesia, since this surgery would be much more invasive than the last one. He'd already mapped out his plan for removing the tumor. It would involve taking out a piece of her stomach, but this particular organ was amazing in that it could stretch and adapt to the needs of the individual.

"Let's begin. Scalpel."

As in previous surgeries, Lindy anticipated his every need, placing the instrument in his gloved hand almost before he asked for it. Except this time, he was hyperaware of her fingers connecting with his. As much as he tried to tune it out, he couldn't. So he ignored it instead.

He found the tumor on the wall of Tessa's stomach and carefully clamped the blood supply to it. "Preparing to dissect." His hand was remarkably steady as he made his way around the border of the tumor, marking positions on a chart so that he could tell how the tumor had been situated. He would need that in case the pathology came back with tumor cells within the dissected edge. If he left cells behind, there was a good chance the tumor would grow back. Then he lifted it out and placed the growth in a stainless-steel basin that Lindy held up for him. "I need that taken to Pathology to see if the margins are clean."

One of the other nurses took the specimen container. "I'll be right back."

This was the waiting game. Pathology would do a quick scan to see if they could detect abnormal cells along the border, listing where they'd found them, if they did. If that happened, he would know exactly where to remove more tissue, which would then be rechecked.

There was no music. Zeke preferred to work in a quiet space, and his team knew that, keeping all conversations minimal and in low tones so as not to distract him. Lindy's eyes met his above the mask. "It looked good."

"Thank you." He glanced up at the anesthesiologist. "Everything okay?"

"She's in good shape."

The clocked ticked down the seconds and the sound seemed to ping in Zeke's head, time dragging out until it seemed almost a surreal dream. But it wasn't. This was a girl's life and he didn't want to close her without knowing it was safe to do so.

Ten minutes later the phone to the OR rang and one of the nurses picked it up. She looked at Zeke and gave him a thumbs-up sign then hung up. "All clear."

A series of pleased murmurs went through the room. "Let's close her up."

He sutured the stomach with small careful stitches, not wanting to risk a hole or a leak that could bring with it the danger of peritonitis and a second surgery or worse. As soon as he had that done, he sewed the abdominal muscles back in place and finally the layers of skin.

And then he was done. He glanced again at the clock. What he'd expected to take four hours had taken three. Part of that was due to the skill of his team, and specifically Lindy, who'd performed her duties brilliantly. He might have had a couple of rough patches, but she'd sailed through without a hitch.

"Good job as always, people. Let's wake her up. Anyone up for coffee?" He made sure he asked early enough that Lindy wouldn't feel put on the spot if no one else opted to go.

A couple of the other nurses indicated they could go and when he glanced at Lindy, she hesitated as if trying to decide where this fit in that whole personal versus professional discussion they'd had. Finally she nodded.

Relief washed through him like a flood. Maybe they were going to be able to get through this after all. Or at least he was. Maybe she'd misread his intentions as much as he'd thought she had. Or at least was willing to give him the benefit of the doubt.

And sometimes that was all he could ask. But from now on, no more movie nights with Lindy and her daughter, and no more nights of any kind with Lindy. For his own peace of mind.

Daisy ran down the hospital corridor and latched onto his leg before he could back away. Zeke stood stock still before looking down at the tyke who'd attached herself to him. Marina used to run up to him and do exactly the same thing, looking up at him with her sweet smile.

But this wasn't his daughter. And she never would be.

Lindy hurried down the corridor and caught up with Daisy. "I'm so sorry. I didn't realize she'd slipped away from me until it was too late."

He swallowed. The same could be said of Marina. He hadn't realized she'd slipped away either, until it had been too late. And realizing she was never coming back again had taken even longer to sink in. And when it had…

Clenching his jaw, he forced a smile that probably looked as ghastly as it felt. "It's fine."

"Daisy, you need to let go of him." She pried the child's fingers loose and then swung her up into her arms.

Daisy looked right at him. "Can Zeke come?"

"No, not tonight."

That's right. It was Friday night. A full week since the last disastrous one, when he'd taken Lindy home and made love to her.

She hadn't asked him to come. In fact, she'd made it clear she didn't want him to. It was good, because that way he wouldn't have to turn down the invitation. Which he would have. Right?

"What's the film?" he asked out of curiosity, not because he was going.

"*Princess Diaries*!" Daisy's answer was immediate, the delight in her face obvious.

He couldn't hold back his grin. "You still like princesses, huh?"

"Princess!"

When he glanced at Lindy, her face was tense. "Don't worry. I won't come."

"I didn't mean…"

"I know you didn't."

Even so, she seemed to hug Daisy tighter as if closing him out of their little circle. That stung, and he got his first whiff of what it was like to be shut out. "I don't want my parents to get any funny ideas, which they might if it became a regular thing."

His brows went up. The thought of movie night and all that went with it becoming a regular thing made something inside him perk up. He quickly put it right back in its place. Not only because of work but because of how right it felt having Daisy cling to him.

"I don't want them to get any funny ideas either." He forced himself to give Daisy's nose a light-hearted tweak. "Even though I'll miss the princesses."

Realizing how that sounded, he added, "The ones on the screen."

Well, that didn't make it much better. He seemed determined to make a mess of things, even when trying to straighten them out. All the more reason to leave things where they'd left them.

Daisy laughed and hugged her mom tight before giving a loud wheezing cough.

His chest gave a sudden squeeze. "Is she okay?"

"Yes, just an allergy or something. She gets them periodically."

An allergy. Or something. Hadn't he said those very words?

"Have you had it checked out?"

Lindy looked up at him with a sideways grin. "I'm a nurse, remember? Yes. I checked her out. And I had her pediatrician check her out. Nothing to worry about."

A few of his muscles relaxed, even though he'd been a doctor at the time that Marina had fallen ill and had missed the signs. Another reminder of why getting involved with someone with a child was not a good idea.

He was happy the way he was, his job giving him all the love and fulfillment he needed.

At least that's what he had told himself time and time again.

Was he starting to doubt that?

Maybe he was, because he felt a little flat, knowing he wasn't going to be spending the evening in the company of Daisy and her mother.

Lindy was evidently a whole lot better at compartmentalizing than he was.

"Well, I'm glad she's okay."

"Speaking of okay…" she shifted Daisy a little higher on her hip "…how is Tessa doing? I heard that her parents were really happy about the outcome of her surgery. Any idea when she'll be discharged? I'm assuming she'll still be here tomorrow. I was hoping to run by and see her, if so."

"She won't be discharged for another day or two. I want to make sure her system reboots itself once we introduce liquids and solids back into her diet. And, yes, her parents consider themselves very lucky."

"I'm sure they do. You're a great surgeon."

He hadn't meant about that. "No, they feel very lucky that the tumor was benign." He understood the relief they must have felt, even if he hadn't experienced that first-hand.

"I'm pretty sure they feel lucky to have had you operating on her too. Don't sell yourself short."

"I'm not." He knew he was a good surgeon. But

he sometimes wondered if he was lacking in the empathy department, trying to keep himself emotionally removed from his patients even as he tried his best to save them. The same way he'd kept his wife at arm's length at times. Tessa had somehow broken through that barrier, at least on some level. And Daisy had wormed her way in even further. He was going to have to be careful or pretty soon he wasn't going to have any wall of protection left.

Did he even really need one?

He used to think he did. And now?

"Well, we'd better go. Mom went down to visit a sick friend and was going to meet us back in the lobby."

"Have a good time tonight. At least you'll get to bed at a decent hour." He couldn't resist that little rejoinder. The sudden pink tinge to her face said she knew exactly what he was referring to.

"Well, I guess you will too."

That was doubtful at this point, but he wasn't about to tell her that he'd spent a few sleepless nights remembering what they'd done a week ago. And talking about it, even in a half-teasing way, wasn't going to help him in that area. Better to just drop the subject before it got any deeper. Or he changed his mind about coming to watch Daisy's latest princess movie.

Because the further he steered away from any thoughts of an after-party, the better.

Three days later, Lindy and Zeke were parked outside a neighboring hospital, where they were going to see if its helpline project would fit in with what Mid Savannah wanted to do with a women's center. They were to spend a couple of hours there and then report back to Neil and the committee later in the week. The idea was to jump in and see how things ran.

And if it came to actually answering phones?

Lindy wasn't sure she could bare her soul to a complete stranger. But she'd done it at her other volunteer job, and these were strangers who needed help. And hadn't she bared her soul to Zeke when he'd been practically a stranger? She had, and she was none the worse for wear. Not from that anyway.

Taking a deep breath, she waited for Zeke to push through the door and followed him in. They found the place empty except for two people—one of whom was seated at a desk, a phone in her hand, and the other person, who looked to be a supervisor, was leaning over her. The man scribbled something on a pad of paper and pushed it toward the person on the phone. Lindy's misgivings grew. Was that person on a tough call? She had no way of knowing.

The man motioned them over, where they waited for him to finish helping the volunteer.

The small office looked like it had actually been a large supply closet at one time, so there wasn't room for an army of people all talking at once. As it was, it was a little cramped with just the four of them.

She'd been thinking more along the lines of something bigger. With room for two or three people working at one time. And the ability to take walk-ins off the street if it came down to it.

But one volunteer? There would be no one to pass the client to if whoever was on duty got in over their head or landed in a dangerous situation.

No. That wasn't entirely true. When Lindy had spoken with the person in charge of the service she'd been told they could get on another line and either call 911 or get in touch with one of the agencies that dealt with issues that were more complicated. Or more dangerous. That was a good point to remember when they opened their clinic. The place she used to volunteer at had a panic button that would notify the police in case an irate partner came in. A button she'd never had to push, thank God.

She glanced at Zeke and said in hushed tones, "Have you been here before?"

"No, first time, and I have to tell you this isn't what I had in mind."

"Me neither. The place I worked at had multiple lines and a place where people who were in trouble came to get help."

She went on. "I do have a line on a building that I want to check out after we leave here." She'd felt horrible calling Zeke in on his day off, especially for what had turned out to be such a small operation, but Neil had been getting pressure from some of his board who wanted to see them move on this thing quickly.

Quick didn't always equal better.

She moved toward the pair who were working together on the phone and overheard the other volunteer trying to get an address. The phone was on speaker and the woman on the other end seemed angry.

"I just want to know where I can find a good law-yer to sue my boyfriend. Like I said, he hit me."

The caller's voice sounded belligerent rather than frightened and for Lindy, that sent up an automatic red flag.

"I can't do that, but I can get you some help, if you're in danger. What is your boyfriend's name?"

"I'm not saying." A few choice words came over the speaker, causing the volunteer to glance up at her supervisor with raised brows.

It was then that Lindy saw what he'd written on the pad.

Possible hoax.

It did sound like it and the person's speech sounded almost slurred, as if she'd been drinking or was tak-ing something that impaired her thinking. "Then can you give me your address so that we can make sure you're safe?"

Click.

The caller had hung up. The volunteer sighed. Young, with long blond hair and baby-blue eyes, she introduced herself as Tara Sanders.

"Sorry to have called you in here for nothing," she said to the man, who introduced himself as Todd Grissom. "I've just never had a caller like that before. I thought she was suicidal at first. She didn't ask for a lawyer until just a second ago."

Todd glanced at them. "We find it's better to give people the benefit of the doubt, when possible. But as she hung up, our hands are tied. We can hand the recording over to the police department and see if there's anything in there they can use, and of course we'll keep a record of the cellphone number, just like we do with all our calls."

Zeke glanced around. "I see another desk and a phone." He nodded behind the current volunteer.

"We do have another line. Unfortunately, we don't have enough volunteers to man it. We're probably going to throw in the towel if nothing changes in the next couple of months."

Lindy didn't understand. "Were there enough volunteers when your program started up?"

This time it was Tara who answered. "I've been volunteering for three years and we used to have a lot of people. But people get tired, you know? Burned out. It seems like there's a never-ending stream of people who need help and not enough resources to go around."

Which was exactly why Mid Savannah was interested in opening their own center. Neil said they'd had a plea from another organization saying an actual medical-based facility was needed. People could always come to the hospital, but the tangles of insurance and red tape sometimes kept them from trying to get help. They wanted an actual place with an exam room or two, along with a place to conduct group sessions or one-on-one counseling. The phones would be used as a filter and a way to direct folks to the right place on the right day.

"How many callers would you say you log in an average day?" she asked.

"You mean on this phone or both of them together?"

"Let's say both of them." Even as she said it the phone behind Tara began to ring. Todd went back to get that one, speaking in low tones as he jotted down what the caller said.

"I'd say we get around forty calls in a day."

"So in an eight-hour period there are around five calls an hour." Less than fifteen minutes per caller. "And if someone calls while you're on the line?"

"They'll get a busy signal. Todd only answers if there's no one else available. He knows how hard it can be for some of them to confide in a man. But there are no guarantees the caller will try again later."

"They'll get a busy signal."

Lindy had visions of their lobby flooded with people and not enough bodies to handle them "Great. Thanks so much for letting us come and observe."

"Do you want to try taking a call? We have a book with prompts that help a lot. You told me you volunteered at Gretchen's Place, didn't you?"

"I did."

"Did you do phone work?"

"Yes. It was pretty busy as well."

The difference had been that their volunteers hadn't petered out.

Tara reached under her desk and hefted a large three-ring binder, setting it on the desk.

Okay, wow, that was bigger than anything they'd

had at Gretchen's Place. "How do you find anything in there?"

"It's all alphabetized."

Todd was still in the background on the phone. It sounded like he was trying to get someone to turn himself in.

Lindy glanced at Zeke. "We'll go as soon as I try this, okay? Unless you want a turn as well."

Zeke shook his head. "I do better in person than on the phone."

She certainly understood that. Was that true? Or was he quickly realizing this was going to be more involved than simply empathizing with at-risk women and trying to get them help, the way she herself had once needed help?

"Gretchen's Place had a log that we entered all calls into."

Tara flipped to the first page of the binder. "We have that as well. And you'll need to record the call and notify the person on the other end that you're doing so. You'll assign the recording the next number in the sequence. Doing that will automatically save it to the computer, and we can retrieve it at a later date along with the actual recording and time stamp. It helps us cover ourselves in the event that someone challenges our version of a conversation."

She was impressed. From her initial impression and the tiny size of the office, Lindy hadn't expected the helpline to be as sophisticated as it was, but it sounded like they'd started off well and things had just fizzled out, for whatever reason. It was a good reminder that you couldn't grow complacent about the mission or it would lose its momentum.

She'd never known Mid Savannah Medical Center to do things in half-measures. Not that she'd been there all that long, but from everything she'd seen, they liked to stay on top of things. The hospital she'd worked at before her marriage had also paid attention to the little things, but it had been a much smaller facility and it was doubtful they would have had the resources to open up a place even as small as this one.

And somehow she couldn't imagine her and Zeke trapped in a tiny cubicle for two or three hours. His lanky figure already ate up a great deal of the available air space. And he was rapidly taking up a great deal of her thoughts as well. He'd once said he couldn't work with her if she couldn't maintain that separation of professional and personal. Well, it was hard enough in their huge hospital. In here, it would be impossible.

Friday night movies hadn't been quite the same without him, however, and her mom had insisted on keeping a sleeping Daisy for the night yesterday. If only she'd done that the Friday before, maybe she and Zeke would have never had their encounter. Except she had enjoyed her time with him, was glad for it no matter what else happened.

She glanced at Tara. "Anything of crucial importance inside that book?" Maybe she could treat it like her other hospital's helpline. Surely it couldn't be all that different.

She slid into the chair and looked at the open

screen on the desk. Tara grabbed a second chair and sat beside her. "There is, but you won't have to deal with most of it." The other woman flipped a couple of tabs and opened the page to a list of phone numbers. "These are the organizations that you'll want to keep track of. They're also on one of the screens."

She leaned across and clicked an icon labeled "Resource Referrals." A page identical to the one in the binder popped onto the screen. "It's here, so the book doesn't have to be pulled out every time we want to give someone a phone number. And of course 911 is exactly the same."

Tara continued. "Mostly you want to listen and make sure the caller isn't in immediate danger, like we said earlier."

"If I suspect someone is in danger, even if the caller claims she isn't, can I still call and report it?"

"Absolutely. That's happened more than once, and we'd much rather be on the safe side than risk someone's life."

"Once you disconnect, the computer will ask you if you want to save or delete. You'll always want to save. Periodically, one of the other board members will go through calls that were marked non-urgent and cross-reference them to other calls. If it was a one-off and there was a satisfactory resolution, such as finding the appropriate place to send her, then we'll delete the actual recording to free up space. But the phone number and time stamp will remain to help with writing grant requests."

"Okay, got it."

She glanced up and caught Zeke's eyes on her. Damn! How was she going to concentrate on a caller when he was looking at her like that?

Like what?

She wasn't sure. But she liked it.

Their night together almost seemed like a dream now, a surreal combination of physical and emotional reactions that could have belonged to someone else. Only they didn't. They belonged to her and she did not want to give them up. Not yet.

That sexy mouth went up in a half-smile that made her stomach flip.

"What?"

"Nothing. Just anxious to see you in action."

She gave him a sharp look, but there was nothing there to indicate the words had any other meaning.

Was she the only one having trouble wiping those memories from her skull? If only it was as easy to zap them away as it was to erase the call files from the computer. But like Tara said, even if that happened, there would probably still be some kind of record, a mental paper trail that would remain with her forever.

And that's probably the way it should be. Every experience in life brought an opportunity to learn and grow. Though she wasn't quite sure what she'd learned from that night other than to be more careful about letting her sexual urges run amok.

That made her smile, because it perfectly described what had happened. She'd let them out for the first time in ages and they'd gone a little wild and crazy on her.

Wild and crazy. Like her toenail polish. She remembered using those words. Remembered him saying them back to her. As if he knew exactly what she was thinking about, his dark eyes dropped to her mouth for a brief second before swiftly returning to her face as a whole.

Tara cocked her head. "Something funny?"

Somehow her smile had frozen in place. She wiped it away as quickly as she could. She needed to get control of herself. "No, sorry. What else do I need to know?"

Instead of Tara answering, it was Zeke. "You already know enough to get you into a whole lot of trouble. I don't think you need to know any more."

Um, what kind of trouble was he talking about?

Her mind had swung onto a detour. And he knew it. Knew what he'd done to her with those few simple words.

Tara smiled. "He's right. There's no reason to try to stuff everything in your head for one caller."

She was right. About the helpline. And about the other stuff?

What she would like to do was admit that she wanted his mouth back on hers. But that wasn't going to happen. Not now. Maybe not ever again.

The phone suddenly rang, making her jump. Oh, Lord, could she really do this?

Tara rubbed her hands together. "Okay. It's showtime. I'll be right here if you need me."

Unfortunately, it wasn't Tara she needed. It was Zeke. And she was very afraid that he already knew

exactly how he affected her. And that there was no
way in heaven or on earth that she could let him know.
Because Zeke wasn't offering a lifetime. He wasn't
even offering to repeat their last encounter. So she
picked up the phone and gave a shaky greeting and
waited to see who was on the other end of the line.

CHAPTER NINE

SOMEHOW ZEKE GOT through the next two hours of visiting the call center and then a building a few blocks away. It had been one thing to be cramped in a tiny space when there'd been other people around, but to be standing in a large open warehouse with no one but a realtor, who politely waited outside while they looked around, was much worse.

At the call center he'd been a brave man teasing her when he'd known they could do nothing about it. But he'd sensed her wound so tightly in there that he'd been afraid she might burst.

Afraid to be back in that world where there was fear and denial. So he'd tried to lighten the atmosphere and had ended up almost setting himself on fire in the process.

He had a feeling that he and Lindy had something in common besides a single night of sex. And it wasn't nearly as fun.

Could she have PTSD from her experience? Of course she could. Just as any of them could from a deep-seated trauma. Including him.

That sex, though, had blotted out everything for a brief period of time. It had been like an addictive drug that when used once hooked the user for the rest of his life. Zeke already found himself wanting more. Only they'd both agreed that wasn't happening.

She finally finished looking at the building. "Well, I think this one's a possibility."

"A lot of money to revamp it to fit our purposes, though."

"I think anything will be."

They got back into her car and she switched on the ignition.

Touching her shoulder, he swiveled in his seat to face her. "Are you okay?"

"I think so. I'm pretty keyed up right now, though. I probably won't be able to sleep for a while. Do you want me to drop you off at home or at the hospital?"

Since it was only seven o'clock, he doubted she would go home and hop right into bed. Besides, she had Daisy to deal with, unless she was sleeping over at Rachel and Harold's tonight.

"Do you have to pick up Daisy?"

"No, Mom is keeping her."

"Good. It probably would be a good idea for you to unwind."

"After sitting for the last two hours? I feel like I need to be up doing something. I need to burn off some energy."

It wouldn't be dark for a while, and he didn't really feel like going home to an empty house either. But what else could he do? Just then he saw a poster hanging on a street sign. It was the perfect solution. "I don't know if you're up for it, but Savannah hosts a jazz festival every year. I just saw a sign for it. I'm pretty sure tonight's is in Forsythe Park. It's probably partway over, but it's free, if you're interested. Otherwise drop me off at the hospital so I can get my car."

"I remember those, although it's been ages since I've been to one. You're thinking of going?"

"I thought I might. Care to join me?"

Zeke wasn't quite ready to go home, and the thought of going to the concert by himself was depressing.

He'd given up on finding Marina's age progression pictures but, then again, he hadn't really tried. He kept putting it off. And maybe that's what asking her to a concert was about as well. But sitting on a blanket listening to live music appealed to him. Like Lindy, it had been ages since he'd gone to one of the events, and tonight seemed like the perfect night. It would give the rapid firing of neurons in his head a chance to slow their pace.

And music? The perfect stress reliever. Well, almost perfect. The only thing better would have been...

Nope, not going there. He was going to have to find his endorphin fix in a different place.

"The jazz festival sounds perfect. I think I have a blanket in the back of my car from when I took Daisy on a picnic after we moved back, if you don't mind sitting on the ground."

With her? That sounded like heaven, and he still

wasn't sure why. Maybe the snatches of memories from their night together were holding him enthralled. Well, that would diminish with time. Maybe if he was with her in a non-sexual way, his body would get used to the idea that he wasn't going back to visit again, that it was firmly part of his past.

Like his ex. And Marina.

A bucket of pain sloshed over him, but he ignored it, pulling out his phone and saying, "I can't think of a better way to listen to one of those concerts. Let me just check to make sure it's at the park and not the theater." The concerts were sometimes split between the two venues. If it was inside, seating was limited. Scrolling down until he found today's date, he nodded. "It's at the park."

"Great. That settles it, then. Do you want me to drive?"

He smiled, his heart suddenly light. "How about you provide the seating, and I'll provide the transportation? Does that sound like a semi-equitable trade?"

Within five minutes they were on their way in his car, her blanket folded on the backseat. He was glad she'd agreed to come, the tiredness of mind and body dissipating almost immediately and warm anticipation taking its place. As hot and humid as it was in the summer and early fall, September was the beginning of a modicum of relief from the constant heat. And right now, with the sun starting to descend, the weather was comfortably balmy, if not cool.

Finding a place to park proved to be a bit of a challenge, since they'd arrived after things had already started. The plaintive sound of a saxophone reached them, even through the closed windows of his Jaguar, the one real luxury item he'd allowed himself.

Pulling the blanket from Lindy's more sensible car had made something inside him warm. He had imagined her and Daisy having conversations as they drove to the store or to Rachel and Harold's place. It had set up an ache in him that he'd tried to banish but he hadn't been entirely successful. He'd pushed it back, but it was there hovering in the background, waiting for another opportunity to make itself known. It actually would have been nice to bring Daisy out here, the three of them sitting together.

The ache took a step forward, but Zeke clenched his jaw and it retreated once again.

There! Someone was pulling out of a spot. Just in time. He slid into the space and shut the car off.

"This is great. Thanks for thinking of it. I wasn't looking forward to going home to an empty house but didn't want to admit that to my mom when she suggested she keep Daisy for the night."

"That makes two of us. The thought of sitting at home staring at the walls didn't appeal to me either. So we'll enjoy some good music and even better company."

They got out of the car and he retrieved the blanket. Lindy's light floral scent clung to the fabric. Folding it over his arm set the scent free, and he breathed deeply. He almost said the words "Next time…" but somehow called them back before they left his throat.

Why would there be a next time? He might have

coffee with her periodically after a shared surgery, but he wouldn't be sitting in the office of the women's center week after week. He didn't have time to, first and foremost, and secondly he was pretty sure that Lindy would find it odd if he somehow managed to appear each and every time she volunteered. So he'd better take advantage of tonight and enjoy himself. Because he wasn't sure when he would get the chance to do something like this again.

They wove their way between people, and Zeke glanced at the stage periodically. The saxophone was still playing, the light notes spiraling from the stage to their intended target, his ears absorbing the sound.

There they went…those muscles in his neck. They were starting to soften and relax, and his headache began to ease.

"How's this?" He'd found a spot big enough to toss open the blanket without hitting anyone and where they wouldn't feel like they were sitting on top of those surrounding them.

"Perfect."

Zeke shook it open and spread it on the ground, waiting while she kicked off her shoes and eased her way down, knees bent, arms wrapped around them. She arched her neck way back, while tilting her head to the right and left as if she had a few kinks of her own to get rid of. Her dark hair touched the blanket behind her, sliding back and forth as she continued to work at it.

"Sore?"

"A little. I'm not sure why."

Maybe the music had lulled him into a false sense of security, because when her hand went to her nape, as if trying to tackle the ache on her own, he couldn't resist.

"Here, let me." He toed off his loafers and sat beside her, one hand sliding under her hair and massaging the muscles he found there with firm strokes.

"Mmm, that feels good, thanks."

Focusing on the stage, he let the music wash over him as he kept ministering to her nape and the sides of her neck, his thumb gliding up and down her soft skin.

When he glanced over at her, her eyes were closed, but she wasn't sleeping. What he hoped she was doing was enjoying the feel of his fingers pressing deep into her tight muscles and loosening them up, one section at a time. What he was doing probably wasn't obvious to anyone around them and even if it was, it wasn't any different from what any man might do for someone he loved.

Only he didn't love her. He needed to remember that. So what *were* his feelings toward her?

Hell if he knew. But one thing was for sure. The feelings weren't platonic. No matter how many times he might lecture himself or how many examples of friendship he might hold up, he knew there had to be a third option. Something he hadn't quite reached or achieved. Some deep transcendental realm that he needed to find.

As if reading his mind, she took a deep breath and let it out on a sigh before leaning to the side slightly.

"Thanks. I'm good." She stretched her legs out in front of her and leaned back on her elbows. The polish on her toes had changed. The glittery silver had been replaced by some kind of opalescent purple that seemed to shift colors each time she moved her feet, which she was now doing, one foot moving sideways, keeping time with the beat.

"More wild and crazy?"

She glanced at him and then looked at her feet and laughed. "Oh, yes. Everyone should have at least one wild and crazy side."

He'd been the recipient of another wild and crazy side, then shut that line of thought down. They were here for the music and nothing else.

Planting his hands on the blanket behind him, he forced himself to settle and relax as the quick notes continued to dance around them. Low conversations were taking place as dusk enfolded them in shadows, and as he looked, he saw all types of people, some on lawn chairs, some on blankets like they were, and some simply sitting on the grassy expanse. But one thing they all had in common was a love of a way of life that was both old and new. Savannah had a charm that he hadn't found in many other places.

And Lindy fit right into that charm. Being away from her hometown hadn't killed it, although there was a solemnity to that wild and crazy side that had probably come from what she'd endured.

As it had a couple of times before, anger rolled up his gut. How could any man do such damage to someone he was supposed to love? And worse, not care whether or not his child was around while it was happening. Thank God, Daisy had been an infant at the time. He could not imagine his daughter seeing such an ugly side of human nature, and Zeke had a hard time understanding what could generate so much rage that someone would lash out at another person.

He wouldn't. And most people he knew wouldn't, although he did know that abusers could come across as great people when you met them on the street or worked with them. It was only those at home who saw the truth.

That was the dangerous side to compartmental-izing, the very thing he'd told himself he needed to do in regard to the night he and Lindy had spent to-gether. But making love hadn't hurt anyone. Except maybe his "want to," which he now kept locked up. And that guy needed to stay there. At least when Lindy was around.

So he settled in to enjoy this side of being with her. And actually he had probably seen Lindy in more settings than he had any other woman at the hospi-tal. He'd seen worried Lindy, competent Lindy, con-cerned Lindy…and sexy-as-hell Lindy. And those facets were all rolled into one fascinating woman. It was no wonder he wanted her.

And she'd wanted him. At least she had for one night.

"He's so good." A soft voice came from beside him and he tensed at first, confused as to what she was saying, then he realized she was referring to the musician.

What had he thought? That she was muttering something about him under her breath? Not very likely.

"Yes, he is. I don't think I've heard him before but, like I said, it's been years since I've been to one of the festivals. He might have been in diapers the last time I came."

She gave a light laugh. "You're not quite that ancient. If he was in diapers, then you probably were too. He can't be any older than thirty-five or -six."

"How did you guess my age?"

"You have that look about you."

That made him frown. "What kind of look is that?" It didn't sound exactly flattering to hear her say that.

"That crinkling around your eyes from laughter."

"So I have wrinkles, do I?"

"Not wrinkles. Crinkles. There's a big difference."

He suddenly found himself wanting to know exactly what that difference was. "Explain it to me."

"Wrinkles are caused by worry or stress. Crinkles are caused by happiness."

They were? He didn't normally feel happy. But maybe she saw a side to him that he'd missed. His job made him happy. Could that actually express itself in the way lines were woven into the fabric of someone's skin? Maybe.

"You have crinkles too."

"I do? Where?"

He leaned over and touched a finger to the bridge of her nose and let it slide down the side nearest him.

"Here. When you smile, the skin here crinkles. I remember the first time I saw them."

"Really?"

"Yes. You were in the operating room and you had your surgical mask on. I could tell whether or not you were smiling by the lines—or lack thereof—on either side of your nose. It was damned attractive."

"Wow. I didn't know. And I certainly can't imagine that looking good. To anyone."

"Well, it does." He had no idea why he was admitting any of this, except that she'd brought up the subject by explaining what she thought so-called crinkles represented. He liked her thinking of him as being happy. He couldn't remember the last time someone had said that of him, even his mom, who was carrying some long-term grief herself over the death of her husband of thirty-four years. Marina and his dad had died within a few years of each other. He guessed it really was true. Grief had no expiration date.

Or maybe it could have. If he let it.

What exactly was the problem with him and Lindy being together? He'd made it into such a big thing in his head, but maybe it wasn't. As long as she didn't want promises of forever—which she'd never even implied she did—and probably didn't honestly, after what she'd been through. But maybe being with her had caused some of his wrinkles to make the shift into crinkles.

Or maybe he'd been generating them all along. But suddenly he thought that coming to the concert was the stupidest idea he could have come up with. Why hadn't he just taken her back to his place and done what he really wanted to do?

Was it because of the whole "bad idea" thing? Or was it because he'd thought she might reject him? Maybe it was a little of both, but he was about to test one of those theories. Whether the other was tested or not depended on her response.

"Lind, how interested are you in staying for the entire concert?"

That got her attention. Her eyes met his and she seemed to look at him forever, although it was probably only a few seconds. Then she smiled...and there they were: crinkles. On either side of her nose. "I think I could be talked into slipping out a little early."

He leaned over the blanket and gave her a gentle kiss. It was the only way he could think of to make his intentions known. And when she curled her fingers around his neck and held him there for a second, he had his answer. He stood, reaching a hand down to help her up and then whipping the blanket back over his arm. There were some looks of confusion from those around them, but a couple of other folks knew exactly what was going on. After all, jazz's smooth, silky notes made it the perfect intro for what was on his mind. From the moment he'd suggested coming here, things had been moving in this direction, only he'd been too stupid—or maybe too smart—to admit it to himself.

And now he didn't care.

He tossed the blanket into the back of his car. The second they were in the car his lips were on hers and it was all he could do to pull away from her and put the car in gear. He didn't want to take the time to go all the way back home, wanted to do it right here in this car. But it was very probable they'd be arrested before they got to the best stuff. And that was definitely not the stuff crinkles were made of. So he added gas and eased off the clutch and headed back the way they'd come.

His apartment was on the far side of town and it took them almost a half-hour to get there. The whole time Lindy's palm had been splayed across his right thigh, and with each shift of gears, each time his foot came off the gas pedal, it seemed to slip a little bit higher. He wasn't quite sure if he was causing it or if she was purposely moving her hand. Whatever it was, he was hot and hard and was having a godawful time concentrating on the road in front of him.

But he'd better, or they were going to crash into one of the posts along the highway, and if he survived, he'd have to explain to law enforcement exactly why he'd been driving while distracted. He didn't think Lindy's parents would approve of him putting their daughter in the hospital. So although it took a monumental effort, he glanced over at her. "You go much higher with that hand and I'm going to have to pull off the road and find a bank of trees to hide away in."

"Would that be so bad?"

"No." He laughed. "Not bad at all, but I'd rather have you in bed, where I can do anything I want to you."

Her hand edged higher. "Does that mean I can do anything I want to you too?"

"Yes, baby, you can do absolutely anything your heart desires."

And there went that hand yet again. He gritted his teeth and prayed for mercy.

They hit what must have been Zeke's apartment door with a rattle of keys and her back pressed against the solid surface as he kissed her again and again. She never would have believed she could be so turned on by a car ride where they'd barely touched, but anything and everything had been implied, even without saying it outright.

His pelvis pressed into her in the deserted corridor as he tried to fit his key into the lock beside her. She laughed and slid sideways to let him have better access.

To the lock. And to certain regions of her body that were hoping to get a little satisfaction. The door swung open without warning and she careened backward, only just barely missing falling by him grabbing hold of her wrist. That didn't stop her from knocking over a bookshelf that was next to the door. Papers and framed awards sprayed in every direction. She gave a horrified murmur and turned to clean up the mess.

"Leave it." He was still holding her hand, coming up behind her and turning her to face him. "They're just things, Lind. Nothing to worry about."

God. She wanted this man. Wrapping her arms around his neck, she went up on tiptoe. "In that case, we're either going to spend some time on the long leather sofa that I see on my right or you're going to take me to your bedroom and show me exactly what you meant earlier when you said I could do anything I wanted."

He bit her lip. "Did I say anything? That term might have been a little too sweeping."

"Uh-uh. No give-backs."

"Maybe you'd better tell me what you have in mind, then."

He leaned his head down and in a sudden boost of confidence she whispered the naughtiest thing she could think of in his ear. The thing she'd thought about last time as he'd rolled his condom over his length.

His answering laugh was rough-edged with what sounded like disbelief. "I'm pretty sure that's not going to happen. I don't intend this to be a party of one."

"But you promised..." Talking like this, freely, without shame, was the biggest turn-on of all. She couldn't wait to get this man in bed and feel him in her, over her. Once had definitely not been enough. Especially since there was some kind of raw emotion twisting its way out of her. Something that made her look at him—at everything that made Zeke who he was. And it was just...

God. Oh, *God*! She loved him.

Loved him. Loved his laugh. Loved his crinkles. Loved his wrinkles, even. Loved the way he made her feel.

How was this even possible? She didn't know, but

she gloried in realizing it was possible to feel something profound. Something that felt sacred and good. And whether it worked out or not, she owed Zeke a debt of gratitude, and she intended to start paying it now.

She didn't have to wait for the bedroom. The party could start right here. Right now. With hurried hands, she reached for his belt and undid it, and the button of his slacks, then his zipper. She was wild for him, wanted him to take her now, as all the foreplay she'd needed had happened on the way over here: in the car, in the elevator, at his front door.

Then she had him out, his hard length in her hands, glorying in the heat coming off his skin, in the hiss of his breath as she tightened her fingers around him and pumped.

"God, Lindy." He cupped her face. "What are you doing to me?"

"If you won't do it, someone has to." She stretched up and bit his lip. Hard, letting him know she was not afraid of rough, because she knew he wouldn't hurt her. Not really.

She let go of him long enough to push her own slacks down her hips, her undergarments following quickly. She needed him. Right now. They could slow it down later.

Zeke got the idea and eased her down to the floor, making short work of finding a condom and sheathing himself. But this time, instead of thrusting into her, he rolled over so that she was on top, the way they'd ended the last time. Only this time they were just beginning. Just getting started.

She lowered herself onto him, that luscious sense of fullness so very perfect. Just like him. He took hold of her hips, but instead of guiding her, he let her set the rhythm, simply gripping her as she took him all the way in and then lifted off him.

Closing her eyes, she concentrated on the sensations that were washing over her and slowly building. She picked up the pace, vaguely hearing him mutter something under his breath. Whatever it was, it sounded like he approved. Her world was spinning in on itself, becoming denser and more compressed the faster it whirled. Her hands went to his shoulders, using his body as leverage as she rose up and came down again and again, the feeling of power it gave her heady. Her movements sped up as she got closer and closer to the zenith, a searing heat growing in her belly. And then it hit. Hard and long, her brain losing its ability to process for a second or two. Zeke shouted beneath her as he followed her into oblivion.

An oblivion that was more beautiful than anything she'd ever experienced.

She loved him. God. She couldn't get enough of those words, wanted desperately to say them aloud, but she didn't dare, clenching her teeth around them and keeping them inside.

Then it was over. She pulled in a breath and then another, her fingers reaching to sift through his hair. And then he opened those gorgeous brown eyes of his, and she was lost all over again.

"That was…incredible." He reached up and cupped the back of her head, tugging her down for a kiss. And then another. "I can't seem to get enough of you."

"I think you just did."

One side of his mouth went up in a smile. "You only think I did. But that was your turn. And now it's mine."

Then he turned onto his side, dumping her off him. "Hey!" Her brief attempt at a protest ended in a laugh as he climbed to his feet and reached down a hand.

"This time we're going to bed. You don't have to go home, and I already am home, so you're going to spend the night."

He didn't ask, which made her smile. "What makes you think I'll say yes?"

"Remember that thing you wanted me to do? The one I said no to?"

A spark ignited in her belly. "Are you saying…?"

His smile grew. "Tell me you'll spend the night, and you'll find out."

"I'll spend the night. Gladly." He didn't have to coax her. She would have stayed even without the hinted promise.

"Then, my dear, you're about to get your wish. And I'm about to get mine." With that he led her through to the bedroom and shut the door behind them.

CHAPTER TEN

ZEKE WOKE UP in a swirl of confusion, unsure of where he was. For a panicked second, he thought he'd forgotten to go to work before realizing it was still early. He glanced at the readout on his phone. Barely six.

He heard some kind of scraping noise, like furniture being dragged across the floor, and tensed before the events of the previous night came flooding back.

Lindy had stayed with him and they'd made love… He tried to count and failed. The events were pretty much a blur. Except for the fact that his muscles were loose and relaxed, so much so that he wasn't sure they were going to let him get up.

But where was Lindy?

Had she left?

He frowned before hearing the same sound he'd noticed a second ago, a little louder this time.

That had to be her. But what was she doing? Trying to leave before he woke up?

He didn't like that. Last night, just before he'd dropped off to sleep, he'd had a vague plan of getting up, cooking her breakfast and then having a long talk.

Cranking himself out of bed, protest of muscles or not, he somehow made it to his feet and headed into the other room. He was afraid that if he stopped to get dressed, she'd be gone before he could stop her.

He made it through the door and came to an abrupt halt. She'd righted the bookcase and was in the process of putting the spilled contents back on it, gathering papers and giving them a tap to neaten them.

"You don't have to do that."

She whirled around. "Good morning to you too. And I wanted to. It's a good feeling to know that I can knock over a bookcase without making someone angry."

"Never. I take it we're talking about Luke."

"Yes. That last day with him was…" Her eyes skated down his length. "It's really hard to talk to you when you're standing there naked."

He gave her a slow smile. "Okay. Give me a sec."

He went and pulled on a pair of sweat pants and then arrived back in the room. "I want to hear the rest of the story. This is the day you got away?"

"Yes. Remember I told you he opened credit cards in my name? Well, I found out and confronted him. He flew into such a rage, screaming that I knew nothing about him. I'd seen him angry before, but this was different, and I knew I had to leave. But when I went to get Daisy, he blocked my access to her. That scared me. I backed away and went into the kitchen, dialing 911 as I went.

"I barely got out my name and address when I felt him behind me. His arm wrapped around my neck and suddenly I couldn't breathe. I knew I was going to die. All I could think about was Daisy, how I should have left long ago, how I should have protected her. Then I blacked out. There must have been a police officer right around the corner, because when I came to, somehow I was alive and Luke was on the floor. There was blood everywhere. They told me he grabbed an officer's gun as he was being arrested, and they'd had no choice but to shoot."

Zeke took a step forward. "I knew it was bad. Hell, Lind, but I didn't know it was that bad. I'll be honest. I'm glad he's dead, because I'd be tempted to put him in the ground myself."

Lindy went back to picking things up, setting another stack of papers on one of the lower shelves. He went over to stop her, to make her turn around and face him, when he recognized something she had in her hand. A small pile of printer paper that was stacked together. He saw her look at it and frown, her head tilting in question.

"Who's this?"

She turned it toward him and there, facing him, was a picture of his daughter. And not just any picture, it was one of the ones he'd been avoiding looking for. They hadn't been in his desk after all, they'd been on that bookshelf.

Every ounce of pain that he'd felt after seeing that picture roll off his printer returned in full force, and he felt himself shut down, even as her question hung in the air. What the hell was wrong with him? She'd just opened up to him and told him about the worst day of her life. So why couldn't he tell her about his?

Because he couldn't.

Maybe it was some character flaw in him, maybe he was just not built like normal people, but he knew he wasn't going to talk to her about it. Wasn't going to suggest they start seeing each other. He didn't want to watch Lindy go through what he'd put Janice through. Especially not after what she'd endured with Luke. She needed someone who could be open and honest and give her that new life she deserved. That person wasn't him.

And Daisy should have someone who wouldn't constantly compare her to a ghost or wonder what his own daughter might have looked like. He'd known all along this was a bad idea, and Lindy had shown him just how bad it could get.

"It's Marina. I used an age progression program to see what she'd look like as she grew up." He took the sheaf from her and set it on top of another stack of papers. When Lindy was gone, he was going to shred them and be rid of them once and for all.

Thank God she'd found that picture before he started something he now knew he couldn't finish. So he needed to finish it in another way.

"Listen, Lindy, about last night..." He didn't want to hurt her, although he wasn't sure that what he was going to say would do more than sting. Maybe he'd been wrong, and she really didn't care about him as a person at all. Maybe she was just experimenting with something she'd never been able to experience as a married woman.

He swallowed hard. Just a few minutes ago, as he'd lain in bed, he'd actually contemplated attaching a permanence to their relationship that had been so premature it was laughable. Except no one had ever felt less like laughing than Zeke.

"What about it?" She was watching him, a wariness in her eyes that hadn't been there a minute or two ago. Then her face cleared even as all the color drained out of it. "I see."

For several seconds no one said anything. As he was formulating the words that would make the smallest burn circle possible, she beat him to it. "Were you afraid I was going to expect something out of you because of what we did here? If so, don't. You've already seen that I'm a neurotic mess. And that won't change." She pulled her hair over one shoulder. "I have no intention of getting involved with anyone ever again. I have a daughter to protect."

The use of that last word felt designed to cut and maim, which it did. Especially since part of his reason for breaking things off was Daisy herself.

What if someday he resented the fact that Daisy was alive, and she figured out why? He couldn't do that to her. Couldn't do that to Lindy. And he definitely couldn't do it to himself.

Only he didn't need to say any of it, because Lindy was telling him she had no interest in pursuing something more. Well, that was perfect. It was win-win for both of them.

"I know you do. And I was going to suggest basically the same thing. Whether it's our timing or…" He cleared his throat. "Whatever it is, it's obvious neither of us wants a steady relationship right now. This was great. I enjoyed it. But I think we were right the first time around. It's better if we keep our relationship strictly professional."

Lindy's expression had gone very still, and he wondered for a second if he'd only heard what he'd wanted to hear. No. She'd said specifically that she had no intention of getting involved with anyone. Because of Daisy.

Well, that made two of them. He couldn't get involved with her. Because of her daughter. And because of him. She thought she was a neurotic mess. Well, his neuroses beat hers hands down.

He was suddenly wishing he'd finished getting dressed. He felt naked and exposed even with the important parts covered.

"Right. Now that we've both cleared the air and found that we're in agreement, I'm going to go. I need to pick up Daisy from Mom's house, and I have some errands to run."

Errands that didn't involve him. The sting of pain that caused made him grit his teeth for a second or two.

"I thought she was staying with your mom for the night."

"I've changed my mind."

Because of him. A wall of hurt rose up, towering over him. "I'll get dressed and take you."

"No!" She stopped and then lowered her voice. "I really don't want them to see you pull up. It'll just give Daisy an opportunity to talk to you, and I think we both know that's not a good idea. I don't want her getting attached, only to have... Only to have to tell her that she can't see you anymore."

"I understand." His heart felt as hard as a rock. She wasn't going to let him see Daisy again. Well, why would she? It was true, Daisy had launched herself at him almost every time she'd seen him. It was better this way. For both of them. "I can at least take you to the hospital to get your car."

"Thank you, but I'd actually rather take a taxi. I've called them already, in fact. They should be here any minute. So I'm going to go down to meet them."

She glanced at the paper lying on top of the stack. "Your daughter would have been very beautiful, Zeke. I'm so sorry she's no longer with you."

And with that, she went out his front door and quietly shut it behind her.

As he stood there, staring at the space she'd once occupied, he wondered if he'd somehow just made the biggest mistake of his life. And somewhere inside the answer came: yes, he had. Only he'd realized it far too late.

Lindy got through the rest of the week in a daze. Every time she looked at the board over the nurses' desk and saw her name on cases other than Zeke's, she realized he'd shut her out. Not only out of his personal life—it also looked like he'd shut her out of his surgical life. She missed working with him. Missed talking to him. Missed making love with him.

But those were no longer viable options. So she needed to do one of two things. Suck it up and make the best of things or quit a job she'd come to love and try to find another position at one of the other hospitals in the city. It wouldn't be hard. Nurses with her qualifications were in high demand, from what she'd heard. She'd had four offers before settling on Mid Savannah Medical Center. She'd chosen the best of the best.

In more ways than one.

And it looked like she wasn't going to get to keep any of them.

What about the women's crisis center?

She'd personally asked Zeke to be involved in it. Volunteering there would be torture, although she doubted he'd put in another appearance if she were in the room.

The strange thing was, Zeke had come into that living room naked, but he'd been a much softer man than the one who'd re-emerged in briefs and affirmed every reason she'd given for them not being together. Neither of them had talked about love. She'd had to assume that Zeke felt nothing for her. That had stabbed her through the heart, and she'd been unable to catch her breath for several terrifying seconds. It was like being strangled all over again. Only this time it had been caused by her own stupidity.

She could have sworn, though…

When she'd told him she couldn't think with him

standing there, he'd given her this smile. This sexy, *oh, really?* kind of grin that had given her a boost of confidence. That confidence had been short-lived. Because the next thing she'd known, his face had gone stony and cold, and she had no idea why.

It had been right after she'd picked up that picture of his daughter.

Was he mad that she'd touched it? No, it hadn't seemed that way. Shocked was more like it. Well, she'd been shocked too, because the face in the top picture on the stack had looked like Zeke. So why…? Then she realized it had to do with Daisy. She was about the same age as Marina when she'd died. But what if Zeke had realized the same thing. From the look on his face it had been a while since he'd seen those pictures. Maybe he'd thought he'd lost them. They'd been mixed in with all those scattered papers.

So? How did standing here agonizing over the whys change any of it? It didn't. So it was better just to make a decision and then stand by it. The way she had as she'd stood in his living room. She was not going to go back and beg him to be in a relationship with her. The old Lindy might have done exactly that. But the woman who looked back at her in the mirror every morning was no longer a pushover who would lie down and let people wipe their feet on her. She'd made it through a terrible ordeal. This was a walk in the park compared to that.

She had a feeling she was comparing apples to oranges, but it didn't matter. What was done was done and there was no going back. For either of them.

The sooner she realized that the better. With that, she opened her computer and jumped from website to website, searching for the perfect position. One that was as far from Mid Savannah Medical Center as she could get.

CHAPTER ELEVEN

HE COULDN'T BELIEVE she would leave the hospital over what had happened between them. But who could blame her, honestly? He'd done nothing to convince her to stay. He hadn't even put her on his surgical schedule. If that wasn't him telling her she wasn't wanted, he didn't know what was. He hadn't meant it that way.

No, Zeke. You never do.

But where the hell was she? The thought of her going back to California made him feel physically ill.

Why? It should make everything a whole lot easier for him, but it didn't. He was more miserable than he'd ever been, actually.

He jiggled his pencil between his fingers and tried to reason through things. Tried to take them apart and examine them one piece at a time. When he came to the one in the middle he stopped. Stared at it with eyes that finally had the blinders stripped away. He loved her.

It was that simple. And that complicated.

That was why he'd taken her off his rotation. Why

he instinctively knew that things could never go back to the way they used to be. It was far too late for that. It was either all or it was nothing. And for days now he'd teetered between two worlds. The present. And the past. He could only live in one or the other.

Which did he choose?

The possibility of living with a deep well of pain with a margin of happiness? Or living with a deep well of pain and no happiness?

Did he want wrinkles? Or crinkles?

Did it even matter? She was gone. He'd driven her away with his stupidity.

There was only one thing to do. He walked out of the hospital, got into his car and headed home. Once there, he took the thin batch of papers and stared at them one by one, inspecting each change with a surgeon's eyes.

They weren't his daughter. They would never be his daughter. In holding on to something that wasn't real, he'd probably destroyed the best thing that had happened to him since Marina's death. Lindy. And Daisy. He loved that little girl. He didn't know how or why, but he did. And, by God, he loved her mother too.

Marina would be horrified at how long he'd held on to those fake pictures. The ones he needed to cherish were the ones that were real and depicted her as she had been. A sweet, kind soul who hadn't deserved what had happened.

And neither had Lindy. She hadn't deserved what he'd dished out. Or what he hadn't dished out, actually. His silence about the real issue had spoken volumes. And he'd been wrong.

What could he do about it now?

For one thing, he would get rid of these images. Even as he thought it, he turned on the shredder and slowly fed the manufactured photos through it.

Then he could learn to talk. Even when he was in pain. So what if he didn't want to. It was what adults did, and if he couldn't figure out how it worked, then he'd better damn well find a therapist who could help him get there.

One thing he did know. He wanted his future to include Lindy and Daisy.

And if he gave in and begged Lindy to come back, what then? What if Daisy got sick and died? What if Lindy was hit by a car? And died?

Was the hurt of that possibility worse than the hurt of losing Lindy forever?

No. It wasn't.

So he needed to find her and quickly. Before it was too late. And he knew just where to start.

Lindy sat in the waiting room of a step-down hospital on the other side of the city from Mid Savannah. She hated it. Didn't like the people, didn't like the feeling she got when she came through those double doors. She knew it had nothing to do with the hospital, though, and everything to do with her.

Because she hadn't liked any of the other four hospitals she'd applied at either. Two of them had offered to hire her on the spot. But she'd held off. She'd know it when it was right.

Or at least that's what she'd told herself.

She wasn't as sure as she'd once been. After all, she hadn't been willing to go back and confront Zeke about what had happened in his living room a week ago. And it was too late now. She'd already resigned from her position. She doubted they would take her back, since she'd given hardly any notice. But she'd barely been scheduled for any surgeries either. She didn't want to just sit around and do nothing. That wasn't the way she operated.

Ha! So she operated by running away from her problems? Since when? Lord, she hadn't run when she should have, and now she'd run when she shouldn't have. She'd run away from a man who meant the world to her. Who had shown her life in a whole new way. He was the best thing to ever happen to her. And she'd crumpled up her broken heart and tossed any chance of getting him back out the window.

Except he didn't love her. He'd practically said it himself.

Only he hadn't. She'd ended up doing most of the talking, putting all kinds of words into his mouth, which he'd merely repeated. And she'd never said the one thing that might have made all the difference. If he didn't love her back, then she'd have to accept it.

But what if he did? What if, like her, he'd just been afraid to admit the truth?

Dammit, she should hunt the man down and tell him how she felt about him. If he didn't feel the same way, she'd be no worse off. She could just keep job hunting and hope that she would one day get over him.

But only if she got actual closure. Only if she heard the words come out of his mouth.

A woman came out and called her name. It was her turn to be interviewed. She stood and looked at the HR person and gave her a smile and a quiet apology, and then she turned and walked back the way she'd come. For once in her life she was going to face down her fears and kick them in the butt. And then she was going to go and confront Zeke.

As she went through the exit, she was so intent on getting where she was going that she didn't see a man coming up on her right until he said her name.

The voice was familiar. Too familiar. She turned in a rush and saw Zeke standing there. How in the world…?

Maybe he was picking something up. He might not have come looking for her. But hadn't she been about to go try to find him?

Well, here he was.

She was just going to do it and to hell with the consequences. Up went her chin and when she spoke her voice didn't quaver. Instead it was solid with conviction.

"I was actually getting ready to go see you."

He smiled. "Well, that's pretty convenient, because I was coming to see you."

"What? How?"

"What do you mean, how?"

"I mean how did you know where I was?"

He reached a hand out and then seemed to think better of it. "You weren't home and weren't taking my calls, so I went to the one person who would know where I could find you."

"My mom."

"Yes, but don't blame her. She wasn't sure about telling me at first, but Daisy vouched for me."

That made her laugh. "Of course she did. She probably ran up to you and gave you a kiss, didn't she?"

"How did you know?" He shoved his hands in his pockets. "I did something bad, though, while I was there. I told Daisy a secret."

Foreboding swept over her and then came tears, her voice breaking as she forced out the words. "Don't you make her fall for you the way you made *me* fall for you. Not unless you intend to follow through."

He frowned but didn't say anything. Okay, she'd said her piece. That was that.

"What…what did you say?" His voice was soft and laced with an intensity that sent goosebumps skittering up her spine.

She didn't care. She was going to get her closure if she had to drag it out of him. "I said I fell for you."

There. Digest that!

"What if I told you that I fell for you long before you fell for me?"

"I'd say that was impossible." Her heart warred with her mind for several long seconds before one of them came out the victor.

"Why do you say that?"

"Because I fell for you while we were sitting on a blanket at the jazz festival."

His eyes closed for a second before flicking open and staring at her. "Say that again."

"I fell in love with you." She changed the tense to present. "I *am* in love with you."

"You said you had no intention of getting involved with anyone."

"You fed me that same line."

"I lied." Their voices marched across the space in unison.

This time Lindy got there first. "But why?"

"I lost my daughter. And I was afraid of getting attached to Daisy. To you. And then losing one or both of you too. Or shutting down emotionally and then losing one or both of you. In my mind, the outcome was always the same. I lost you."

"Oh, God, Zeke. When I think of what could have happened…"

"I know. And when you left the hospital, I had visions of you running back to California and realized the real danger of losing you didn't come from the outside. It came from me. I pushed you away before you could leave. And it evidently worked."

"Not quite. Because as I was sitting here, waiting for an interview, I realized that I'm done running. Done being afraid of what might happen. Things happen, they happened to both of us, but that doesn't mean they will again."

Zeke nodded, and he cupped her face with hands that shook. "I think I finally came to terms with that over the last couple of days. I love you, Lind. I want to be with you. Only you."

She pressed her forehead to his. "Yes. I want that too. All of it."

"I don't have a ring yet. There hasn't been time. But I do want you wearing my ring. If you'll say yes."

"Oh, Zeke, of course I will. And yes."

"I want to do it right this time. My ex-wife and I got married young. Probably too young. But you and I have both lived through some terrible circumstances. And I think we're mature enough—and smart enough—to know what we want out of life and to go after it. At least I am."

"Me too."

Lindy drew in a deep breath and held it for a second before allowing all the past hurts to flow out and disappear into the atmosphere. "So are you saying you actually *want* me as your wife, Dr. Bruen?"

"I definitely do, Surgical Nurse Franklin."

He kissed her and then drew her into his arms and held her tight. "I almost lost you."

"No, you didn't. Like I said, I was coming to find you. I was planning to tell you how I felt about you. Instead, you found me."

"Thank God we both came to our senses. Is it too early to tell your folks? To tell Daisy?"

"To be honest, I think my mom already knows. And if I know my daughter, Daisy probably knows you're here to stay."

"And I am. Here to stay." He wrapped an arm

around her waist as they walked toward the exit. "Come back to Mid Savannah. We all want you back."

"I don't know if they'll have me back."

He smiled and drew her closer. "I'm pretty sure you'll be welcomed back with open arms. By Neil. By our team. By me. *Especially* by me."

As the automatic doors swept open, dropping them right into the heat and humidity that defined Savannah, she couldn't think of any place she'd rather be than with this man. And now that she had him, she was never letting him go again.

They deserved a fresh start and a happy ending. And it looked like this gentle southern city was going to give them exactly what they wished for.

EPILOGUE

LINDY AND ZEKE, along with the hospital administrator and a few other key folks, gathered around a wide red ribbon that stretched across a white-pillared porch. What had once been a genteel old house a few blocks from the hospital was about to become the Mid Savannah Women's Crisis Center. Neil, scissors in hand to cut the ribbon, awaited a signal from somewhere off to the side.

Zeke wrapped his arm around his wife's waist, uncaring that there were photographers snapping constant pictures. His hand splayed over the side of Lindy's belly, thumb tracing over the taut surface, where a new life was rapidly making its presence known. The first three months of marriage had been exciting in more ways than one. The pink "plus" symbol that had appeared on the pregnancy test had come as quite a shock, but after a few minutes of blinding panic, he'd welcomed the news wholeheartedly.

Caleb Roger Bruen would be well loved. There were no guarantees in this life—for any of them—but Zeke had decided that fear and guilt would no longer take up residence in his heart. He had been given a second chance at love...one he probably didn't deserve, but he was not going to take it for granted, or waste a single precious minute of their time together.

"Ready?" Neil's voice called him back to the present. "One, two, three." He sheared the ribbon in two as cheers from the onlookers went up all around them.

The hospital administrator had wanted to name the place after Lindy, but she'd refused, saying that that part of her life was behind her. That while she wanted to help as many women as she could, she would rather not have a constant reminder of what she'd personally gone through. She needed to move forward with her life. Plus the fact that she wanted to be able to tell their children at a place and time of her choosing and not because they'd seen her name on a sign.

Once the pictures were done, he leaned down to her ear. "Feeling okay?"

"Perfect. You?"

"More than perfect."

She turned and faced him. "I love you, Zeke."

"I love you too."

She peered to the side, where the crisp white porch gave way to huge magnolia trees that stretched down the road almost as far as the eye could see. The blooms were magnificent. "This is my favorite time of year."

"Is it?"

"Mmm..." She put her hands on her belly. "It's the perfect time to be pregnant."

She seemed to like that word right now, and he could see why. He liked it too.

"I hadn't realized there was a perfect time."

"There isn't, but I just love the way the magnolias bloom."

He dropped a kiss on her mouth. "I love the way *you* bloom. You are glowing."

"It's the heat."

No, it wasn't, but he wasn't going to argue with her. He'd asked her to hold off working at the center until she'd had the baby, but Lindy, in her calm unruffled way, had sat him down and told him that she needed this. Needed to continue what she'd started when she'd first returned to Savannah. She promised not to take any unnecessary chances and would take a break once she hit her seventh month.

Zeke would have to trust her. He *did* trust her. She wanted this baby as much as he did. And so did Daisy. She couldn't wait to meet her new brother.

"What time do we need to be at your parents' house?"

Her head tilted to look at him as the reporters moved on to their next story and people began clearing away the ribbon and the rest of the paraphernalia that went with the grand opening.

"Not until six, why?" She gave him a smile that could only be described as wicked. "Did you have something in mind?"

He hadn't. Until she'd said that. It didn't take much to start him thinking along those lines nowadays. Then again, Lindy had been pretty amorous herself.

"Always." He glanced down at his watch. "It's three. Does that give us enough time?"

She laughed. "Are you feeling a little ambitious today?"

"I'm 'ambitious' every day, when it comes to you."

"Well, then, I'd better put all of that ambition to work." She stretched up on tiptoe and gave him a slow kiss that made something start buzzing in his skull.

He pulled away, his breathing no longer steady. "We'd better get going if we're going to reach the house. Hopefully there are no emergencies."

She slid her fingers into his hair. "The only emergency right now…is me."

So Zeke took her hands and kissed the palm of each one, before towing her behind him on their way to the parking area. He couldn't wait to get her home. Where he could show her just how much she meant to him.

And where he would renew his vow to be the best husband he could. Because Lindy, Daisy and now Caleb deserved the best of everything. And he was going to see that they got it.

Each and every day of his life.

* * * * *

COMING SOON!

MILLS & BOON

Coming next month

HEALING THE SINGLE DAD'S HEART
Scarlet Wilson

None of this had been planned. When Lien had appeared at the door it had seemed only natural to call her over to say hello to his parents. He'd half-hoped it might give them some reassurance that he and his son had actually settled in.

Instead, it had opened a whole new can of worms.

He felt his phone buzz and pulled it from his pocket. A text from his mother. Three words. 'We love her.' Nothing else.

Guilt swamped him. What was he doing? As soon as Lien had sat down she'd fallen into the family conversation with no problems and been an instant hit with his parents.

He couldn't pretend that hadn't pleased him. He'd liked the way they'd exchanged glances of approval and joked and laughed with her.

But it also – in a completely strange way – didn't please him.

Part of him still belonged to Esther. Always had. Always would.

He'd found love once. He'd been lucky. Some people would never have what he and Esther had.

How dare he even contemplate looking again?

His mother had pushed him here to start living again. Not to find a replacement for his wife.

The thought made his legs crumple and he slid down the wall, his hands going to his hair. For a few seconds he just breathed.

He was pulling himself one way and another. Guilt hung over him like a heavy cloud.

He knew why he was here. He knew he'd been living life back in Scotland in a protective bubble. It was time to get out there. That was why he'd accepted the tickets and climbed on that plane.

But what he hated most of all was that he did feel ready to move on. He was tired. He was tired of being Joe, the widower. It had started to feel like a placard above his head.

But part of him hated the fact he wanted to move forward. He was tired of being alone. He was tired of feeling like there would never by anyone else in his, and his son's life. He was tired of being tired. Of course, he had no idea about the kind of person he was interested in. The truth was, the few little moments that Lien had caused sparks in his brain had bothered him.

It had been so long and he couldn't quite work out how he felt about everything yet. Of course he'd want someone who recognised that he and his son were a package deal. He'd want someone who could understand his usual passion for this work. These last few weeks had mirrored how he'd been a few years before. Every day there was something new to learn. Someone new to help. It was what had always driven him, and he knew that, for a while, he'd lost that. But Vietnam was reawakening parts of him that had been sleeping for a while.

Continue reading
HEALING THE SINGLE DAD'S HEART
Scarlet Wilson

Available next month
www.millsandboon.co.uk

MILLS & BOON
MEDICAL
Pulse-Racing Passion

Set your pulse racing with dedicated, delectable doctors in the high-pressure world of medicine, where emotions run high and passion, comfort and love are the best medicine.